THE MEN

THE MEN

Also by Sandra Newman

The Heavens

The Country of Ice Cream Star

The Western Lit Survival Guide

Read This Next

Changeling

How Not to Write a Novel

Cake

The Only Good Thing Anyone Has Ever Done

THE MEN

A NOVEL

SANDRA NEWMAN

Grove Press
New York

FIRST EDITION

Published simultaneously in Canada
Printed in the United States of America

This book was set in 12.5-pt. Garamond Premier Pro
by Alpha Composition & Design of Pittsfield, NH.

First Grove Atlantic hardcover edition: June 2022

Library of Congress Cataloging-in-Publication data is available for this title.

ISBN 978-0-8021-5966-3
eISBN 978-0-8021-5967-0

Grove Press
an imprint of Grove Atlantic
154 West 14th Street
New York, NY 10011

Distributed by Publishers Group West

groveatlantic.com

22 23 24 25   10 9 8 7 6 5 4 3 2 1

The gods who came into existence in the beginning, being few in number and overpowered by the multitude and the lawlessness of earth-born men, took on the forms of certain animals, and in this way saved themselves from the savagery and violence of mankind.

—Diodorus Siculus, *Bibliotheca historica*

1

When the men disappeared, it felt like nothing. I was camping in the mountains of Northern California with my husband and my son. It was dusk, and the sky was all one color: grayish violet, silken, dim. The lime-green leaves of the alder above me were trembling and luminous, brighter than the sky. In the tent, my husband, Leo, was reading on an iPad and letting our five-year-old, Benjamin, who had night terrors, fall asleep against him. Through the tent's mesh window, I could make out the iPad's light. I was lying in a hammock, putting off joining them. It was August, hot even up here in the mountains, and I had an idea about watching the stars come out and feeling wild and solitary, bound to no one. I wanted to indulge my fantasies of escape, of being a prima ballerina in Japan or sailing solo around the world—fantasies in which I'd never married and had my whole life free.

Still, I felt my husband and son there and loved that they were there. I was in love with them. I didn't want to be single and childless;

I wanted to fantasize about it with them there. I wasn't worried by their long silence. There had been times I was frightened in the world, bad times. This was not a bad time and I was happy.

At 7:14, an intense nothing happened, an elation that wasn't of the nerves or the brain. I would later recall it as being "like drugs." When it passed, I felt Leo and Benjamin were gone but quickly dismissed the idea as foolish. Mood swings were normal for me and often accompanied by bizarre ideas. I looked to the tent and saw the tablet's light, a vivified spot. I didn't call out. I didn't want to wake Benjamin. I went back to my thoughts.

At about eight o'clock, I fell asleep. Down the mountain, in the world of people, women were already calling the police. They were running through their houses screaming names. They were pounding on neighbors' doors for help and finding their neighbors running through their houses screaming names. They were driving to police stations and discovering them lit and empty with the doors left open. Small aircraft were falling out of the sky.

I went to sleep on the mountain while the world fell apart. I slept right through till sunrise.

Their living voices, gruff and deep. The sound of a man in another part of the house. Boys hanging from branches like monkeys, hooting and kicking out at each other. How three boys could sound like ten. Drumming on a table. Whistling. Masculine, unselfconscious noise.

Gone.

Too few women on this committee. Another board of directors with no women. Men making decisions about women's bodies. Gentlemen's clubs. Men's rights. Women's magazines. Feminism. Gone.

Watching a boyfriend play computer games. Laughing at a man's story, then another man's story. Bracing yourself when he shows you something he made; the relief when it's not bad. The girl act. Putting on a little-girl voice. Wearing flat shoes to make sure he's taller.

The big hand on your shoulder. Him telling you it's going to be okay. "You're beautiful," said with that authority. Letting him take over. Letting him drive. Letting him decide. Him carrying you to bed. The rush of being sexually helpless before it. Being an object of desire for men.

Gone.

The suffocated feeling of being talked over. A man putting on a high voice to mock you. At a party, a man's eyes passing over you to find a younger woman. Him answering your question but addressing it to her. Two men talking for a young woman's benefit; she mutely attends as if judging a contest. You say something and all three wait impatiently for you to finish. No one hearing you because they don't want to look at you. Standing at a mirror in a public restroom and seeing what they see.

Him getting scary. Him punching the wall. Keeping your head down and letting it pass. Being ashamed you set him off. Being proud you didn't. The moment you realize you're not in control; all the magical thinking falls away and you're a body being killed. Or just coming to a group of men at a street corner. Them falling silent and staring as you pass. Not at your face. Footsteps behind you in the dark. Big hands on your throat. Not being able to stop him.

Gone.

Your father. Your brother. Your friend. Your son.

Meeting your husband for the first time.

For me, Leo.

Leo's friend had come to look at a car my father had restored, a '91 C4 Corvette. Leo tagged along, a nondescript blond man with a slight foreign accent. He leaned against the garage wall, slouching in a way that suggested boredom. It made him seem teenagery, although he was actually thirty-eight. Out of nowhere, he caught my eye and smiled.

That was my worst period, just after Alain. I had panic attacks, psoriasis, a broken foot that had had to be reset twice. I was harassed everywhere I went. I'd moved home with my dad because living alone wasn't safe anymore; I got death threats taped to my apartment door. Nineteen years old and damned—that was the word I always thought in my head.

But I smiled back at Leo. There was that instant rapport.

He came over to me with the gangly, good-natured friendliness of a dog greeting another dog. He said in that accent, "Hi. I'm Leo."

I said, "I'm a Leo." Then I added awkwardly, "But I don't really believe in astrology."

He smiled but didn't answer. We both looked back at the Corvette. It was low to the ground and built to look agile, a car that appeared to be gathered to pounce. Royal blue. Leo's friend was sitting in it now, and my father was bent over by the open door, explaining the work he'd done on the engine. I'd helped him work on the car and loved it in a way that was painful with loneliness. I sometimes spoke to it when no one was around. When Leo looked at it now, I felt how it didn't matter to anyone else. The friend might or might not want it; there were other cars. Leo gave the impression of finding sports cars silly, an opinion I had once shared. It wasn't even true that I'm a Leo; I often tell foolish lies when I'm nervous. I knew Leo and his friend were both biologists at UC Santa Cruz, and I wanted to tell him I'd had a life once. I'd been a ballerina, a professional dancer. I wanted to tell the whole story in the self-justifying way I'd avoided so far. Of course, he might know it already. He might be about to turn to me and say, *You're* that *Jane Pearson, aren't you? How does it feel to know those children will never be the same?*

When I looked back at him, he was looking at me. We were standing very close together, and it felt as if we were about to kiss. Leo blushed—he was a man who easily blushed—and I was out of my depth, smiling foolishly, a girl. I couldn't think of anything funny to say. Then I'd looked away without meaning to. Now he would leave and I was never going to see him again.

He said, "I'm glad you don't believe in astrology."

Four months later, we were married.

I fell asleep on the mountainside. The sun went down. The stars blazed as my dreams blazed and flowed, guided subtly by the changes of breeze on my face. My husband and child were gone forever, for hours. I slept straight through till morning. When I woke, the sun had already risen. The sky was clear, colossal, robin's-egg blue. I had no premonition. When I found the tent empty, their shoes still there, my husband's phone and car keys still there, I assumed they'd gone to pee in the woods. Leo felt at home in the forest and might not see the need for shoes. I made coffee and heated a pan for eggs. Time passed, and the terror grew slowly and then very suddenly, like roaring in my ears. It became so bad, I couldn't feel anything. I saw the forest and the sky like a very bright movie. I was trying to breathe so I wouldn't pass out. I began to scream their names.

I don't know how long I stayed there, breathing in as deeply as I could, then screaming. I know it became hard physical work like digging. A few times, I tried 911, but my phone had no reception. While I screamed, I began to search the woods, moving outward from the campsite in a daisy pattern, finding nothing. No place they could have fallen. No tracks. I tried to guess what Leo had been thinking: why he might have taken Benjamin somewhere alone, how they could have gotten lost. But Leo wouldn't get lost; he studied forests for a living. He wouldn't let me wake and find them gone. He was responsible above all things.

Once I swooped down on a Kit Kat wrapper, even though we didn't eat Kit Kats and the wrapper was already faded and brittle. Still, my body believed it meant something. I crouched there, thinking of mountain lions, of Leo having a stroke and my boy running off in the wrong direction. When I stood up again, the sun had risen clear from the trees, and I had the vertiginous sense that it had risen while I was squatting by the Kit Kat wrapper.

Here I hit a threshold of terror and started back down the mountainside. Halfway to our car, I got a phone signal and dialed 911. As it rang, I was already relieved. I was pacing in a circle like a victory lap, thinking it would be all right. This was why Search and Rescue existed. They found lost people all day long. It had only been a couple of hours, and Leo and Benjamin weren't wearing shoes, so they couldn't have gotten very far. There would be a harmless explanation. I'd panicked before and there was always a harmless explanation.

When the phone picked up, I stopped pacing and straightened as if standing to attention. The phone clicked through to a recording: "Don't hang up. We are experiencing heavy call volume . . ." I held still, trying not to lose my temper, my breath loud with the phone against my ear. I thought, *My son is wearing red Avengers pajamas. It's the Diamond Lake trail in the Siskiyou National Forest off Route 199. Benjamin is five years old. We don't know if he's allergic to bees.* Then the recording cut out, and I stiffened as if I'd gotten an electric shock.

A woman's voice said, "911. Is your emergency regarding a male?"

The question didn't make sense so I ignored it. I said, "I need Search and Rescue, please." Saying it made me start to cry. I said louder, sobbing, "Both my son and my husband are missing. It's the Siskiyou National Forest off 199. They're out without shoes. It's been hours now."

The woman said, "Both missing persons are male?"

"What? It's my husband and my son. Yes, they're male. Yes."

"Ma'am, now I'm going to read you a statement. Try to listen, because this is all we're able to do for you right now. As of seven fourteen P.M. Pacific time on August twenty-sixth, there is a mass disappearance situation affecting men and boys. The scale of the crisis makes it impossible to respond to each problem individually, so we're asking people to stay calm and watch news sources for updates. We have no other information at this time. Please do not call emergency services again—"

I said over her, "Just put me through to Search and Rescue. Please, this is a five-year-old child. A little boy. I need Search and Rescue."

"Ma'am, you don't understand."

"You have to put me through. It's your *job*."

"As of seven fourteen P.M. on August twenty-sixth, there is a mass disappearance situation—"

I hung up the phone. I checked the recent calls to make sure I'd really dialed 911. I called 911 again and got the recording. That alone made my body crazy with fear, but I waited, pacing and sobbing and muttering. When at last the phone picked up, a different woman started reading the statement before I could speak. "As of seven fourteen P.M. Pacific time on August twenty-sixth, there is a mass disappearance situation—"

I screamed, "Will you listen to me? Will you please fucking listen?"

She said, "Is this about a female?"

"No," I said, and she cut the line.

I called 911 again, sweating and sobbing, and got the recording. I swore and threw the phone to the ground, then scrambled after it. Above, the trees rustled, loud and close, then subsided into silence as the wind died. No footsteps. No sound that could be footsteps. I would die to save Benjamin. That had to make a difference. I sat on the ground and tried calling my father, but he didn't pick up.

Then I wanted to call my husband, even though I'd taken his phone from the tent and had it in my pocket. In my mind, there was still a small chance he would answer and tell me where they were. I didn't give in to the temptation. If I wasted time now, that could be the thing that doomed them. I got to my feet. I went back up the mountainside.

2

Ji-Won Park was alone the night of August 26 in her apartment in Raymond, New Hampshire. She had the television on while she worked on a project. On the East Coast, it was after ten, but Ji-Won often worked very late. She was an artist—an unsuccessful artist who made dioramas and collages that no one saw. She had a day job in a hardware store, and when she got home, she made art.

At 10:14, she was busy gluing while MSNBC showed breaking news about a political scandal, a senator caught insider trading. On the left of the screen were two video-link boxes with talking heads; on the right, a still photograph of the senator leaving the Capitol Building. His mouth was agape in what appeared to be a snarling denial. One talking head demanded repercussions. The other wondered who could cast the first stone. Ji-Won wasn't listening closely. The scandal was so run-of-the-mill, it was difficult even to notice: one speck of dirt in a dirt terrain. The senator and the talking heads were all male, another thing then very difficult to notice.

A talking head fell silent in the middle of a sentence.

Ji-Won was concentrating on the thing she was gluing, a googly eye that was part of a googly-eye-covered frame she'd been constructing for a mirror. She'd been happily away in her thoughts and not inclined to notice external things. But the TV remained completely silent. When she looked back, only twenty seconds had passed and already it felt jarring. The still photograph of the politician was there, but in the talking-head boxes there was only blue background. For the first time she consciously noticed that, though the shades of blue were alike, one was wallpaper and one was evening sky.

She glued one more eye and nothing had changed. She looked again at the TV and stood up, her palms already sweating as they easily did. When another minute had passed, she got the remote and flipped through channels. All seemed normal until she came to one that showed an empty football field. Even the stands were mostly empty, and the scene was unnervingly silent. As with the news channel, what was strangest was that nothing happened. No announcer explained what viewers were seeing. The camera angle didn't change. No music. A few people stumbled around in the stands, apparently heading for the exits.

Ji-Won realized the broadcasts affected were live. Whatever this was, it had so far affected only live TV. Something terrible was happening right now.

The person she thought of was her best friend, Henry Chin. Normally she would have texted, but the television's silence frightened her.

She called him on the phone. As it rang the first time, she felt better because she was about to talk to Henry. By the second ring, she was nervous again. By the third, she knew there was something wrong. It went to voicemail. She called back and it went to voicemail again.

Henry always picked up the phone for her. He would pick up during a fight with a boyfriend. He would pick up during sex. He had even left a theater in the middle of a play to pick up for Ji-Won. One time he didn't pick up because he'd left his phone downstairs, and when she finally got through to him, crying, he didn't find her reaction strange. He apologized fervently. He cried too. They'd only been living apart for a month then and both of them were fragile.

So she called and called and was sick with fear. The last call dropped out in the middle of a ring. When she called again, the phone wouldn't connect, even though she had three bars.

What she remembered later about that moment was knowing Henry was gone. He wasn't at the other end of the phone. He wasn't anywhere. She didn't yet believe it, but she knew. She stood clutching the phone to her chest, afraid to leave the room and all the little safe things that happened here. The football stadium was now entirely empty.

Her memories began again fifteen minutes later, when she was driving to Henry's house and hit a traffic jam in Epping, New Hampshire, a one-horse town that never had traffic, that couldn't demographically have traffic. Still, as Ji-Won braked, more cars arrived. She was instantly boxed in. The traffic wasn't moving at all, and already all the cars were honking. A pickup veered into the breakdown lane but traveled only a few car lengths before hitting an obstacle, an SUV that had crashed into a tree. The SUV's front doors were open, its lights still on. A woman leaped out of the pickup's driver's side and ran forward between the lines of traffic, her face bright pink and shiny with tears.

Then Ji-Won wanted to get out too. She wanted to go to other cars and pound on the windows and demand to know what was going on. She got her phone from her bag and called Henry again, but again the call wouldn't connect. She thought of checking the internet but didn't. The traffic might move. She had to get to Henry. When she looked up, two other women had gotten out of their cars and were standing in the road excitedly talking, patchily lit by headlights. If Henry were here, he would go talk to them and come back to tell Ji-Won what they said. She tried to imagine getting out herself, but it only made the panic worse. She turned on the car's heating, a thing she often did, even in the summer, because the hot air on her feet calmed her. Only then did she think of the radio.

When she turned it on, there was nothing but static. She went through the stations, and the static dipped into silence, then climbed hills of static and dropped into silence; again and again, a dozen moments where the world's heart stopped. She caught at last on a woman's voice saying, ". . . not yet clear if it's global in scale, but we have reports of mass disappearances in Europe and China. In America tonight, every region is affected, with government functions at a standstill and fires raging out of control . . ." Ji-Won listened, breathing shallowly, gripping the wheel. Years seemed to pass while she worked to understand. The woman talked about nuclear power stations left critically understaffed and gave a number for experienced workers to call if they could come forward. She said the Speaker of the House was expected to address the nation in the next ten minutes, with the president and vice president still missing. The woman's voice sounded anxious but brave, and Ji-Won was reminded of how a female voice on the radio often sounded vulnerable to her, like a brave child reciting in the dark. Around her, more women were leaving their cars. They were hugging in the bleary haze of headlights. A little girl among them turned and looked directly at Ji-Won.

The woman on the radio was losing control now, her voice deformed by tears. Ji-Won was crying as the woman was crying as the women in the headlights were all crying, and she realized they were all part of something, something strange and malign and enormous like a war. They were all brave children together. They were children who would never be happy again.

Alma McCormick spent the day of August 26 at the mansion where her brother, Billy, worked. He was a personal assistant for two doctors who'd bickered for years about getting married and now had really wed and were on honeymoon in Tuscany. The mansion was a plantation-style house in a rich neighborhood in Los Angeles. It had rosemary hedges and a massive jacaranda and a pool with a Spanish-style cabana and a statue of Poseidon where a diving board normally went. Billy was left to keep an eye on the gardeners and take care of the greyhound, Fred.

Letting Alma come over was bending the rules, but Alma was depressed, because Evangelyne, because bitches broke your heart and just fucked off, and of course the bitch in question was an academic star and Alma worked the counter at a burger joint, so Alma should have known, but no, she'd fallen in love. But she'd promised she wouldn't drink tonight and she kept all her promises to Billy. It was also her fortieth birthday, though they weren't allowed to mention that. Instead

Alma talked about their mother and her sudden fascination with her Mexican roots, when all the time they were growing up they had to be *Americans*, no hyphens allowed. And did Billy remember that girl in their school who was also half Mexican but had blond hair, and gross dudes told her, "You're too pretty to be Mexican," and she'd whine to Alma about it? But what Alma got was a girl sitting next to her in math class writing a note to a friend saying, "I'm sitting next to La cucaracha. Ewwwww." Bitch was writing in purple Sharpie, but she switched pens and wrote "La cucaracha" in black. Just the kind of thing Mami taught them to deal with by saying, "I'm American! Melting pot!" Not that Mami had even been in touch with Alma. Like, Alma knew she hadn't been the greatest daughter, but what ever happened to fucking forgiveness? No wonder Alma was still waiting tables at forty with a bachelor's degree. No wonder they were both so depressed.

Billy said, "I'm not depressed. I'm just fat."

"That's the most depressed thing I ever heard, dude."

Billy laughed gently (he was always so gentle) and said it wasn't easy for their mother either. People did the best they could, and she would come to forgiveness in her own time.

But Alma raged and became unhinged and insisted you didn't just drop your kids, even when those kids were broke-ass drunks, and she stalked along the edge of the pool, inveighing against the shittiness of fair-weather parents who could burn in hell. On and on, while Billy laughed and splashed water on her and booed when the insults got too ugly. The sun was setting, and part of the horizon was dramatic orange with liquid sun, the spidery high silhouettes of palm trees black against it. There she went, and she saw herself in her mind's eye, a buzz cut avenging angel, handsome, all black tattoos on her noble, thick arms, with the greyhound, Fred, dancing after her, activated by her wild voice. At last she yelled, "And Evangelyne!" At that moment, the dog peeled off, sprinting up to the main house and triggering the motion-detection lights so the mansion flashed white. A little lean coyote was silhouetted against its wall.

The coyote briefly ran toward Fred, then thought better of it and wheeled and vanished. Fred barked ecstatically in all directions, doing a victory lap of the lawn, so fast his racehorse legs were a blur, then veered back and belly flopped into the pool, splashing Billy so thoroughly he had to get changed.

It was a good, good night. It could have made up for everything. Alma hadn't had a drink. It was cool.

And Billy came back out from getting changed, padding through the soft grass (these luxuries they shared with the rich because Billy rode on charm and she got in on Billy's good love); Alma high on it all as her brother came toward her and she opened her arms to hug him deeply, to say it was a good, good night—

when it changed. She couldn't focus. The great night shrank, and all the rich, wide lawn became nothing, uninteresting. Something else pulled her mind. Captivating thing, thing that wanted her to notice it. Billy seemed very unimportant. Far away.

She fought. She needed her brother. She fought for Billy with all her mind. Tears came to her eyes. It was a nightmare where you couldn't move, couldn't wake. Fred raced around the lawn again, yipping and frantic, and the movement of the dog was hypnotic. She fought it. She fought it and the orange in the sky had gone. Time gone. Billy wasn't there at all. She was alone.

She knew. She started running and fell and got up. She ran calling him, the greyhound close at her heels, both afraid. She hunted the front and back lawns, screaming. She went inside and went through the mansion, all the forbidden rooms as well as the open rooms: the pink marble bathroom, where she tore the shower curtain open; the music room with the grand piano; the bedroom with the massive bed awash in pillows that she threw all around, while Fred barked and whined—Billy was gone. He wasn't anywhere at all. She was alone.

Then she called Evangelyne. Then she found the liquor cabinet. She rampaged through the house again with a bottle of bourbon in her hand. She knew. The third time up the stairs, she went on hands and knees and stopped in the middle and sat there drinking, snot running down her face from the tears.

Then she had a last hope and ran out the front door. She sprinted out into the night, tore the front gate open, and ran down the street in bare feet, yelling, and as she ran past the other assorted mansions, she heard other voices calling through the night, screaming, sobbing, as if they too knew Billy was lost.

For Ruth Goldstein, it began in the afternoon, when her eldest son, Peter, came home unannounced. He was then thirty-four and had had another breakdown, an acute depression with flashes of euphoria, which ended in his catching a flight to New York and knocking on Ruth's apartment door to say he was escaping from his sister, Candy, because he didn't feel safe around her anymore. Candy had only let him stay to have someone to manipulate, to punish whenever she felt cruel. He'd often suspected this, but now he was sure, though he couldn't be absolutely sure because he was so fucking borderline.

And if he was wrong, that would be so shitty. He was always hurting everyone who tried to help him. He knew coming here would upset Ruth; it would upset his half brother, Ethan. It would really piss off his stepdad. And what if this was all more fucking insanity? (By this point he was crying.)

Ruth said, "You don't have any luggage with you, sweetie."

He laughed nasally and said, "I didn't take anything because I didn't want Candy to know I was leaving? But then I called her from the airport to say why I went. I'm sorry. I'm so crazy!"

And Ruth said, because this was the point of it all, "Do you need to stay here a few days?"

Then (as always happened when she let Peter stay) his misery magically vanished. Ethan came out and was overjoyed to see him. Peter laughed and hugged Ethan and did a dance of happiness. Just like that, the place was filled with a pajama party atmosphere, a home-for-Christmas atmosphere. Peter was returned to childhood. Eleven-year-old Ethan was returned to an earlier stage of childhood. Ruth became the mother of children she'd once been, a slovenly and satisfied giantess, indulgently admiring their antics. Peter and Ethan sparred with Nerf swords, then made a Bundt cake together while Ruth chopped vegetables for dinner. Peter cleaned the kitchen and began to fussily tidy the cabinets, which Ruth always left in uncoordinated clutter—she didn't see the point of making neat rows of cans when she knew where everything was. Now Peter carped about her "degeneracy" happily and got up on a chair to dust, while Ethan gazed up at him with the openmouthed marvel of a little dog in love with a big dog. And it was the spellbound peace of the apartment, the old CD of *The Nutcracker Suite* that Peter always put on, her boys padding around in their bare feet. A bliss, a reprieve—what Peter came home for, and what she couldn't stop giving him, even if she worried that it wasn't good for Ethan.

Then, while the cake baked, she and Ethan made dinner. Peter showered and came out wearing Ruth's floral bathrobe. Ethan said, "You look *ravishing*," and they all laughed.

Peter said, "How much would Tom hate it if he saw me in this?"

"Don't be ridiculous," Ruth said. "He's not such a caveman."

That got her twenty minutes of caveman jokes, with Ethan making "oog-oog" noises and Peter teasing her about the allure of *Homo erectus* men. Peter set the table for dinner, talking about how he was going to get a horticulture certificate, because he now loved gardening. He believed that plants were love. Ruth listened and made approving noises, though she couldn't help thinking this would end like all the other things: the Jungian therapy abandoned after three sessions; the training to be an aromatherapist; the sign language classes; the three girlfriends and two boyfriends; the $10,000-a-week rehab for alcoholism he didn't have; the rescue dog he'd adopted, then brought back to the shelter the same day, after which he went home and took ten Xanax and slashed his wrists and called 911.

Then Ruth's husband, Tom, came home. Peter ran to the bathroom to change before Tom saw, but Ethan said to his father immediately, giggling, "Peter's wearing Mom's clothes." Tom looked at Ruth and said, "Peter's here?"

Later, Ruth thought they should have disappeared then, when it could have all ended on an okay note. But it happened at the synagogue later that night, after three hours of fights and tantrums, of Tom saying he would throw Peter out if she didn't, of Peter saying, "Why not just kill me, Tom? You're too much of a coward, that's the only reason," of Tom telling Ruth, "Tell your son to have some dignity," of Peter telling Tom, "Your problem is you can't stand your stepson being a fag," of Tom saying, "You're not even gay. You're a fake. You're a fake and a goddamn parasite," of Peter saying, "I knew you were just this bigoted. And in case you didn't know, you're racist too."

And Ruth screaming, "Stop it!" and sobbing, pushing in between them physically, calling them assholes. Ruth shutting all the windows so the neighbors wouldn't hear. Ruth shrieking, Ruth swearing, Ruth out of control. It was what came with Peter, or what he brought out in them. Ruth's fault for letting him in.

Ethan hid. He vanished into his room. That was the worst of it. She couldn't even think about Ethan. She would die. At one point she was coming back from the bathroom, and Ethan cracked his door open, whispering, "Mom?" but shamefully she waved him away. Choosing Peter. She was always choosing Peter. Her fault.

At long last Tom went out, not saying where he was going. By then she was late for synagogue. She'd signed up to make sandwiches for the soup kitchen. They were always shorthanded, so she couldn't not go. But Peter couldn't be alone, and there was Ethan. So they all three went, and in the taxi they were hit by euphoria again, that feeling of playing hooky from trauma. Peter mimicked Tom and they all giggled, though Ruth knew she should put a stop to it—but the sun was setting over the Hudson and the windows were open to the summer air and she was weak. She was human. She could not be all things.

Then of course all the synagogue people loved Peter. Ethan basked in his reflected glory as Peter held forth about his life in California, talking about his job as a gardener and how people always spoke to him in Spanish, and once when he explained to a man that he was not Latino but Sephardic Jewish, the man said, "Oh, so this is your house?" Peter's voice was manic, too loud. Ruth suffered, though the other people didn't seem to notice. Meanwhile, it was already after nine thirty. Ethan would be out too late. At last the man who was donating the cheese arrived, and they all went into a back room furnished with folding tables and plastic chairs, with sagging posters on the walls: MIDRASH AND MOVIES. THINKING OUT OF SHABBOX WITH RABBI GOLD.

At the long tables making sandwiches, Peter calmed down. He said, "This is what I should be doing with my life. I'm so selfish."

Ruth said, "This is your life. This is what you're doing."

"Okay," he said, "but—"

Then Ruth lost interest. Didn't hear what was next. It was as if she were freed to coast in the soft light of her thoughts. It peaked, and she was more than alive. She was touched by the glowing-hot fingertip of God, ignited—a frank bliss she'd never felt in synagogue. She'd never really believed in God. She'd been a fraud and she needed to think about that right now. She closed her eyes.

When she opened them, time had passed. The feeling was gone. She was in the ugly light of any church hall. The room seemed colder. It was now half empty, with a messy scattering of vacated chairs.

The women in the room looked at one another, all wearing bright, besotted smiles that rapidly faded into puzzlement. Ruth knew right away that all of them were female. There was—had always been—a characteristic feeling to a female room. It took more time for her to grasp specifically that her sons were gone.

Blanca Suarez was fourteen years old and having emergency cardiac surgery when the surgeon and the anesthesiologist went. All over the hospital, doctors went. There was panic throughout the surgical unit, women coming out of operating theaters yelling names of missing doctors and demanding help with their ongoing surgeries from others needing help with their ongoing surgeries. In the end, a resident completed Blanca's, with a nurse anesthetist she had to share. It took longer than planned. Blanca woke in the middle to find the resident sweating, hunched at the long stalks of laparoscopes protruding from Blanca's punctured chest. The resident and Blanca were alone in a blinding white place, at a great height of horror and impossibility, Blanca's body looking like a macabre bagpipe. There was no pain, only weight and a mouselike tugging so far inside, Blanca couldn't be sure it was her. Then the resident noticed the change in her breathing and yelled for the nurse anesthetist, who came in already weeping, said, "Oh, my poor lamb," and made it go away.

When Blanca woke again, the noises were wrong. Normally she liked waking up in recovery. She was a veteran of surgeries: born very premature, with complications, she was always in a hospital, engulfed by a machine, getting bloods taken, holding still, opened up. Waking in recovery meant she hadn't died, and her father would be there. He would have taken the day off and brought her candy and books. There was the beeping of machines that sounded underwater somehow, the pain that meant she was brave and exceptional. It was a place where you didn't have to sleep in the dark.

But Blanca woke alone, and the noise was all wrong. It was sobbing and ranting. ER noise. A nurse came and topped up Blanca's morphine before she had time to figure it out. She lay there drifting in the morphine's wake, very sleepily and slowly absorbing the news from the terrified babble around her. Two kids in other beds were telling each other what had happened, fighting anxiously about the details. When she understood what it meant to her, Blanca started to cry, but in a morphine way, a fairyland way that was almost pleasure.

Her father had been her only person in the world.

She lived in the Texas Children's Hospital for a month, recovering and waiting for her aunt María José to come from Las Cruces. There were various adventures in that time: the day the power first went out, the day the hospital was invaded by drug addicts, the water contamination crisis, a mother who tried to stab the doctor she blamed for the loss of her son. In the second week, there were fires in the city, and Blanca was able by then to go to the window to see the distant plumes of smoke, looking firm in the air like cats' tails. Some mothers came to the children's hospital twice a day to eat, because the grocery stores were out of food, while the hospital was getting donations from a network of well-wishers all over the state. It had emergency generators and volunteer guards; it would stand when the rest of society fell. The volunteer guards wore red scarves or bandannas to identify themselves and carried a motley assortment of weapons: hunting rifles, handguns, baseball bats.

In the third week, Blanca and a band of other unclaimed girls went feral in the corridors. They slept on the carpet in a waiting room, making tents of stolen sheets and whispering for hours, elaborating a folk belief in which they alone knew where their fathers had gone. They saw it in their dreams: a prison city on a snowbound island, guarded by winged demons. The girls were planning to kill the demons through white magic and get their fathers back. Some of them were probably only pretending, but Blanca really did have dreams where misshapen birds and animals patrolled a dead landscape, smiling human smiles. On the horizon, she saw a mass migration in which she knew her father marched. If she could only figure out what was happening, he could still be saved.

One night, long past any possible bedtime, the girls crept into the hospital chapel to speak to God and ask for His help. The oldest girl, Akeisha, got them to kneel down, holding hands, and picture their fathers. The chapel was nothing but a carpeted room with three rows of wooden chairs facing a cross. Fluorescent light from the hall came murkily through two stained-glass windows. Blanca wasn't used to staying up late; to her, it felt like an uncharted hour that possibly no one had seen before, a time when anything at all could happen. Ghosts could be real, or God could appear. The night could last forever. It didn't matter that she could hear the elevator dinging and footsteps passing outside. Those were adults. They no longer counted. They hadn't known how to stop this from happening. Blanca prayed though her chest was aching. The pain was powerful. She was almost there.

But the next day, one of the guards brought in a box of donated toys and electronics, and the other girls started playing video games. When Blanca tried to talk about the demons again, Akeisha called her stupid.

The last week, Blanca went to the chapel alone. By the time her aunt came to pick her up, she was praying to her father.

3

On the tenth day I came down the mountain, stiff-haired, red-eyed, madwoman-looking, and drove into the world on a two-lane highway that seemed to flow into blackness, the thick trees burying and burying the road. I'd spent those ten days searching the forest, praying, screaming their names. By then I knew what had happened, of course, but the emergency made no sense, so I thought it might capitulate to prayer and sacrifice. If miracles were happening, there must be gods. So I lay in the dirt and chanted at the sky. I didn't wash myself or change my clothes. For the last three days, I had no food. My body was covered in mosquito bites, some of which I'd scratched down to the blood.

The nearest town was a little tourist place that was just one street of stores. Both ends of the street led to mountains that rose in layers of dark green forest and bleached brown rock, until the farthest peaks were misty blue, as if heaven were visible from this town and its citizens could just walk out their front doors and hike into the afterlife. There was no one out and nothing was open. No cars. I drove through the streets alone.

I stopped first at a supermarket, an Albertsons whose glass door had been broken in very thoroughly and carefully, all traces of glass cleared from the frame. I stepped through the missing door with the feeling of stepping into a mirror. Inside, it was cool and dim. There was no food whatsoever on the shelves, and it had the grandiose emptiness of a cathedral in a nation where faith has waned. Nonfood items remained in patches: colanders, party balloons, hundred-packs of plastic spoons. A few wilted, liquefying shreds of greenery clung to the produce bins. In one aisle, a jar of pickled beets had smashed, and shards of glass and little round beets lay scattered on the tiles in a bright magenta stain. Automatically I looked around for Benjamin, to stop him from stepping in the glass. When he wasn't there, I felt the ordinary panic of having lost sight of my son in a grocery store. Part of my dazed mind jumped to guessing where in the store he might have strayed. When I remembered, the pain was incandescent.

I did lose Benjamin once in a supermarket when he was four years old. While hunting for him, I had calmed myself by imagining he'd been kidnapped by a kindly spinster who would adore him and care for him better than I could. When I told Leo about it later, he thought it was hilarious. He named the woman "Miss Brasenose." After that, he sometimes threatened Benjamin that, if he didn't keep up, Miss Brasenose would get him. Benjamin would roll his eyes and say, "Miss Brasenose isn't real." But he would catch up; you could see he was a little concerned.

Now I sank to the supermarket floor. I was praying out loud and not noticing the words. With the idea of expiation, I planted one hand into the shards of the jar, crushing broken glass into my palm: an intolerable bright singing pain that was clean. When the hurt became a bone-deep throb, I let go, shook glass from my hand, and picked away a few shards that had embedded themselves. I wasn't crying anymore but huffing strangely, trying to expel all the air from my lungs, a thing I've always done when I'm very upset.

For a while then I was eating the beets, meticulously clearing the bits of broken glass from them with my fingernails and fingertips. They were still moist in their centers and the moisture was calming. My hand was bleeding but not dangerously. That was good; I still had to find Leo and Benjamin.

When the beets were gone, I got to my feet and walked back through the deconsecrated Albertsons. When I got out to the parking lot, I was at first struck by the quiet in all directions. There was no sound of traffic at all, an absence like a deafening noise. Only slowly I noticed a faint, sweet clamor of voices in the air. When I turned my head at a certain angle, it seemed to be coming from the sky. It was high-pitched, festive. It almost had a melody. Many children playing, was my first guess, though I also thought of the God I'd been praying to, of the choirs of heaven.

The sound seemed near and far away at once, and I wondered if it was delirium. But I guessed at a direction and walked, and when I turned the first corner, I saw them. They were two blocks away, in a parking lot in front of a strip-mall pizzeria. They weren't angels or children. It was the sound of a hundred women with no men.

A few were standing, but many had blankets spread and were sitting eating pizza from take-out boxes. Some wore dresses and high heels, while others wore pajamas or sunbathed in their underwear. Everyone was drinking Bud from cans, and they all appeared to be talking. One shrieking little girl was chasing another, menacing her with a long white feather. Through the voices, I could hear a groaning generator and a speaker playing "Goodbye Yellow Brick Road." A teenager was singing along with Elton John, that you couldn't keep her in a penthouse, while three younger children giggled and danced in splay-armed circles around her.

In that moment, I was struck by how profoundly a scene was changed by the removal of a masculine element. It felt very sweet and fantastical: a world of lambs with no wolves. At the same time, it was oddly reminiscent of a rebel encampment on the eve of a raid.

Now a herd of little girls raced toward me, filtering effortlessly through the women. They came at a gallop, parted around me without pausing, and continued full tilt down the middle of the street. No one got up and chased after them. No one yelled at them to stay in sight. There were no men. No cars in the street. The little girls were all set free. A chill went over me, thinking of the broken glass in the supermarket, of bears—some risk I needed in order for the world to seem substantial and real.

The women had all taken note of me as the little girls passed. Most looked away, perhaps alarmed by my appearance, while a few still held my eye and smiled. It was as if they were volunteering their faces. I hadn't seen anyone in ten days, and the emotion was indescribable, a very powerful mix of relief and fear. Here was my salvation, I thought; at the same time, I knew they might turn on me if they realized who

I was. I reminded myself I was probably bigger and stronger than all of them. I was six feet tall. I'd been a dancer. If they tried to hurt me, I could probably escape—though of course I wouldn't. I'd be torn limb from limb without a struggle. That was one thing I'd learned from the business with Alain.

As I thought this, a very gaunt white woman with blackish hollows around her eyes and wispy iron-colored hair—a woman with a face like a horse's skull—detached herself from the others and came toward me. As she passed, the other women flinched and looked away. A teenage girl even got up hurriedly and went into the pizzeria, as if fleeing an impending scene.

"Ma'am?" the horse-skull woman said to me. "Ma'am, if you think they're going to help you, you should just turn around now. They only want your gas from your car, and they won't even let you charge your phone. Here the generator's only for medical equipment. Or that's what they told me."

My hand was throbbing. Blood seeped ticklingly between my fingers. I couldn't help looking at the open door of the pizzeria, where music was playing, presumably from some electricity source, but she wouldn't follow my gaze. She said, "And even if something else is running off the generator, that's just part and parcel. There's plenty of capacity for something *Holly* wants. Holly's the owner here."

I said, "I don't need to charge anything."

"Holly acts like she's your friend, but whatever she tells you, she just wants to siphon your gas and then you're stranded here. That's what they're like here. You'll see."

At that moment a woman rushed out of the pizzeria—a heavy, middle-aged white woman in a purple dress designed to be floaty and shapeless, with long, floaty, shapeless hair. She was smiling in welcome like an emissary from this female realm.

She said to me, "Hello, stranger. I'm Holly. You look like you need something for that hand."

The horse-skull woman said to her, "I've been telling this lady you're not an inexhaustible resource. Or that's what you told me."

"Julie, are you okay?" said Holly.

"I'm fine," said the horse-skull woman. "What are you talking about? Are *you* okay? I'm fine."

"Listen, Julie, I'm going to take care of this lady. If you want, you could go ask Micah for a Xanax. There's some lemonade left to drink it with."

The horse-skull woman snorted explosively, turned on her heel, and stalked off, muttering to herself about controlling people, toxic people who were going to be sorry. She walked through the other women and went on, keeping carefully to the edge of the road though there was still no sound of cars.

Holly watched her go and sighed. She said, "I'm real sorry about that. Should we go get you cleaned up?"

She led me into the pizzeria, which was suffocatingly hot and dark. The pizza oven was on, but the lights and air-conditioning were turned off, presumably to keep from overwhelming the generator. Contrary to what the horse-skull woman had said, there were power strips plugged into all the outlets, with other power strips plugged into those, and a chaotic overgrowth of charging cords and cell phones and laptops. A huge fan on the floor was creating a wild turbulence that stirred even my dirt-stiffened shorts. On the tables were boxes of local produce:

tomatoes and dirty potatoes and eggplants. A sign taped to one box said: ASK BEFORE TAKING. WE ARE RATIONING! The wall above the one booth was covered in HAVE YOU SEEN flyers with printed photographs of men and boys. All the flyers fluttered manically in the breeze from the fan, as if desperately waving to attract attention. The teenager who'd run inside before us was now at the booth working on a jigsaw puzzle. She looked up and asked, "Things go okay?" Holly said long-sufferingly, "It's just Julie."

Holly took me to the utility sink in the pizzeria's kitchen. She said I could use it exactly like a bath, and don't ask her how she'd figured that out, but she did ride a bike five miles to work and in the summer it got ugly. She brought a hurricane lamp. From a cupboard, she got down a pail filled with bubble baths and washcloths, then a very faded but clean beach towel with a print of the Puerto Rican flag. She pointed out a carton of old clothes on the floor, which she said people had been donating all week, and she'd thought, *Who's going to need clothes?* but here we were. She made me show her my hand by the lamp's flame and clucked and said she'd get a nurse to take a look. She had the soothing despotism of a mother of young children, and when she left to give me some privacy, I missed her. I imagined how people must have first been drawn here by the free pizza and the generator, then were held by Holly's maternal pragmatism, until she became the de facto chieftain.

On the other hand, it struck me as plausible that Julie was right about Holly wanting my gas. That generator had to be running on something. There would also be ambulances and fire trucks. I couldn't imagine myself refusing if Holly said she needed my gas for an ambulance, not in front of all these people. That may have been how it began for Julie.

I thought all this in the loosened, post-horror trance of washing away the blood and dirt, immersed in a sink as deep as a tub, lavender bath foam getting in my hair, my blood appearing bright on a white washcloth. I contorted myself to rinse my hair underneath the streaming faucet. Elton John had now moved on to "Bennie and the Jets." The steel bottom of the sink buckled slightly with my shifting weight, reminding me I was really here. And there was a moment—I was hearing Holly's voice outside, gently telling some little girls they couldn't come in and being drawn into a good-natured argument about whether *they* would like it if people walked in on *them* in the bath, which the little girls insisted they would—when it struck me forcefully that the new world was better. Already, it was better. I liked it here.

I began to cry at the thought. In my head, I told God it *wasn't* better. Anyway, nobody cared if it was better. I told God I wouldn't want to live in a world without men, even if my own family was somehow spared. It would lack a whole dimension of experience. I told God whatever I thought He needed to hear to make Him bring them back, crying stupidly for Benjamin and Leo and pressing the wet washcloth against my face to try to stop the tears.

By the time I had cried myself out again, the bath foam bubbles were flat. Outside, Holly was talking now to two adult women, laughing pleasantly as if it were a normal day. With their soothing muffled voices in the background, I dried myself and found clothes. I came out barefoot on the warm, dusty tiles to find two middle-aged Black women sitting with Holly at the booth. The three of them were focused on the jigsaw puzzle, leaning forward in a staggered array so all their faces could catch the fan's breeze.

One of the women was majestically fat, the other only plump. The fat woman had a grand crown of chestnut braids and wore a lacy sundress. The plump one had a short cap of grizzled black hair and wore faded scrubs. It was clear they belonged together, however, because they were identical twins.

The sundress twin was eating pizza with a fork and knife. The scrubs twin was focused on the jigsaw puzzle and hadn't looked up. The puzzle was a photo from a national park, and all the pieces were blue and green. They'd finished the waterfall but seemed to be getting nowhere with the foliage.

Holly got up to introduce us. The sundress twin was Maya, and the scrubs twin, Micah. They'd run out of gas here driving south to San Jose, where they both lived. Maya had a daughter there, who'd been staying with her dad while the sisters went camping. The girl was now alone, just ten years old. "So I'm seriously losing my mind about now."

Micah was a nurse. As I sat down, she produced a first aid kit from beneath the table and said, "Let's see." Holly went and brought me a slice of pizza and a can of Tecate. I ate one-handed while Micah tweezed grit from the wounds in my palm and bandaged it. There was an atmosphere of commonsensical nurture, women getting on with the business of life. With my wet hair in the breeze from the fan, it was just cool enough if I didn't move at all.

Meanwhile, they went on talking. At first, it was about the local gas issue. The twins were saying they'd give anything just to be able to fill their tank and asked Holly if there was a plan going forward. Micah said the crisis might end soon, so maybe some supplies could be spared for private use, while Holly took a conservative line. Briefly Micah looked mutinous, then reconsidered and sat back, tired. Maya said she guessed everyone was suffering, and God would have to grant them the serenity.

Then they talked about the world and its chaos: the tankers and container ships adrift in the ocean; the oil refineries that had exploded and burned on unchecked; the horrifying stories of passenger aircraft that couldn't be landed when the pilots vanished, because the planes had reinforced locked doors on their cockpits, and how an Aeromexico flight had taken out a whole residential block in Buenos Aires. I drifted off and thought about how to find Leo and Benjamin. So far, I'd been proceeding on the assumption that the disappearance suggested the existence of God, so the solution must be irrational. One should search even when it made no sense. One should starve and sleep in the mud and pray. But perhaps, even though the problem was supernatural, one should proceed as if it weren't, since God helped those who helped themselves. Perhaps what was needed were the skills of a scientist or a smart politician who would fund research. I was a stay-at-home mother with an English degree whose only skill was ballet dancing. My husband and son would die without help because I was worthless, because I'd wasted my life.

By then, my silence had become a hole in the gathering, a hole that had accumulated mass and began to suck the comfort from the room. I hadn't even helped with the jigsaw puzzle. The women's talk came to a natural pause and all three looked at me.

Holly said, "You're looking better. You've got some color back. You were in a real state when you came in."

"Yes," I said.

Holly looked dissatisfied, so I added, "I was looking for my husband and my son. Up on the mountain. We were up there camping."

"I figured as much," said Holly. "You don't have to talk about it if you don't want."

Micah said, "I wouldn't like to have gone through that in the woods, that's for sure. That's scary."

Maya said, "Bad enough in a car. And we had each other."

Holly said, "We're here for you if you want to talk. You might find it helps. A lot of people here are finding it helps."

There was perhaps an animosity in her manner. I never like people to attend to me closely. Holly was just the kind of person who would entertain suspicions about a stranger, and pursue those suspicions until proved right. My appearance hadn't substantially changed since my crimes were a national news story. I'd told them my name was Natalie, but I couldn't lie about my face.

Then I remembered how, in the corps de ballet, the girls always said the quickest way to make a woman like you was to say your boyfriend was cheating.

I said, "I'd just learned my husband was unfaithful. That's what I'm really struggling with. I saw him with another woman, and I never got to talk to him about it, and now he's gone."

This is the story I told about Leo's infidelity, which I warn you ahead of time is not true.

There was a rising-star biologist at Leo's university whose wife was a voluptuous Greek American woman who cheated on the rising star with all his colleagues and also bullied him, often berating him in their Mini Cooper in the parking lot where anyone could hear her bellicose voice, insistently sexy and throaty from cigarettes, the roar of the sexual lioness. Then the doors would open and they both would come silently out. The wife's name was Cleopatra; the husband's, Micky. That alone gave their relationship a comical aspect. Leo and I liked to gossip about them as a way of confirming we would never cheat. I privately pitied Cleopatra, though. Perhaps she couldn't help cheating. Many people drift into a false position. I envied her too, for her power, for using men and dominating them: a fuck witch. Then at some point we stopped gossiping about them. I told Holly and the twins, "That should have been a red flag."

I then explained that I have an uncanny, one-in-a-million capacity to recognize faces. For instance, if I left the pizzeria that instant and didn't see Holly again for ten years, I would still be able to spot her instantly in a crowd of a thousand people. I could also spot the twins and be able to tell them apart, regardless of weight change, clothes style, aging. Each face is unique in my eyes and I never forget. I can't go on vacation in Paris without recognizing some random American. Sometimes I recognize a person I last saw in my early childhood—a friend of my parents' or a kindergarten teacher—though I have no narrative memories from that period of my life. The people have aged thirty years, of course, so these encounters are depressing, sometimes even macabre.

Because of this freakish ability, I told Holly and the twins, when one night I was driving home on the coastal road and passed a lit-up restaurant at speed, I had no trouble recognizing Cleopatra at a table with my husband, Leo. She was touching his face and crying.

"I didn't want to stop because my son was in the car," I said. "Then I put off mentioning it to my husband because I was so afraid he would lie. It would be so tempting for him to lie. People never believe I can be sure I've recognized someone from a glimpse like that. I'd only met Cleopatra once. But I know. I have this freakish ability."

When I finished, Holly and the twins looked politely skeptical. Of course no one really believes your claims about your freakish abilities. The freakish ability, however, is real. I was not at all embellishing the freakish ability. It was the rest of the story that was fabricated. There was a Cleopatra, but Leo never met her, and she had no connection to his place of work. As far as I know, she never married.

Holly said carefully, kindly, "It might not have been what it seemed like. Even if they were there together, they were only in a restaurant. It could have been innocent."

I said, "No, I'm sure."

"We all know how that is," Micah said. "When you know, you know."

"Still, it's hard to see from a car," said Maya. "Looking into a restaurant? From a car? You're seeing through two different windows. Just thinking about the glare."

"Yes," I patiently said. "It's harder to see from a car. That's true."

"Hey, speaking of cars," said Holly, "if you have your car here, we'd sure appreciate you sharing your gas. We're trying to keep up basic services. We've been providing the ambulances with gas, then there's also what we offer at the pizza place here. But of course we can talk about that later. Just putting it out there. I know you're wiped out."

I instantly felt resistant to surrendering my gas, though I knew I would ultimately give in. An ambulance was an ambulance. I didn't even have anywhere to go. I couldn't very well claim I needed my car when Maya and Micah were right there, and Maya's daughter alone in San Jose. It was at that moment that I cast my eye up and spotted the ComPA flyer.

It was pinned among the HAVE YOU SEEN printouts, seeming absolutely ordinary there. I looked away instinctively, getting chills all over. Still I saw it in my mind's eye: the neat red flowers along its border; the plain font we used to call "Arial-Leninist"; the logo of a crossed knife and fork that was a joke about a hammer and sickle, but no one ever got it without being told. I'd spent so much time designing similar flyers, but I hadn't seen one in years and had no idea they still existed. I'd certainly never expected to see one outside the cafés of liberal college towns.

As my initial shock subsided, it struck me that there was nothing incriminating about my interest in the flyer. It had nothing to do with Alain.

I had let my eye stray back to it, and because Holly was that kind of person, she noticed and guffawed. "Oh, that? Those people came through this morning, and the kids here are totally infatuated. But I think I can take that down now. Maya, can you reach that, sweetie?"

I said, trying to sound nonchalant, "Can I see it?"

Maya took it down and handed it to me. Holly started explaining, saying what people always said about ComPAs: they were crazy, cultlike, fanatical, Stalin killed more people than Hitler, who's going to pay for all that free stuff. "They're taking advantage of the crisis now," said Holly, "acting just like a mafia and taking over neighborhoods because there's a power vacuum. Well, some people fall for that kind of thing."

The ComPA flyer began with the typical rabble-rousing, slightly altered for the new era. It had all the old promises—better this, free that—but also the suggestion that a feminized society would be more equitable and less violent. More surprisingly to me, there was a past-tense section that listed the ComPAs' achievements in the ten days since the disappearance. Working with local authorities, they'd reinstated bus service in Greater Los Angeles, cleared major streets of abandoned cars, restarted the Scattergood Generating Station. Thanks to them, garbage collection in L.A. County was back at 100 percent. Now they'd taken their program to San Francisco and points north. They welcomed all local input.

It included an address for "Northern California Operations" in San Francisco. It was signed: "Founder and National Director, Dr. Evangelyne Moreau."

I got to my feet as if I'd been stung and walked blindly to the open door with the flyer in my hand. I stopped in the doorway, trying to breathe, pretending that Holly and the twins weren't staring. I was eerily calm and exalted: one of the great moments of my life.

Outside, the sun had begun to set. The women in the parking lot talked softly on their blankets, pacified by the growing dark. The lack of cars made the town sound huge and windy and unsettlingly natural. There was that murmur of women like forest noise and the uneasy quietness all around. We were a seed adrift on the ocean. With the power outage, there was a shift in the balance of light to the advantage of the heavens, and it looked as if the still-living sky were drifting away and leaving a black dead Earth behind. I was looking at the sky. It was all so clear.

I had thought every person I loved was gone. But here was Evangelyne, Evangelyne who I believed in above all people, who could find my son if anyone could. And I was frightened but euphoric with the ease of a trajectory. I didn't have to find God or reinvent myself as a scientist or a politician. I only had to get to Evangelyne.

Holly said, "Natalie, honey? Are you okay?"

I turned and saw them again, with a flood of contrition and wistful generosity. Maya and Micah were watching me with faint irony, their tired faces uncannily the same. Holly looked sincerely worried, primed to rush to my side and help. Good people—and the last piece fell into place with one impulse of love.

I said, "I do have gas in my car. But I just keep thinking about Maya's daughter. I was headed to San Francisco myself, so I was thinking, Maya, Micah—do you want a ride home?"

4

Ruth Goldstein spent the night of August 26 walking back and forth between the synagogue and her apartment, hunting for Peter and Ethan. She even looked for Tom, whom she hadn't missed yet, whose disappearance still felt like a theory. It was what you had to do, or you would never forgive yourself, even though Ruth was exhausted to the bone, to the point of pain. It felt like dying from old age.

That night it seemed every woman in New York was on the streets, and Ruth stopped sometimes to join a knot of heated strangers: people saying UFOs had been sighted over Washington, D.C.; people saying a volcano had erupted in Hawai'i that emitted a strange green light; people saying all the men had been abducted by China. Once Ruth was caught up in a rush to the Hudson, where someone thought she'd seen a man swimming, but it turned out to be a drowned woman. Later, Ruth walked up Broadway with a young Pakistani woman who'd been diagnosed with stage 3 ovarian cancer just last week, and now this.

The woman said that in Lahore, where her mother was, thousands of women were praying in the street in rows, while the rain poured down and it was sweltering. "So at least I am spared that." Ruth walked her to Mount Sinai, in front of which a long line of grim-faced women were waiting for admission. It turned out the woman could go straight in. The line was for people who had lost their babies. At the moment of the disappearance, every male fetus had vanished from the womb.

There was no traffic moving, and the altered noise of the city was eerie: countless footsteps and a blur of voices, like being in a colossal amphitheater before a performance. In the first hour, there were occasional explosions as aircraft fell out of the sky. By midnight, that was over, and the streets had turned into a vast impromptu block party: little groups sitting on car hoods drinking wine and playing music through portable speakers; people dancing on abandoned cars or openly sobbing or both at once. One girl sat on a mailbox nursing an infant while shrieking that she wanted to die. In the park by the river, a circle of women were holding hands and singing a hymn, while in the bushes just beside them, others squatted to urinate.

Like everyone, Ruth hugged total strangers and babbled about the event, the disappearance, the catastrophe, the miracle. Like everyone, she ranted that the world was ending, the other shoe was about to drop, but who cared, let it all go, good riddance. Like everyone, she was superstitiously afraid of the sky, of the air, of reality, which might dissolve at any moment. Like everyone, she stared at passersby, inspecting them for signs of masculinity. A scene that later haunted Ruth: a trans man surrounded by an angry mob, his jeans having been pulled down to his knees, his face beaten purple, his beard plastered to his chin with blood. One woman, perhaps his girlfriend, was screaming and trying to pull the others off, while a flurry of hands grabbed at his vulva. Ruth balked just as the man got an arm free and struck out, cuffing an attacker in the head. Just like that, the mob lost its nerve and receded in one motion, like a simple organism deciding something wasn't food. A red-faced woman screamed gloatingly as she stalked away: "I hope you get murdered, you delusional cunt!"

Ruth never thought to intervene. She was paralyzed by the idea that transgender people were still here. Peter was gay—he was bi or gay. He could even be trans, or at least nonbinary—one of those things that kids were now. He'd never said he was, but since when did children tell their mothers everything? No one would ever call Peter masculine. He could still be here.

Even at that moment, Ruth knew there was something wrong with this theory. Nonetheless, a hope took root in her mind that she could never entirely be rid of afterward, even after she knew that whatever it was had removed every human with a Y chromosome, everyone who'd ever been potentially capable of producing sperm.

The last time Ruth arrived at the synagogue, just before dawn, she found it on fire. The facade was stone, so the flames weren't visible, but the door was open and thick black smoke was pouring into the street. A group of Jewish women were standing outside with tears streaming down their faces, their arms around one another, singing the Shema Yisrael. Ruth was so tired it took her a minute to think that someone had already blamed the Jews. Of course! It was the answer to all life's problems! Ruth started laughing, and an old woman standing nearby said, "Laugh. Why not? This is the icing on the cake."

Another old woman said, "Who cares? We had enough God. What God?"

Ruth said, "I'm impressed. A girl firebug."

"You're easily impressed," said the first woman.

Then Ruth's phone rang for the first time that night. She went hot all over. It was Peter. It was Ethan. They hadn't called before because the phones weren't working, but they'd been there all along. They were at home now.

The screen said *Candy*.

As the days passed, Ji-Won never went home. She left her apartment and all her possessions and joined the crew of women who were clearing the roads of abandoned cars so traffic could get through, so goods could be delivered and ambulances could arrive; the women who never went home. She slept in her car. She ate donated meals and took bathroom breaks at the houses of local women who hosted the road crews. The routine work was a solution like a road; it led you forward so things made sense. You didn't have to want to live.

Still Ji-Won made no friends. She was the weird fat girl who couldn't meet your eye, who didn't speak at all or spoke too loud. But she made herself useful, would silently appear to help with any work requiring manual dexterity. She was the one they counted on to siphon gas or swiftly jimmy a car door. For her, it was good to be a mascot figure, a role she'd always been glad to play. It made other people feel powerful. They expanded to fill the space and accepted her while demanding nothing from her. With that and Henry, Ji-Won had always been able to be completely happy.

The day they cleared the road as far as Henry's exit, she left her crew to drive to Henry's apartment. She found his shower left running, the rooms all damp. The water had long ago gone cold, but she stripped and took his freezing shower. She brushed her teeth with his toothbrush and got into his bed—like when they'd lived together here and shared a bed and sometimes showered together, when no one could believe it wasn't sexual, before he lost all the weight and decided their relationship was holding him back.

Then all the world's male humans vanished. This felt related, though it probably wasn't. She lay in the bed but didn't sleep. She'd met Henry for the first time when they were fifteen, when he was on his way to Ji-Won's neighbor's house for a piano lesson. Ji-Won was standing on her front step, hanging a wreath she'd made from green tulle, cedar boughs, and orange roses. Henry stopped dead in the street and scream-gasped. He said, "Oh my god, that's the most gorgeous thing! Where did you get it?" When she said she'd made it, he scream-gasped again and said, "Are you from *heaven*?"

Then the inseparable years, then the day he'd said, "But I'm gay, and our relationship is kind of unhealthy. I mean, I want real love," and Ji-Won didn't understand. She didn't know what else love was.

Now she lay in his bed and whisper-sang "I Will Survive," the song they'd sung to each other on the phone the night she first moved out. Then she got up with her hair still wet. She roamed around the apartment for a half hour, not crying, not knowing what she wanted. At last, she took a carton of Henry's discarded fat clothes, labeled BIG BOY DUDS, put it in her back seat, and drove south. When she hit a jam, she joined the clearance crew there. By the time they'd cleared the road to the Massachusetts border, she was wearing Henry's clothes.

Blanca was picked up from the hospital by her California aunt, Christine. Christine was the aunt who was only twenty-five, the third wife of her uncle Carlos. Blanca's family had never liked Christine, who came to family events in tight T-shirts that showed off her big breasts and once laughingly mentioned that her mother had told her she was brave to marry a Chicano guy because they always cheated. Blanca didn't really know Christine and would have fought going with her if there was anyone left to fight, or if her real aunt, María José, hadn't told the hospital she couldn't take Blanca, or if Blanca didn't have stitches in her heart. If everything was something else.

On the train from Houston to L.A., Christine kept saying that Blanca didn't have to talk if she didn't want, and she totally got it if Blanca was angry because there was a ton to be angry about, and she sure wished Blanca's dad could be here. Meanwhile, town by town, the train filled up. Soon there were women packed together on the floor, sleeping miserably on top of one another and snoring. Blanca kept her seat, still weak, but Christine gave hers up to an old Native lady and chatted cheerfully with the woman, unaware that Blanca was hating her, that Blanca couldn't stand sitting next to strangers, that feeling this angry could *kill* Blanca. Then a white girl across the aisle asked Christine if Blanca was adopted, and instead of telling the girl to fuck off, Christine told Blanca's whole tragic story, while the dumb girl kept saying, "Oh. My. God." After that, all the train women cosseted Blanca, gave her cookies and offered her pillows, and Blanca couldn't help feeling loved and soothed while hating the women and hating herself.

Then in the night, all the women started talking to each other. It began as pure shared grief, everybody crying openly and telling stories about their husband, father, son. Blanca cried too, swept into the grief, and tried to memorize the stories and mentally told her own, although she never actually spoke. A conductor kept pushing through, interrupting to say what was happening with the journey—the train would move again when the driver woke; they were waiting now on a fuel delivery—and the conductor too once paused to talk about her nephew and stood there crying, women reaching up to soothingly touch her arms and offer her tissues on both sides.

But at last one woman said it wasn't all bad. Her violent ex had been stalking her for years, and now, for the first time, she felt safe. Then everyone talked about the men they wouldn't miss: the deadbeat exes, the groping bosses, the abusive stepdads. The conversation drifted to the world outside: the communist loonies taking over California; the mass protests in Brazil and the Philippines against their acting governments; how Kiev was burning to the ground and they only had a single solitary woman firefighter. They talked about the rash of self-immolations—so far, they'd identified forty-seven women who'd set themselves on fire on August 26, and the suicides included the Danish prime minister's niece. Then on through cycles of weeping and laughter; through the churn of passengers getting on and off; through tense hours when the train stopped altogether and the air-conditioning got shut down; through cheerful hours when the train was in motion, chugging past different flavors of desert and fields of seesawing oil pumpjacks and low towns that bristled with fast-food signs. Everywhere the electricity was out, so it looked as if humanity had died overnight, but occasionally there was a woman walking casually on the benighted streets, and once a girl on a scooter, kicking methodically through the starlit dark.

Blanca joined the conversation only once, when the train was stopped in an electrical storm that built and thickened so the stars all vanished and the sky was seamed with continuous lightning. Thunder crashed all around, and the women fell silent. Their faces flashed in the darkness, exalted and afraid. At last someone said, "This can't be connected?" and people laughed nervously here and there. A few said, "No, no, no," in a way that made it clear it had crossed their minds too. Christine said, "Well, who knows? One thing, I totally believe in God after this." Blanca blurted out, "But do you *like* Him?" At this, all the women really laughed, and though Blanca hadn't meant it to be funny, she couldn't help grinning and feeling flattered, feeling like an adult, feeling a surge of love. The world of only women could be okay. Blanca would never stop missing her dad, but maybe she could still be happy here. That was probably what he would have wanted.

But when the train terminated at L.A., all the women just left, already focused on the next thing. No one even said goodbye to Blanca. In a minute that community dissolved into nothing; the people just went and dwindled and vanished into the blinding noonday sun.

After Billy went, Alma drank all night. Undone, unmanned. In the house where it had happened. Dawn caught her flat out on the wet lawn, weeping into that thick grass where he'd been taken. The landline rang in the house then stopped. There was a broken bottle beside her head. At its reek of tequila, she shut her eyes and weakly, undramatically retched. Billy gone.

And she remembered the one time she'd met the doctors whose mansion it was, Arkady and Patrick. She'd been invited with Billy for dinner, and one of the other guests was a pathologist, a tiny Filipina woman who'd arrived preoccupied, red-eyed, demanding a double martini, then told a story about a cadaver that had come in that day with a burst appendix: a homeless man with severe schizophrenia who hadn't understood what the pain was from. He'd been taken to the hospital much too late and died before they could prep him for surgery. When his body came to the pathologist, the first thing she saw was a Band-Aid on his stomach. At this point in the story, the pathologist started to cry. She said, "He was trying to fix it." Then Patrick took her empty martini glass and cocked it, saying, "Another Band-Aid?" Alma resented him for making light of the story, then herself for being an uptight bitch, and only loved Billy, who was crying too and holding the pathologist's hand.

The grass wheeled underneath her, and she wheeled underneath the sky, and there was no one. Somewhere a coyote howled, maybe that same coyote from that night. No sirens now. No cars. No noise, and she was grateful to everyone for keeping their mouths shut, that was really decent, just another way women were better than men, except Billy. If they'd only left Billy. And she argued with Them, told Them all the reasons Billy wasn't who They meant. They could erase her abusive shitfuck dad, erase the two guys who'd raped her behind a liquor store and kicked her in the face and called her a dyke, erase all the scum who beat on women and kids—and who'd also bullied *Billy*. If They had any justice, They should give back Billy. Then the sun was high overhead and she'd slept. She must have struggled in her sleep; her hands were covered in dirt and grass. Her phone pinged in her pocket: *Mami*. She raged and wanted to smash the phone, fucking throw it in the pool, but couldn't. What if Billy. Its battery was low, so she went inside to charge it. Lay dirty on the rug there, sunburned, dizzy. Billy gone.

Another night and day passed. The lights went out. The phone died. Just one more limb cut off. Time blurred until the day she got up dehydrated, stood light-headed at a kitchen counter, turned the faucet, and nothing. No water. She cried out, and the dog came over with an itty-bitty eager scuffle of claws on the tile floor. His cold nose at her hand, seeking. Whiskers stiff against her fingers. Had he had any water that day? But his nose was still wet. She turned off the faucet, turned it on again. Nothing. They would die here together. Die of thirst.

There was a case of Pellegrino right there at her feet, and she laughed so hard when she saw it. Looked out the window where the Olympic-sized swimming pool sparkled in the sun, and laughed.

The dog drank the Pellegrino just fine. This house: she would never live anywhere else.

On day eight, when the lights and water came back, Alma took a shower while her phone recharged. She came out and checked the phone, and her hands were trembling despite herself. Nothing from Billy or Evangelyne or anyone. Just ten identical emails from her mother's email address. She would never know for certain if her mother had sent them or if the email had been hacked. Although she didn't know it yet, her mother was dead.

The email messgess all contained a link to the same website: www.themen82019231.com. The subject line was: *Baby crees que e verdad.*

THE MEN (8/27 5:15:03 GMT)

1. The first clip on the website shows the dusty street of a favela in São Paulo: weather-beaten houses, litter, one edge of a graffitied wall.

There's no sound. It's one continuous shot and the angle never changes. The image is poor and the colors are strange, too bright. Some parts of the screen are obscured by glare. These features will be constant in all the clips.

As this clip begins, men and boys are already flooding from the houses and walking down the street, all heading to the left. Their movements are languid and labored, as if they're walking underwater, but the fluttering of their clothes and hair in the breeze is normal. The men never look at each other and no one speaks. The camera remains trained on the street as they dwindle until the road is empty. Another thirty seconds pass and one last man walks by with a baby in his arms.

2. A man and woman sleep intertwined in a bed flanked by night-stands with matching lamps with conical shades. The furnishings are so generic it's impossible to tell what part of the world they're in. It's possibly a Hilton or a corporate apartment. Again, the colors are off, the darkness an oversaturated mustard yellow with splotches of black.

The couple lie unmoving for a full minute. Then, with no apparent transition, the man gets out of bed and walks out of frame. The woman sleeps on undisturbed.

This clip had a second life as a reaction GIF on social media, used to suggest someone leaving in disgust when a line of stupidity had been crossed. A woman who claimed to be the woman in the clip went through a futile legal process, attempting to stop people from posting it.

3. This clip is an aerial view of a prison with watchtowers and a perimeter fence. As it begins, a seemingly enormous fluttering creature passes the lens. It's all white feathers: a fluffy, festive thing like a quinceañera gown. Closer to the ground, a flock of such creatures flaps past in a little pale stream. In a much slower stream on the ground, a line of men are leaving the prison. They move laboriously as if wading through mud. This clip goes on for several minutes. The camera angle never changes. The men flow from the prison and out of frame.

4. A dozen nude men stand in a field of tall grass. Their mouths move, but each man seems unaware of the presence of the others. On more careful inspection, their mouths aren't making the movements of speech but the jerky, stylized speech motions of Claymation. As in all the clips, there is no sound, so it's unclear if they're vocalizing.

The men stop "speaking" and kneel. On their knees, they are perfectly, unnaturally still.

Another figure enters the shot. Its face appears human, but its body is feline. It's covered in short, pale fur. It walks on all fours queerly, like a human on hands and knees, if such a human were preternaturally graceful. It's roughly the size of a horse. It towers over the men.

In the background, several larger shapes parade along the horizon: blurred, lumbering figures seemingly too large to be any earthly creature. A lilting, sinuous movement suggests an elephant's trunk; perhaps they are elephants. Their exaggerated gigantism could be an optical illusion or an artifact of the film equipment being used.

This clip is followed by credits. These consist of a simple list of names in three alphabets. The names are in no apparent order: 802 male names.

5

The drive was uneventful. We three talked. It has always astonished me how women talk. Men talk, but women talk as if engaged in research, talk in no direction, pondering, investigating, acting out scenes, asking open-ended questions, spinning a life like a spiderweb and dancing upon that woven life.

I'd had no friends for many years. There was Leo, then the wild, undifferentiated world. It took me time to speak. But a thick rain began after Redding, and we were snug in the car, my same safe car from times before. They told me about their week with Holly. They talked about the men and boys they'd lost. They talked about grief, and how losing their mom to a heart attack was like this but different. They said maybe God did this to teach us, and maybe it wasn't right or wrong but a thing like an earthquake, a thing God saw very differently in His front-row seat in eternity. They talked about recovery from loss, how Maya was good at it, but Micah wasn't.

Here I opened up and talked about an old Chinese novel I'd once read, in which the daughter of a family becomes a concubine of the Chinese emperor. For years, her family is no longer allowed to see her because her status is too exalted, but at last the emperor graciously allows his concubines to go home for a family visit, but only if the family builds a suitable palace. So the girl's family builds a palace with courtyard gardens and grand pavilions, and composes couplets to engrave on the doors, and imports a troupe of actresses to perform in the theater of the palace, and builds a monastery, which they fill with twenty Buddhist nuns and twenty Taoist nuns. At last, all is ready, and the daughter arrives with countless imperial eunuchs preceding her in formation to carry her court costumes, and the concubine herself is borne by eunuchs on a silk-upholstered sedan chair. She climbs out in the palace's central courtyard and bursts into tears and says, "We must be happy now. Who knows when I will be allowed to see you again?" And I said I wished I could build a palace for every person I'd lost—for every person Maya and Micah had lost—even if they could only weep with us for an hour because we might never meet again.

Saying this, I was building a palace of a kind, or making a palace of the rain-bound car to weep in with Micah and Maya. And they cried with me as we imagined all the palaces women would build on this orphaned world. Meanwhile, the sun set. The land dimmed, became secretive. The mountains had given way to a dark, vast plain, a quietness in which our voices lived. Sometimes headlights or tail-lights swam past in the rain, very few and dazzling, like tropical fish. They trailed reflections as our voices boomed, became music, were a color in the dark.

I didn't tell them my story, the story of Alain. Still I'll put it here, since it felt so present to me in that raining night. It's the story I might have told if I were innocent, if I hadn't told them my name was Natalie, if I hadn't spent my whole life lying and avoiding the consequences of my crimes.

The story begins very tragically, with my mother's death from cancer, a terrible death where she was angry all the time from the pain and fear, from being surgically mutilated, trapped in a hospital, facing her own extinction, and she took it out on me and my father. If we told her we loved her, she said, "And what good does that do me?" If we brought food, she said we should have known she was always nauseous. If we asked if she wanted anything else, she said, "Yes. Not to die." If we talked about our lives, she cried and called us selfish, because all that was lost to her. She also bitterly complained that we never said we loved her, never brought her anything or asked what she wanted, never told her about our lives. The cancer had metastasized to her brain, so there was no one to blame. I was a kid, and it was maybe reprehensible that my father took me to see her at all. But it was that or I didn't see my dying mother.

When she first got sick, I was eleven and had just gotten serious about ballet. When she was dying, I was often absent, at classes or rehearsals or performances. My father wanted us to cope by going to church, where I offended him by surreptitiously watching ballet on my phone. Once my mother died, I almost never went home. That's where Alain begins.

As everyone knew at one time, but has now mercifully forgotten, Alain Cornyn was the founder and director of the Baltimore

Youth Ballet. BYB was created to allow young dancers, ages fourteen to eighteen, to dance professionally and get exposure, experience, and a paycheck early in their careers. All the principal roles were danced by teens. There were tutors for all school subjects, and I know there must have been classes sometimes, but I have no conscious memory of them. Alain was from a very rich family, and the company was funded by their wealthy friends. It was prehistoric white Baltimore money, some of which derived from the transatlantic slave trade. Alain liked to confess this, making much of the Arab side of his heritage and talking about black sheep. BYB championed diversity, of course, and had a program that recruited disadvantaged kids from countries like Brazil and Kenya. Many people in the dance world hated Alain, but at the time, he was untouchable: a hero of the arts.

When I joined, BYB still had a full-time manager, Cleopatra Daniels, a voluptuous Greek American woman who was clearly sexually involved with Alain and bullied him in front of everyone, often berating him in her Mini Cooper in the parking lot where anyone could hear her bellicose voice, insistently sexy and throaty from cigarettes, the roar of the sexual lioness. Then the doors would open, and they both would come silently out. They had an open relationship. So said gossip. She'd once been a principal dancer but had had a spinal injury and now walked with a cane.

While Cleopatra was there, Alain was always tête-à-tête with her. On his few forays among us, he would announce that he'd escaped her clutches. He wouldn't stay long and would receive a continuous stream of texts from her, texts that made him look flustered and exposed. Then one day Cleopatra was gone. That barrier was lifted, and everything changed.

Before I go on, I want to remind you this is a ballet story; it lives in the flight and the adrenaline, that cross between a Disneyland ride and a superpower, all wrapped up in a princess fantasy: a very young girl's idea of sex. It's also a lot of sweat, pain, boredom, and long bus trips to cheap hotels—but the soaring was always about to happen. We were the children of the air. There was no one like Alain for evoking that fairyland, for weaving its highs into everyday life, so our gossip felt like court intrigue, and a drive to the hardware store at night was black tulle on an enchanted lake. He was also that thrilling adult who invited teenagers back to his house, a house that had real art, real antique rugs, a real library with leather-bound books; who let us have one champagne cocktail and drove us home at two A.M. Who made that feel like love. When any of us had an injury, Alain dispensed painkillers from his stash, while telling cautionary tales about ODs, and how once in Thailand he and Cleopatra got addicted to a certain white pill they bought from a dealer who went by "Mickey Mouse," who spoke no English but "Hey" and "Mickey Mouse," and they never did find out what the pill was.

Alain was handsome but a little peculiar-looking. His heritage, he said, was "Mayflower-Algerian": sharp Scottish features and green eyes with olive skin and black hair. He'd once been cast in a movie as an elf, but was fired by the director because he made the other elves look too human. Or that's the story he told; that might be one of the ones that wasn't true. He was small. At six feet, I was much taller than he was, and almost all the boys were too. He liked to call himself "the detestable little monkey," a thing he was called once in a review. In his youth, he'd "whored around," he said, with both men and women, had been the toy of a count and a celebrity chef and a South American dictator's daughter. These friends had given him a Patek Philippe wristwatch and a motorbike and various items of emerald jewelry to match his grass-green eyes. These tokens he called "hunting trophies." The jewelry was now in a safe-deposit box because he didn't want to pay to have it insured. Naturally intimate with everyone, on tour he was in and out of hotel rooms, barefoot in the corridors, eating french fries off our room-service trays, bearing tales, playing favorites. He'd briefly been a dancer himself and was dexterous, graceful, and surprisingly strong. He could do any physical thing, like a musician who can pick up any instrument and play. He was also highly cultured in the casual way of the rich. He was always making us watch Russian films, explaining the symbolism of cathedrals, expressing his contempt for some overrated artist none of us had heard of. Once he gave Beckett's *The Unnamable* to a sixteen-year-old dance jock, and the poor kid read it from cover to cover, comprehending nothing, for love of Alain. Everyone was in love with Alain. Alain didn't like to work with dancers who didn't seem infatuated at the first interview. He said art was a child of love. He himself was asexual, he liked to say, with one hand on a fourteen-year-old's nape, the fourteen-year-old lit up like a jack-o'-lantern, ready and not ready. We all dreamed of seducing him. One night, a group of us discussed what we'd be willing to do if Alain would be our boyfriend, vying to best each other with the sacrifices we were willing to make: *Would you give up dancing? Would you be in a wheelchair? What if he never even fucked you? What if he fucked you, but then you had to die in ten years? Five years?*

He would say, "If God had wanted us to be good, He wouldn't have made us beautiful." He would say, "If I'm a monster or a genius, if I'm anything, it's because I'm lonely." When someone asked what he did in the company, he said, "I am the atmosphere. I am the air."

Once Cleopatra Daniels was gone, he singled me out very quickly. One of the first things he told me was that Cleopatra wasn't her real name. It was the name of Alain's very first assistant, from twelve years before, but he could never be reconciled to any assistant who did not have that lovely name. An assistant was a boring pest; a Cleopatra was an intoxicant, a helpmeet, a captive child of faerie. The name transcended personality. An assistant inhabited the name, just as a dancer danced Giselle.

I said, "Could I be a Cleopatra?"

At that time, Cleopatra Daniels was twenty-one years old. I was fifteen.

It was *Nutcracker* season, just before Christmas. We'd chartered a bus for a tour of four cities in the Northwest, and we were scheduled to perform in Bozeman, Montana, on my sixteenth birthday. I was already booking our travel then, and Alain told me to book myself a separate room as a birthday present. My family was careful with money, especially since my mother's illness, and the prices of hotels frightened me, so I chose the cheapest place I could find, a dive called the Jokers Wild Hotel and Casino. The casino part consisted of a basement room filled with broken slot machines. The floors were concrete, and a deadly chill penetrated the thin brown carpet. There was truck parking out back, and eighteen-wheelers pulled in and out all night, groaning deafeningly, shaking the walls. This time, unlike any subsequent time, Alain laughed indulgently about my mistake.

I don't remember that night's performance, but I remember how it always was: the dusty vastness of small-town auditoriums; the outer-space feeling of winter parking lots whose silence is broken by a slamming car door; us play-fighting as we walked to the bus, a girl happily trapped across a boy's shoulders, shrieking as he lazily spun around. We were too young to do much in those towns. We would walk to a supermarket and spend an hour there wandering as if it were a mall. Sometimes we went to a restaurant and only ordered dessert. There were occasional drunken escapades when someone had a fake ID, which typically ended with clandestine puking and whispered terrors of being fired from the company. And of course there were the red-hot crushes and spats, the incestuous tribal emotional life, all magnified by an athlete's body chemistry, so it felt hypersignificant, sublime, immense, like the final events in the world. We were all so beautiful in those towns. We were the flowers of the dumb gray world.

Dancers, like waiters, keep late hours. We got back from the theater after eleven, and then the night began. That night of my sixteenth birthday, everybody came back to my private room, all the dancers and some locals, including a local boy Alain had met at intermission. We had a supermarket cake with candles I blew out, but the party never gelled. The bathroom door in my room wouldn't close all the way, so people had to pee with the door a little open, the urine stream audible. If someone farted, the conversation in the other room paused. We laughed about this, but it made the atmosphere stiff. The company dwindled rapidly, until there was only Alain, the local boy, and me.

Now Alain brought out wine, two bottles. We drank from the bottle, the boy and I laughing, young enough to be conscious of what our parents would say if they knew. They didn't know, and that felt like nothing else. Alain had brought a portable speaker and was playing raga music and telling stories about his time in Mumbai while we drank the second bottle. The boy fell silent, staring at my breasts. I kept thinking Alain might kiss me if we could just get rid of the boy, a thing I'd been fantasizing about since he first called me Cleopatra. Then Alain told me I needed a shower. He used the word "stinking"—not as harsh as it sounds; all dancers sweat buckets every day and it stinks. For me, there was a flattering intimacy in the word. It was the boy who blushed.

Showering, I was aware of the translucent shower curtain and the unclosing door, of what someone would see if they came in. I knew they wouldn't come in. I was aroused nonetheless. The music came to an end and wasn't replaced. The silence in the other room grew. I came out at last in a bathrobe to find Alain and the boy playing cards on the floor and smoking weed. They'd both taken off their shirts. It wasn't that, but the silence.

They looked up. Alain said, "Sean has something he wants to ask you."

The boy was like the later boys: smooth-faced, with the clean, natural muscles of youth, very beautiful and very heterosexual. For him, I was an unexpected way to get laid, and at that age I was attractive in an obvious way: blond, with long, smooth legs; breasts large for a dancer; all brand new. Alain behaved, winkingly, as if the boy were a last-minute birthday present and I part of his louche world of emeralds and dictators' daughters, where a casual fuck was nothing, a penny. I did want sex. I thought about it all the time. There was no clear decision and I'd said yes. I was mainly afraid they would see how inexperienced I was, that I'd never done more than kissing.

Once it began, the feelings were too big to identify. We grappled clumsily and our teeth kept knocking together, but when the boy touched my nipple, it dizzied me. The bottom fell out of the night; I was kissing the boy and self-consciously moaning, worried this wasn't how adults moaned. I felt the boy's erection against me, and it was amazing proof such things did exist; they weren't just a dirty kind of science fiction. I let him pull off my bathrobe and was proud that it was easy for me, that I wasn't ashamed of my strong body. Still, when he parted my legs, I instinctively resisted. Then, when I gave way, I felt my cunt as a blazing light. He angled his cock against me clumsily, and at first there didn't seem to be an opening. I was a freak, my hole too small. Then he'd found it and forced his way inside, and the pain was too much. I was going to die. Scattered all around us on the bed were red paper plates with chocolate crumbs and smears of pale blue frosting, pastel candles piled dirtily on one plate. The plates all trembled with the motion. This was the last place I would ever see.

Almost instantly, the boy stiffened and shuddered. He pulled out, and I was left disgustingly wet, ashamed, my body full of strange lights and grief. I hadn't died, and when I put my hand to my crotch, there was only a slight trace of blood among the semen. I could do it. I could make a man come. I was safe now. Still, a terrible fear was loose in me. More than anything, I needed the boy to leave.

Alain smoked a cigarette. He watched us frankly. I was only aware much later that he'd planned it for the night I was first legal.

Alain was a voyeur. He didn't like being touched. Despite all that's been said, I never saw him do anything sexual to a boy. None of the boys ever saw him naked. The fucking was all me, a fact that would later make him difficult to prosecute.

He also prompted me to find the boys. Sometimes he made an introduction, but sometimes he just talked insinuatingly about being bored and said, "But I know I can count on *you*." After a while, I became a professional. I giggled and flattered and touched boys' chests; it was easy when it wasn't my idea. Once a boy was alone with us, however, I fell into a wordless state where I couldn't do anything without direction. The boys too were crippled with embarrassment, and it's still remarkable to me how subtly Alain could manage us. A hint dropped here, an assumption made there, almost always achieved his desired result.

He made me part of his game of "corrupting youth" and openly talked about preferring young boys. I played along; I would huddle with him in corridors and laugh about our "Ganymedes." He led me to agree there was just no challenge in fucking an eighteen-year-old "man" and taught me to see sex with a fourteen-year-old as a hilarious gotcha to the uptight world. He talked about "raiding the international program," saying American dancers all lived in the pockets of "Mommy and Daddy," while the age of consent in most countries was fourteen and no one batted an eyelid. Still, I noticed that, after I'd fucked an international boy, Alain always found some reason to fire him and send him back to his home country.

If I failed to attract a boy Alain wanted, he was furious and wouldn't speak to me for days. I cried and believed he didn't love me anymore. I believed no one would ever love me and thought about jumping under a train. Then the change would come: Alain's conspiratorial smile across the studio, him calling me to sit beside him in a café, his eloquent touch on my shoulder in passing. I would light up to my fingertips, restored from death to life.

Although he didn't have sex with other people, Alain was not asexual. After each boy left, he liked me to stay in the room while he masturbated. He didn't mind if I looked at a magazine, but if I tried to leave, he became enraged. One time he told me not to "fuck him around." To me, those masturbation scenes more than anything had the power of nightmare. I remember them as if I were screaming and trying to escape. Nonetheless I used to fantasize about them when I masturbated myself. I also used to fantasize about two teens performing sexually for an older man. Once, just once, Alain stroked my vulva, encouraging a shy boy to follow suit, and I was disgusted, prudishly shocked, and hated myself for having a cunt, this gross thing that made gross things happen—but I also came. It's possible this has no meaning. It may just be a twitching of nerves and firing of synapses in response to stimuli. But it's one of the reasons I will never be whole, I can never feel good. It's why I need sex too much, though it can make me feel terrified, ashamed, disembodied, so it's like being beaten even as I come. I will never know what sex is like for other people.

At the same time, there's so much I can't remember that I don't really know what it was like. I remember one boy's strange name, Sylvanus, but I can't remember which one he was. There was a boy who cried afterwards; the reasons are gone. I remember the Brazilian international student very well and how, when we danced together, he hummed the music to himself with a dopey, faraway expression. I remember he was the youngest boy I fucked, thirteen and eleven months, and Alain congratulated me for breaking the "fourteen barrier," and I remember bruising my knuckles by punching a door when he was sent home. I don't remember fucking him. I remember flashes of obscenity accompanied by emotions I had much later, like narration dubbed in. I remember all the boys' faces. Of course, when I fucked them, we were about the same age. Now they all look like children.

I was never entirely docile, and Alain and I had ugly fights. Once I refused to fuck a boy, and when Alain pressed the issue, I called him a pimp and he slapped my face and I slapped him back. When I found out Alain had fired the Brazilian boy, we had a fight that stretched over three days. I shrieked in rage and didn't care who heard. I berated him in his BMW in the parking lot where anyone could hear my hysterical voice, made hoarse from too much screaming. I found out one day he'd told the new kids I was twenty-five, and they thought it was "weird and unfair" that I was still getting cast when it was meant to be a youth company. That was another three-day fight. Once I called him a child molester, needing him to deny it, but he saw through this and taunted me by saying he'd always been a pedophile, the younger the better. I jumped out of his car at a red light and pounded on the hood, screaming the word, until he drove away.

I still don't know what people knew. I do know the dance mistress hated me and warned the younger children to avoid me, which made me cool and forbidden and probably made recruiting boys easier. Dancing with them not so much. I did always have friends among the dancers, though I couldn't tell them anything important. At the end of the day, the only person I could talk to was Alain. Alain and I had habits together, inside jokes, favorite songs we sang in the car. We talked for hours every day, and we did discuss very seriously whether we were harming people. We argued about it, and he listened to me, although I couldn't change his mind. I dictated rules to him, which he then broke, and we discussed what made him do that. There was also a night I realized I'd never be a real professional dancer, with the undeniable truth of intuition, and Alain spent hours calming me down. He stroked my head while I wept. He said being too tall wasn't such a blight and people could choreograph around it. He said the technique would come. He said that, even if I was right, he'd gone through the same, and look at him now. When I sobbed, "Then I should kill myself," he graciously laughed and said, "Oh, you'd never really be like me." So I want you to know I loved this person. Looking back, no part of it feels right, but at the time I was inside of it and it was my life.

And I was still a part of the company, the spats and crushes, the tribal life. Alain could still come among us and be a beloved pied piper figure, and in that role, he was innocent and loved us; we were all one flesh. Even now I can conjure a night in Vermont, where it was lightly snowing, and we all walked from our hotel across an empty highway to a supermarket lit up like Christmas. Ours were the only footprints in the frail tissue of snow on the road, and Araceli and Justin walked in my footprints to "throw off the cops" about how many we were; we played make-believe about the crime we'd gotten away with, the murder of a local girl who'd come up after our performance to say, "I didn't know anyone still did ballet." We all shouted, "Dancers will kick your ass!" running and skidding on the icy road. In the supermarket, I bought beef jerky and a paperback mystery to read in the hotel, and on the way back, Alain was walking ahead, on his phone, berating the local contact person, one hand gesticulating all around him, and we started imitating him behind his back. When he wheeled around, suspicious, we all stopped at once, then burst out laughing. Alain made a finger gun and shot at one girl, who pretended to die in the street, falling prettily into the frail snow. It was in some ways the happiest time of my life, when I didn't know right from wrong. Although I did know right from wrong.

And maybe they all knew what was going on, at least knew something. Once Alain took some of us along to his mother's house, and while she was in the bathroom, he told us his Algerian grandfather had been a storyteller in the souk. Just then his mother came back and said, laughing too nervously, "Don't be silly, Alain, he was a judge." Alain said airily, "A man can wear two hats." After that, whenever we suspected him of lying, we kids would say, "Two hats," and he would say, "Oh, babies, you know me too well," and we laughed daringly, adoringly, knowingly. That was the complicity he wove all around him, the way we enjoyed being in on his lies, how his loving mother was jittery and knew it was wrong—but said nothing. Did nothing. And I did nothing. And a year of those boys did nothing. And the boys of all the other Cleopatras did nothing. Some adults spoke to Alain with a visible reserve and sneaked glances at me as if I were a taboo object, a vibrator left on a dinner table. They smiled the whole time Alain was talking, a prurient smile of discomfiture, but said nothing, did nothing. And even when someone did something, it was nothing. One boy asked Alain, "But she agrees? This isn't something you make her do?" and Alain laughed at the idea, but you could tell the boy did not believe, and then it felt very different fucking him. An ethical drama was unfolding in the boy because he thought he was using Alain's slave. He couldn't come and at last announced he needed a Coke from the vending machine. I went with him to show him where it was, and we stopped in the hotel corridor by the glassed-in swimming pool, where a family with young children were splashing and laughing. The colors in the pool behind the glass were very bright—the red and yellow of the little kids' swimsuits and the turquoise water—while the hall where the boy and I stood was a colorless place like a bleached coral reef. The boy said, "You don't have to stay with that man. You're a ballerina. You're really talented. You could do anything with your life." He said I could stay with him and his mom if I didn't have anywhere to go. "Doing that stuff is different for a guy." I started crying and stood there with tears running down my face, hating him. Then we went back and he fucked me until he finished. That was how things worked in that time.

That year was so long, it was a life within a life. It had a death.

We were back in Baltimore for July and August. My father had flown in to see me dance in a recital for parents and donors. I'd had to walk to his hotel in ninety-degree weather, and when he hugged me hello, the stickiness of my skin and the pressure of my sweaty breasts on his chest felt sexual. I was repelled and frightened. I excused myself and went to the ladies' room to cry. When I came out, I saw him standing with his back to me, a dejected and ordinary figure, but his heavy male body looked obscene. I began to shiver in the air-conditioning. I slipped past him and went outside, where I hid out of sight of the windows and lit a cigarette. People passed; when they came near, I started shivering again and was filled with hatred for those people. By the time I got back to my father, he'd been waiting ten minutes and was suspicious and hostile. Then, at lunch, he said he'd been lonely at home, and for a moment I heard it as a sexual reproach and thought he was suggesting I fuck him.

Before the performance, I told Alain about these feelings. He reacted as if I'd brought him a gift and said, "I felt that from him too." I performed with that in my head and fell onstage. I felt my father see it.

A board member brought her nine-year-old son to this performance, and after the show, they both came backstage. The child still had that platinum baby hair, and he'd spent the whole summer swimming in a pool, so the chemicals had tinted his hair pale green. Alain was in raptures over this child, announcing repeatedly that he was hilarious. He kept addressing everything he said to the boy, who chattered importantly and glowed when Alain laughed uproariously at his jokes. At last Alain said he wanted a photograph and got the boy to sit in my lap. He directed us, getting me to put my hand on the boy in various places. All around us were parents and donors drinking wine from plastic cups and laughing. My father was trying to get my attention to leave. At last, the boy detached himself and ran away with the abruptness of a much younger child. Then his mother apologized to Alain, looking flushed and somehow dishonest. In the taxi back to my dorm, this scene kept repeating in my head: the child resisting and detaching himself; my father impatient in my peripheral vision; the mother apologizing with her false smile.

I woke the next morning and still knew nothing. I shared a dorm room then with a girl named Meghan. Our joke was that we always made each other late, and that day too we came to class late. Instead of finding the other kids warming up at the barre, we found them sitting on the studio floor with an unknown white woman talking to them. I remember the shock of the unfamiliar tableau and how the kids swiveled their heads to watch me come in. I stopped in my tracks while Meghan moved on hurriedly, going to sit with the others. Alain wasn't there, and I gradually realized the woman was telling us why he would not be coming back. She used the phrase "misconduct with students." I don't know how long I stood and listened. I remember the woman was wearing pink espadrilles and a chic dress with cheerful red zigzags, and that it seemed undignified in that context. I remember her naming Alyssa Daniels as the person who first alerted the board and how I realized this was the previous Cleopatra. By the time I left I was breathing strangely, trying to expel all the air from my lungs, as would become my lifelong habit when I was very upset.

In the parking lot a man and woman in business suits were waiting for me. They'd either just arrived, or Meghan and I hadn't noticed them on our way in. The woman threw down her cigarette and they both walked to meet me. I was slightly taller than them both and still young enough that that made me anxious. I kept trying to stoop. My first guess was that they were child psychiatrists; I'd had some experience with child psychiatrists after my mother's death. Only when I heard the word "police" did I realize what I'd done, that I was no longer a child who would be helped.

There in the parking lot, they explained Romeo and Juliet laws to me—those laws that mean sex with a minor isn't a crime if there's only a few years' difference in age. Then they named three states that didn't have such laws for victims under fifteen, three states where I'd committed felony rape, including Maryland. Then they read me my rights.

I sobbed wildly as I was being cuffed. In the midst of this, the other dancers came out and, as they passed by us, fell silent. No one met my eye or looked concerned. For me, having friends was over. Some laughed, and I remember it as gloating and malicious, but probably they were just afraid—just children.

The two cops put me in a car and drove me to the station. Only there, in an interview room, did they inform me I might avoid prison time if I helped them convict Alain.

Maya and Micah and I took turns driving all night. It was one of the purest nights of my life, when I talked and listened and nothing happened. I didn't mention Alain. I was Natalie. I talked about my husband and son and wept. Micah talked about her sons. Maya talked about her husband. Dawn came and there were hours when the sun was rising in the middle of nowhere, green exit signs silhouetted against its glare: UKIAH, SANTA ROSA, SACRAMENTO. Everywhere a taste of dust, a brown and indistinct air that came from farms drying up and blowing away, their irrigation systems stilled by power cuts.

Shortly after dawn, we arrived in San Francisco. I told Micah and Maya to go on to San Jose. I gave them my address and said to get the car back to me whenever. It wouldn't be very much use without gas. I'd initially thought of bringing them with me into the ComPA office, thinking their presence might speak for me; they were a good deed I'd just done. But for my plan to work, I had to announce who I was, and I didn't want to see the twins' reaction when they heard the name Jane Pearson. So they got into my car and drove away, waving. I never saw them or the car again.

The ComPA offices were in a mixed-use building. The electricity seemed to be out, and the sliding doors were lodged in the open position. Passing through the empty space, I remembered walking through the broken glass door of the Albertsons supermarket and again felt as if I were stepping through a mirror. I paused there to find my wallet and take out my old ComPA card. The clothes in my backpack stank of old sweat, but I knew these details made no difference. I might be accepted or rejected, but it wouldn't depend on how I smelled. Some parts of the directory in the foyer were already taped over with new names: HOUSING COMMITTEE. PLANNING COMMITTEE. EDUCATION GROUP. At the doorman's desk were two women in red shirts embroidered with black Commensalist Party of America symbols. The red shirts were new, but I knew the symbols—the open hand that meant security committee, the fork and knife that meant officer grade. The ComPAs had devised these symbols out of concern that some members might be illiterate, although in my time we were all college students.

I also recognized the woman with the knife-and-fork insignia, a Chinese woman with alopecia. Her scalp showed through in streaks that made her hair look crudely sketched in. I'd met her years ago at a new members picnic where she was the only new member. She had the beautiful name Luli. At the time Luli had just gotten a tattoo on her calf of a naked woman riding a broomstick, which had sparked a long discussion of why the tattoo was empowering, not problematic. I'd then excited universal hostility by asking how much the tattoo cost. I'd intended to be class-conscious; instead I was a white girl insinuating there was something fishy about a woman of color being able to afford a tattoo. She was also going bald while I had thick blond hair, so the optics could not have been worse. On the other hand, she turned out to be an electronics heiress, so I wasn't all wrong.

The next time I saw Luli, at an anti-eviction rally, she didn't appear to remember me. Evangelyne wanted to introduce us—she was grooming Luli as a donor—but I claimed to be having a PTSD day.

Now again Luli didn't recognize me—unsurprising after seven years, but enduringly strange to me, who has never not recognized a person. The other ComPA was someone I'd never seen before, a white girl with a buzz cut. Her hair and shirt were wet—it must have been raining before I arrived—and I automatically assumed she'd been out running errands for the electronics heiress. Of course this was malicious supposition, but again it turned out I was not wrong.

I walked toward them in what I imagined was a forthright proletarian manner and smiled at Luli deferentially. I took a risk by addressing her as "compañera," and it seemed to still be correct; she smiled. But when I asked to see Evangelyne, her smile went away. The buzz cut scoffed. I had just walked in off the street and demanded to see the chairman of the national party.

"Evangelyne isn't here now," Luli said. "Perhaps one of us can help you."

I presented my ComPA card by way of answer. It was a photo ID like a driver's license. On the back it listed the committees I was on and the trainings I'd completed. I'd once had several of these cards because I was the one who made them up. I liked to work the laminator. I still kept two in my wallet; they made me feel I had had a rich life.

This was my first-ever card, on which my membership number was 005. I put it down with a flourish, like a lucky gambler turning over an ace, and said, "I helped Evangelyne with the first chapter, back in the day. We're old friends."

We all three looked at the photograph, a baby-faced me with bleached platinum hair and Goth makeup, self-consciously raising my chin for the camera. Then the two ComPAs read the name.

"Oh shit," said Luli. "You're Jane Pearson."

The buzz cut hastily said, "I could take you to Evangelyne."

"No, I'll take her," said Luli. "My god. Evangelyne will lose her shit. My god."

"Could we both go?" the buzz cut said.

Luli made a "no" gesture with her hand, smiling at me with a glazed expression, a celebrity expression.

"Thank you," I said. "I'd be eternally grateful."

6

the_men_fan2
I love it but its so fake tho. There like Muppets. Its Actors in cgi suits. Or Actresses even, which makes the most sense.

QueenLeesa83
My sons are with God, not in some exploitive tv show. Whoever made this crap is sick.

Jilly_Sarsparilly
1. how could they make it with actors? use your head. they had to know before the men left and make this whole freaking film with thousands of people. 2. and it can't be women because how do they make the naked ones?

boobydabad
With deepfake now you could make that whole thing and have it all be naked Nic Cages lmao

BBandthebean

WHAT ARE THOSE ANIMALS THO? And the flying things. If that's all a fake? Like it's a freaking entertainment product? WTF?

boobydabad

crazy right? It's like the moon landings

BarbIsCancerFree

I think it's real. With all due respect to skeptics, it's just too complex to be fake. I know it's difficult to accept because it means we live in a very strange cosmos, but if that's the only reason you doubt, ask yourself, how is that more unbelievable than the very fact the men disappeared?

PippiIsTripping

I dont believe any of you realy watched the footage, realy watched it. Those are *women*. It's just pads and binding and fake bears. My sister does costumes at a theater and they make stuff like htat all the time. Look at their "naked" skin in this thing and you can tell its fabric or plastic.

boobydabad

It's fake bears folks

PippiIsTripping

Fake BEARDS. I'm talking about the "Men's" beards. It's a typo for Christ sake!!

Jilly_Sarsparilly

fabric and plastic don't even look alike pippi

crayon4Killa

i saw my dad. i know it's him. he's even wearing the same clothes.

What The Men meant to Alma at first was her sobriety. She watched and fell asleep with the phone in her hand, and when she woke, she had the power to empty all the bottles down the sink because she could watch. After that, she watched all day, every day. She showered with the curtain half open and Patrick's laptop up on the sink where she could watch. She rationed the food in the kitchen, putting off the day she would have to stop watching to go to a grocery store. To save time on laundry, she wore the doctors' clothes. She listened to the news on the radio while watching. She was watching while her mother was buried without her—of course planes were grounded and gas stations closed, so it was hard to say how she could have gotten to Duluth—but she didn't even try. She watched The Men. She called Evangelyne while watching and never got an answer but left voicemails in which she tried to sound mentally stable and cool, never mentioning The Men, never mentioning her mother. She never called work to find out if her job still existed. She never went home.

The footage was all alike: men marching or standing in groups, mouths opening and closing in unison. When they walked, their feet moved with an odd chugging motion and landed wrong, so it looked as if they should just fall over. Weird animals appeared: enormous panthers, pumpkin-headed elephants, beakless birds with human torsos. After every fourth clip, there were credits, a list of names in various alphabets, several of them new to Alma. The men were infinitely varied but their movements all the same. Once in a while, a trans woman appeared among them, and Alma was always outraged. Here was a person unjustly condemned, was the feeling. She would think of her old coworker Toya, who'd gone out drinking with her once, and Alma ended up puking in Toya's car, but Toya just stroked her back and said, "Don't worry! I throw up in this car all the time!" Then there were Pia and Haley, the girls Alma had lived with on the beach her first summer in L.A., when they were teen runaways together. They'd guarded each other's stuff, shared food, sat around a little campfire and told each other they were the hottest, the prettiest, the bravest. Now this: those trans girls gone like men. Just another way God fucked you.

She also spent a lot of time googling, trying to find out what The Men was. Right away there were people freaking out on Facebook and a rapidly evolving Wikipedia page. There was a YouTube channel where someone was archiving all the old Men clips. A fan site called FindThem.com began as a searchable list of all the names in The Men's credits, but grew to include a classified section with ads for meet-ups, watch groups, house shares. Alma also found a Reddit thread where a woman said she'd notified the FBI, but the FBI claimed it couldn't find The Men's makers and then abruptly stopped responding. Other people in the thread had tried approaching other agencies, from the FCC to NASA. The only response they got was that The Men seemed like a very cynical hoax, but it was covered by the First Amendment as long as it didn't solicit money by fraud.

Alma herself didn't always think The Men was real. There were times she was sure it was all CGI, and everybody watching was a giant idiot. Still, she couldn't stop watching. She couldn't stop imagining she would spot some clue everybody else had missed. She couldn't stop thinking she would see Billy. In her fantasies, she'd see him in a favorite haunt that only she would recognize, and then she would drive there at top speed and find him and save him, crisis over. Dumbest of all was her irrational certainty that if she gave up watching, he would come to grief, that only then would he be lost.

In early October, she finished the last food in the house, a potato she smothered in ketchup for the vitamin C. Her car had been running on empty even before the gas stations closed, so she rode one of the doctors' bikes to the supermarket, wearing a massive framed backpack she had found in a hallway closet. After days of watching The Men, the world outside felt absurdly spacious and green. It was dizzying to be riding with the wind in her hair down an eerily quiet Santa Monica Boulevard, with the lines of palm trees tall overhead; Alma was from Minnesota and had never stopped finding them glamorous. Some apartment windows had signs: NEVER FORGET, 3.9 BILLION, THANK YOU EMERGENCY WORKERS! A few parked cars had been turned into shrines for people who'd presumably disappeared there and were covered with dusty candles, wilted flowers, paper hearts with photographs stapled in the center.

Still The Men kept niggling in the back of her mind. Every minute she wanted to stop and watch. What if she was missing Billy? But of course she could check the lists on FindThem. She could find the archived clips. The feeling was suspiciously like wanting a drink, and in fact it kept blurring into wanting a drink, into imagining watching with a bottle in her hand. She decided she wouldn't watch until she got back to the mansion, though the idea of that time without The Men was vertiginous. It was like letting go of Billy.

When she got to the supermarket, it was closed, but its parking lot was full of people and market tents. Many tents were swathed in banners saying COMMENSALIST PARTY OF WEST LOS ANGELES, and Alma saw some posters of Evangelyne smiling broadly, looking prettier than in real life. Alma had heard about the rise of the ComPAs, but somehow never thought she would encounter it personally. Now it felt like a weird dream in which her ex-girlfriend ruled the world. She got some vegan stew from a soup kitchen tent that was covered in ComPA iconography and was pettily relieved when it was tasteless; the Commensalists weren't all that. While she ate, she wandered past other tents—FAST-TRACK TRAINING, REPAIRS, EMERGENCY VOLUNTEERING—and stopped at a Prop 10 stand, where they were registering people to claim abandoned homes. The girl there earnestly explained to Alma that Prop 10 wasn't a property grab but actually a safety measure; it was necessary to prevent fires and decay in empty housing stock. Alma nodded, thinking only of the mansion, feeling crazy with hope. Like, of course it was a fucking property grab, but Alma was totally down with that. She even thought she should have done more with the ComPAs when she was with Evangelyne, though Evangelyne had discouraged it. That should have tipped Alma off that their relationship was doomed. She scanned the QR code to get the Prop 10 application, then wandered on with a feeling of unreality. All around were the improbably beautiful women of West L.A., and Alma couldn't help thinking that these girls were mostly single now. She'd been huddling in a dark room, and all this—but even as she thought it, the urge to watch The Men came back full force. She had to make herself think about something else. Free mansions. Hot girls. Food.

She found a food bank tent and was given a silver pouch of all-purpose egg mix, a cardboard tube of government spaghetti, a loaf of unsliced bread, and a comically huge paper bag of brussels sprouts. Alma flirted with the food bank girl, smiling into her eyes, complimenting her bracelet. On the ride home, she felt unbalanced in a good way, like she might fall in love again and have a new life. She didn't even really want to watch The Men.

Back at the mansion, Alma made herself shower before anything else. Then she rinsed some brussels sprouts and put them on to boil, and was telling herself she might give up The Men. Even if it was real, there were four billion people missing; she could watch her whole life without seeing her brother. And why did she want to see a one-minute clip of Billy marching by like a fucked-up zombie?

As she thought this, she realized her phone was already in her hand. She laughed and looked around, imagining the food bank girl was here to share the joke. Then, instead of opening The Men, she made herself go to the Prop 10 website and start the application process. When she filled in the address, it took her to the mansion's Zillow page and asked if this was the house she wanted to register. Alma got a little rush. She clicked *Confirm*.

A window popped up. *ERROR: This five-bedroom dwelling must be claimed by three or more tenants. Do you want to amend your tenant information?*

Alma stood fuming for a minute, wanting to throw the phone at the wall, to call Evangelyne, to watch The Men. Of course the ComPAs would be too moralistic to let one person take over a mansion. She thought of the liquor cabinet, hating herself for having poured out all the booze.

Then she had an idea and laughed. She opened FindThem.com, went to the classifieds, and clicked *Create a Posting.* She typed in a brief house-share ad, titling it: *Amazing Mansion: Rooms for People Who Aren't Home That Much*. She already had some photos of the mansion: Billy on the front porch, Billy at poolside, Billy cleaning out the flue of the huge stone fireplace. She added these to the ad and posted it.

Then she went and got the laptop from the library with the feeling of reaping a well-earned reward. On The Men, a line of pink-faced white adolescents were jogging through a swamp, the lemon-yellow water around their feet splashing languidly. Alma smiled—she could not have said why—and settled down with it on the kitchen floor. Without looking away from the screen she reached to get the sprouts off the stove and fished a fork from the cutlery drawer. Some minutes later, she remembered to turn off the flame. She ate sprouts and bread, taking bites from the uncut loaf. She watched. She was still there on the floor two hours later when the doorbell rang.

At first, Alma tried to ignore it. In her experience as an alcoholic, people at the door eventually gave up and went away. But it rang again. The bell was a deep ding-dong that came from speakers distributed through the house. It gonged in the walls and hummed faintly in the floor. It rang again, and now went on monotonously; somebody was leaning on the bell. Then, with a jolt, Alma remembered she was still trespassing here. This could be cops.

When the doorbell stopped, it felt like a miracle. Alma breathed and listened through a minute of nothing. Then her body was flooded with peace endorphins. She felt how her shoulders had clenched. She stretched her arms. She noticed the pan in her lap with its now-cold water, the gnawed loaf resting on her knee. The laptop was on the floor in front of her, showing two men and a toddler crossing a grassy expanse, surrounded by immense pachydermous legs. The great legs moved lightly and gracefully, prancing, while the human feet trudged. The child had a toddler's high-stepping gait but ground forward methodically, never stumbling, as if moving along a track. Then the credits came up, and Alma stretched again, gratefully tired.

The doorbell rang. Alma froze. The ringing paused as if gathering breath, then boomed out, seeming louder, *ding-dong, ding-dong*. The person—the cop, it had to be a cop—was leaning on the doorbell again.

Alma leaped up and started ineffectually hiding things: the pan and bread in the oven, a bag of trash in a cupboard, an armful of dirty laundry in the refrigerator. She scooped the laptop up and dropped it off in the library, where she'd first found it. She was sweating as she ran to the door, running all her self-justifying stories in her head, and was there before she was ready, breathless, weak-strong with adrenaline. She had time to think, *Be fucking polite*, before she opened the door too hard.

On the doorstep was a child.

It was a Latina girl who looked about twelve, wearing a black bikini with silver sandals. She was visibly angry, releasing the doorbell with a gesture that said, *About time.* Her hair was in two braids that had been tied awkwardly on top of her head, with two white feathers piercing the knot. But the most striking thing about her was that she had figures drawn all over her bare skin—pentagrams and stars and triangles—in what looked like Magic Marker.

Behind her, the world was still sunlit and peaceful, the neat gravel path between hedges just the same. Through the gate, Alma saw a sprinkler in front of the mock Tudor mansion across the street, flinging white water in the air. No cops.

The kid said, "Hello, I'm your neighbor? Blanca Suarez, from 2110?"

When Alma didn't answer, the girl repeated it in Spanish: "Soy su vecina, Blanca—"

Alma said, "Hi, I'm just the caretaker here. I'm here to look after the house. So I'm not—"

"I just—I need to borrow a phone or computer? It's just to look something up. For like fifteen minutes?"

Alma was already closing the door when the girl added, "*Please*. It's for a ritual."

Alma balked. In her mind, she was closing the door. She didn't. The sprinkler across the street had moved on to the other side of the lawn, where it was visible only as a hazy rainbow.

"A ritual," she said. "What kind of ritual?"

The kid made a stupid-question shrug. "A ritual to find the men. And I know you don't believe in it, okay? I'm not stupid. But I just need to look up a thing online. It's not like you have to believe in it."

"And you don't have a phone?"

"Okay, I have a phone. I don't have it right *now*."

Alma gripped the door. "I'm sorry. If your mom took away your phone, I can't—"

"I don't *have* a mom," the kid said. "She died when I was three. I don't even *have* a mom."

There was a long bad pause then, in which the kid's eyes welled up and she looked ferocious. And now, among the drawings on the kid's skin, Alma suddenly noticed scars, fresh puckered scars on her torso like bullet holes that couldn't be bullet holes, could they? In this neighborhood? They must be some kind of surgery scars, but was that necessarily better? And if the kid's mom was dead, and there couldn't be a father, did that mean the kid was living here alone?

"*Please*," the kid said. "Fifteen minutes."

Alma had intended to leave her in the foyer and go fetch the laptop, but Blanca trailed after her, peering at everything and talking animatedly about her ritual. It turned out to be based on the Burning Girls, an internet conspiracy theory Alma had read about but never found especially compelling, about a cluster of self-immolations that took place on August 26.

"I'm basically researching their Tumblrs and Instagrams," the kid said. "These are actual writings and videos from girls who died? There's a few online, and one has these symbols, like a hexagon with a star in it. So I've been trying to use it in a ritual, but I'm not totally sure which way the star goes. And I know what you're thinking, but I was *just* doing this ritual and it felt like it was working. And it's obvious the Burning Girls knew *something*. If you see the stuff they left, it is. Also, just so you know, I'm not about to hurt myself. That's what freaked out my aunt. She thought I was going to set myself on *fire*."

Alma stopped on the threshold of the library. "Your aunt?"

"Okay, my aunt's the one who took away my phone? I live with my aunt now. But she isn't even my real aunt, she's just the third wife of my uncle Carlos. So it's not like your mom taking away your phone. I don't think she even has the right to take it."

"Yeah, the First Amendment," Alma said. "You should be out here researching lawyers."

The kid laughed then and looked completely different. There was the shock of her perfect teeth, a good indication that she came from money. A rich kid living with her aunt: all cool. Alma thought of ushering her right back out, but the kid now spotted the laptop and went on into the room. Alma followed as Blanca perched seriously, curiously, on a leather Chesterfield, frowning at the screen, where a procession of men in the tattered remains of clothes moved languidly across a lemon-yellow prairie, walking swimmingly, flattening the tall grass.

"Wait," said Blanca. "What *is* this?"

"I don't know," Alma said, caught off guard. "It's The Men?"

"The men? Wait, it's the men now?"

"I guess."

Blanca leaned in closer to the screen. "No, you're saying this is real? This is actually them?"

"I don't know. A lot of people think that. But no one even knows who's posting it."

"They don't? Couldn't someone trace it?"

Alma tried to explain why that hadn't happened but soon got tied in knots. Of course, she knew fuck-all about computers. Instead, she ended up telling the story of receiving ten emails from her mother saying, *Baby crees que e verdad*, and how she'd thought it was a spambot, but finally decided to call her mother. A neighbor answered. They'd just found Alma's mother and cut her down. When Alma had called, this neighbor had been literally holding Alma's mother's phone, working up the nerve to call and tell her.

"So I was just . . . fuck. And of course I had to open the email and click on the link. Right? It's my mother's final message. But, come to find out, lots of people got that same message, and when *they* asked the person it supposedly came from, the person was like,

'Nope, definitely spam.' So it *was* spam. It's just a sick coincidence my mother was . . . yeah."

Blanca looked briefly at Alma, then back at the screen. She didn't say anything, but she had those bright involved eyes.

Alma said, "She hanged herself right after the men went. My brother went, and my mom couldn't handle it, I guess."

"My mom killed herself too," Blanca said, her eyes on the screen. "She had bipolar."

"Sorry. That sucks."

"It was a long time ago. Her family doesn't talk to us now, so I don't even think about her that much. They're in Korea. I mean, that's not the reason they don't talk to us, but just so you know. I know I look totally Mexican, but I'm half Korean."

"That's cool."

"So could I look at the Burning Girls site? I could tell you the URL, if you don't like people touching your computer."

Alma's throat hurt. She wanted to launch into an explanation of why The Men was the important thing, not the Burning Girls. You couldn't just look at The Men and move on. But before she could put it together in her head, the kid said, "Wait. You said this isn't real?"

Alma said carefully, "No, I think it is real. I think."

"Are they in Texas?"

"Texas?" Alma laughed uncomfortably. "Why? Is that what Texas looks like?"

"No, it's just, I'm from Houston, and I know two of those kids?" Blanca pointed at the corner of the screen. "Those boys go to my school."

There was a beat where Alma's heart went batshit. Then she said in a different voice, "Okay. That's good. Do you maybe know their names?"

"Michel and Cooper Williams. They're brothers."

"Cool. That's really cool."

The clip changed, and it was just one man, walking through a forest. Behind him was one of the cat-things, prancing the way they sometimes did.

The kid was still watching with the silly expression of trying not to smile. She said, "What kind of animal is that?"

"No one knows. It only exists in The Men."

Then the credits came up, and Alma wanted to tell the kid to watch for her friends' names, but there they were at the top of the first screen: *Cooper Williams*, *Michel Williams*. Alma pointed to them, and Blanca stiffened, amazed, as if Alma had made them appear by magic. She turned to Alma and laughed in pleasure, her eyes alight with what this meant.

She said, "Damn. My ritual worked."

At that time, Ji-Won still hadn't heard of The Men. She'd finished her highway clearance work, which had taken her by inching stages west to Kansas. There she was recruited to help plant the winter wheat crop on orphaned farms. In the clear cool nights, she lay drowsing in an army-issue sleeping bag, reading with a pocket flashlight, her body so tired it felt gigantic, an ache that radiated far beyond her skin and into the dirty fields.

The book was one she'd taken from Henry's apartment, John Berger's *Ways of Seeing*. They'd read it together once when he was an undergrad at RISD, when Ji-Won was still the strong one, the one who had a job and paid bills. In Kansas, because she fell asleep very rapidly, for several nights running she read the same passage: "Men act and women appear. Men look at women. Women watch themselves being looked at . . . The surveyor of woman in herself is male: the surveyed female. Thus she turns herself into an object . . ."

None of this was true of Ji-Won. She had always been invisible to men and never had any particular awareness of being seen by other people. Henry, meanwhile, had been very visible. Ji-Won had often helped ornament Henry to make him more visually striking to men and women, curating his clothes, sometimes painting his face. This hadn't stopped people from giving Ji-Won advice as if *she* were preoccupied with her appearance, which could be annoying but also nice. She sometimes saw other people as a kind of pixie: sweet, superficial creatures who adorned themselves and chattered in little sociable herds. Now the pixies were thrown into disarray while Ji-Won was much as she'd always been, a little freer perhaps, not so pestered to be "happy."

Then she fell asleep and dreamed of Henry. She was woken several times in the night by the terrifying knowledge that he was gone.

Ruth boarded a flight to Los Angeles, light-headed after a month of crying, in which time the city outside her building had changed and changed again. When she'd come out at last with her two suitcases into a bright September day, there were women sitting out on all the stoops and in lawn chairs on the sidewalks, watching little girls play on 88th Street, which was littered with toys, bikes, paddle pools, and child-sized furniture. On the way to the subway, two people asked if Ruth wanted help, and when she got down to the train platform, for the first time ever it didn't smell of urine. That undid her, and she was sobbing on the train, so furious at the men. Of course you couldn't know their disappearance was punishment, but who didn't think it was punishment? After all the wars, the pollution, the rapes? They even had to piss on the train platforms! They had to keep misbehaving until they got erased. So what if it ruined Ruth's life?

When she got to the airport, it was almost deserted and, of course, all women. The TV screens throughout the terminal were showing an interview with the biotech lady Karen Xi, with the chyron: EMBRYOS FROM SPERM BANKS: 100% OF MALE FETUSES ABORT IN FIRST TRIMESTER. Ruth felt as if horrible news were pursuing her into every moment. Then, boarding the plane, she was irrationally frightened: How could lady pilots fly this enormous plane with their little hands? In the air, all the passengers talked to each other, so that was how she found out her daughter must have paid $10,000 for Ruth's ticket. There were only two planes to L.A. this month, and that was where prices started. She shut her eyes and tried not to feel cornered. You had to keep going if you still had a kid, and if Candy wanted her mom that bad, what other point was there to Ruth's life now?

Ruth slept. Then LAX, then the bus. That feeling California gave her, of being bugged by all that sun. The cars were mostly gone but the roads still there, a million miles of ugly, empty roads, and anyone could see what a blight it was now. She got off and wheeled her suitcase to Candy's old adobe bungalow, painted powder blue when maybe Carter was president, with a U.S. flag and a basketball hoop left up by the previous owner. She used to see all this on the computer screen when Peter video chatted with her. She was going to be sleeping in Peter's bed. She stood on the sidewalk, crying again. That sun. Those roads. All the nothing that it came to . . . until the door creaked open and there was her daughter.

Ruth said, "I'm sorry."

THE MEN (10/16 22:01:20 GMT)

1. An enormous procession of naked men moves gradually, rocking from foot to foot, through a jungle. They are visible only in glimpses through the dense foliage, and their passage doesn't disturb the leaves. It's as if there's a tunnel cut into the foliage whose shape we can't perceive from the vantage point of the camera. On branches above perch strange, broad-shouldered white birds. The birds crane down their necks and turn their heads 360 degrees like inverted periscopes, inspecting the rocking men. They are jarringly identical in size to the men. The behavior of these creatures is avian; they half unfold their wings in response to the men and step from one claw to the other in excitement. However, they have no beaks. When the men have passed and the birds retract their necks, they appear completely headless.

2. This is the last of many clips that are perfectly black with no image at all. In this "black" clip, at the very end, a tiny locus of blackness begins to disintegrate and give way to light and color. It flashes, appearing and disappearing, then abruptly grows and becomes a hole leading to the outside of some subterranean darkness. We see a man silhouetted as he is suddenly revealed by light. Then confused shapes: a cat-thing pulling itself out through the hole, two men, a jumble of extremities. Soon the mass of them blocks the light so it's impossible to tell them apart. In the final frames, a spark of brighter light like a camera flash briefly exposes a man above, holding a baby. Both are nude and entirely begrimed with earth.

3. This is an early anomaly clip. It takes place in a moonlit grassland that will later be identified as the area immediately adjoining the

riverbank. The men are in soiled clothing, proceeding at a faster pace than usual, heading diagonally past the camera. There are roughly a hundred, and in their midst is a single trans woman, one of the first recurring characters. She's appeared in two previous clips and, by the time this clip was first posted, had been recognized by her wife. Her name is Giovanna Fini.

In previous clips, Fini exhibited the same automatic behaviors as the other characters. Here, as she enters the shot, she's already hurrying ahead of the others, jigging erratically, both arms stretched stiffly forward. As she reaches the center of the shot, she stops. The impression given is that she senses the viewer and is shocked by the realization. She raises both arms in the air and rocks back and forth in apparent distress, though her face remains blank, her eyes unfocused. The flood of men parts around her as the clip ends.

This clip was often used to illustrate The Men in media coverage, perhaps because of its cinematic character, or because trans people were a popular preoccupation in those first months. The Men community reacted with fury, feeling this choice encouraged several misconceptions: that trans women in The Men behaved differently from men, that anomalous behavior was typical instead of being a rare exception, that people in The Men were aware of the camera's presence like actors. The online abuse of journalists from some watchers was one reason for the sparse media coverage of The Men in the early months.

4. This is the first clip of the riverbank sequence. It begins with an aerial shot of the grassy bank of a broad, slow-flowing river, seen in moonlight. Eight men, emaciated and in tattered clothing, trot toward

the water. A few yards short of the water, they stop all at once and fall abruptly still. They remain there unmoving. Something breaks the surface of the water, a creature too large and complex to be a fish. It undulates, flashing what looks like a silver elbow, and is gone.

After two minutes of stillness, a second group of men trots into the frame and halts at the same distance from the water. All the men stand unmoving as the clip ends.

As usual, after the fourth clip, there are credits: 182 male names. Here, for the first time, several of the names are followed by an asterisk.

7

For roughly a year, Alain and I were the most famous sex criminals in the United States. Every day, the press came out with new horror stories, many of them false. They were mostly based on the assumption that Alain had raped all the boys with my assistance, an assumption most Americans shared. At first my name and image were only posted occasionally on the internet, but once it was announced that I was being tried as an adult, the media decided I was fair game. A mug shot of me with no makeup, looking shy and vulnerable, smiling childishly, was initially used by news outlets and caused an outcry: Why was this image used for a pedophile? After that, the photo everywhere was of me in sex mode, caked in Walgreens makeup, looking gargantuan and somehow middle-aged, looming menacingly over Alain. Longer articles often described me as the daughter of a banker, and one enterprising journalist dug up a photo of my father posing with a Porsche. In reality my father was a bank branch manager who fixed up sports cars as a hobby, paying for the hobby by reselling them. In the background of the Porsche photo, you can see the mobile home we'd lived in since selling our house to pay my mother's medical bills. All his friends were from the local Baptist church, to which he tithed 10 percent of his income, except for two years when we received tithe money. I once tried to explain all this to someone who was attacking me online. She responded with a picture of a man playing the tiniest violin in the world, and it got 1,800 likes.

The court appearances in my own cases were relatively painless. My prosecutions had been designed to ensure my cooperation as a witness against Alain. I pled guilty and took deals. In Baltimore and in Montana, even my participation in Alain's trials was easy. I stayed in hotels and was escorted everywhere by strenuously thoughtful lawyers. As a minor in a sex case, I was allowed to testify by video link. I never saw Alain.

In Spokane, Washington, all this came to an end. My sentencing hearing was again unremarkable, but by the time I returned for Alain's trial, the prosecutors had received a series of anonymous letters accusing me of new, worse crimes. The letters were from someone knowledgeable enough to seem credible, probably a dancer who held a grudge or one who naively believed the rumors and retrofitted their memories from a desire to see justice done. These letters contained many detailed falsehoods, by which the Spokane prosecutors were wholly convinced. They now believed Alain had had sex with the boys and that this sex was often forced. They believed there were victims as young as ten—that I'd sought out ten-year-old children and held them down with my muscular arms to be sodomized while they screamed and begged. Of course many people believe this still.

In sixteenth-century Germany, there was a legal concept, *vogelfrei*, which literally translates as "bird-free." When an outlaw was pronounced *vogelfrei*, they lost the protection of the law: "His body should be free and accessible to all people and beasts, to the birds in the air and the fish in water, so that none can be made liable for any crimes committed against him." It was one of the ideas I was introduced to by Alain, and when I first read about it, I thought of a rebel living in the woods in defiant solitude and imagined myself the fearless girl who crept out to his bed. Sometimes in the daydream, we lived among a band of the *vogelfrei* in a lawless Eden. In another version, I was *vogelfrei* alone, a noble recluse who drank from streams, set snares for game, and needed no one.

I lived in Spokane for seven months while the prosecutors pressured me to admit to imaginary crimes. All that time I was *vogelfrei*. My father came out to help me find an apartment, then had to leave to get back to work. The first few months, we couldn't afford a mattress; I slept on a towel spread on the carpet. I lived on ramen and supermarket-brand cookies. Early on, I broke my foot trying to dance in the parking lot and had a meltdown at the ER when they said it needed surgery, sobbing that I couldn't afford it, until they sent me home with a boot. As a sex offender, I couldn't be in a school. My probation officer told me I had to get a job, but he had no useful advice for how to do this as a famous pedophile with no high school diploma and a broken foot. I spent most days on my laptop, compulsively scrolling through the obscene comments, death threats, and rape threats I got hourly on the

Facebook account I still hadn't deleted. Thanks to the sex offender registry, all the people sending these knew where I lived. I was also recognized around Spokane. The day I took the GED, a group of other kids followed me out of the building and raided a trash can for garbage to throw at me. Most days, I had to walk to the supermarket, inching laboriously along the side of the road with my boot and cane, and while my fear that people would throw bottles at me from the windows of cars never materialized, men did follow me down the sidewalk. Almost all these men knew my name and used it, interspersed with *bitch whore cunt*. Just once, I went to a movie, and in the dark, two men moved to sit on either side of me, whispering, "You're Jane Pearson, aren't you? Come home and you can fuck me in front of him. Jane?" Another time, a man followed me around CVS, occasionally grazing my ass with his hand: "Jane, why don't you want to talk to me, Jane? Don't be like that. What's the matter with you? Bitch." I'd broken down sobbing by the toothbrushes when another customer, an elderly man, came and told him to leave me alone. The first man kept trying to explain who I was and getting frustrated when it made no difference. "You don't get it," he said. "I'm not the bad guy here."

When I had to appear in court, I was usually driven by local police. These cops were often friendly. I got to sit up front in the police car, and sometimes they let me choose the music. Once a cop took evasive maneuvers to lose a journalist on our tail, and I laughed and laughed and didn't want it to end. For a while, a cop car was the one place I felt safe. This came to an abrupt end on my first day of giving testimony against Alain.

The testimony itself was dull. I was only being asked about real crimes, and most of the questioning centered on a tedious series of texts that established Alain's directing role. The only notable thing was that I saw Alain for the first time since. He looked pasty-faced and heavy and was dressed in a characterless gray suit unlike anything he'd worn before. His hair had gray roots—I'd known he dyed his hair, and yet this somehow came as a shock. Still, when something amused him, his strange green eyes took on a predatory light, and he was suddenly an elfin prince in disguise who would turn us all to stone if the spells of the prosecutors proved too weak—that was the impression. Occasionally he caught my eye and subtly smiled, and I had to fight not to smile back. He never said a word, but all that day I heard his voice in my head.

Jane is the only dancer I have.

Well, someone's looking very Jolly Green Giant.

Jane has a natural beauty. Putting makeup on her is vandalism.

Sports bra, sports bra, sports bra! I can't see anything on this stage for boobs.

No one moves like you. You make breathing musical.

This one! She dances like she's made out of hams.

Here's my Grace Kelly!

Pure Sasquatch.

A song of a girl. A sylph.

A strange, disembodied day, and when I left at last, I was grateful to find a cop waiting to drive me home. I'd never met this officer, who was young with a distinctively goofy face, small-featured and rosy, and prematurely gray hair. He was smiling a lot as he drove, and it made me uncomfortable but not frightened. I still identified police with rules and believed I knew the rules that governed this space. I was likewise uncomfortable but not afraid when he started to ask about Alain.

The questions at first seemed harmless. Had Alain been a bad person in other ways? Did I think he was the way he was because he came from such a rich family? Would I say he was a sociopath? They were questions I'd often pondered, and I ended up talking gushingly, with the relief of speaking after long isolation.

But then the questions changed. Would I do anything Alain asked me to, or were there limits? Did he ever tie me up? Did he make me take on two guys at once? Did I get off on the sex?

Carried forward by momentum, I answered. I was cautiously truthful from the now-ingrained habit of avoiding the risk of perjury, and as I answered the final question—"It was sex. I enjoyed it like sex, sometimes"—I saw his slack and gloating face and knew. The officer took the next exit, not my exit, and soon we were driving through forest. He knew where he was going, a pull-off for logging access, where he could park just out of sight of the road. Presumably he'd taken women there before. He didn't try to dress it up. He undid his belt and said, "I want you to suck my dick, can you do that?" When I balked, he said, "Don't tell me you don't want to. Believe me, don't."

The next day, an attorney drove me to court. Still, by the time we arrived, I'd sweated through my clothes. The sweat had a distinctive acrid smell, a little like a kitty litter box. I gave testimony woodenly, faintly, sometimes having to be asked the same question several times before I understood. I was thinking of when I would have to leave, convinced the cop would be there again. I was worrying that more cops might come. I was thinking they'd been laughing about it together, cracking jokes about what they would do to me. I was thinking about my broken foot and wondering if I could make it to the bus stop, or if some journalist could drive me home. At times, I lost my grip on reality and believed the prosecutor's office was in on it, that I'd be kept indefinitely in Spokane for the use of all the cops and prosecutors and their cronies. Meanwhile I was answering questions about the boys I'd fucked for Alain, with Alain watching as he always had.

But at the end of that day, I was met outside by an elderly retired policeman, a frail, diminutive man who explained who he was without meeting my eye. He said he'd been asked to see me home. As we walked to his car, he kept a careful distance, moving with a certain squeamishness, and it gradually dawned on me that he knew. The blow-job cop must have boasted to someone on the force, and news had spread. Presumably this old man was taking me home because they trusted him not to touch me: there was still a line, and the blow-job cop had crossed it. I started crying, and all the way home I quietly cried in the car's dull heating, too furious and sorry for myself to hide it. Beside me, the old cop slowly changed, his face opening with pity like a flower, suffering. As I got out of the car, he said, "You take care of yourself. You're a lovely girl."

In Spokane, Alain was convicted on two counts of criminal conspiracy and contributing to the delinquency of a minor and sentenced to three years in prison. In Baltimore, Alain was convicted on eight counts of contributing to the delinquency of a minor and six counts of communicating with a minor for immoral purposes and sentenced to twelve years. In Montana, he was acquitted, but he was later convicted in three more states for crimes committed before my time. When he disappeared on August 26, it was from the Shawnee Correctional Center in Vienna, Illinois.

I moved home to California two months after the last trial concluded and went to live with my father in the mobile home, in the bedroom I'd had the year my mother died of cancer. I had to register as a sex offender again in California, for which my father paid a fee. Every morning, my father got up early to be the first to get to the mailbox, which always contained at least one obscene or threatening letter addressed to me. He bought a shredder for this purpose, and I used to wake to the sound of the shredder. In those months, my father let me help him work on cars and never badgered me about my plans. He drove me to my probation meetings and never quizzed me about them, even when I came out crying. Though he still went to church two times a week, he never asked me to go. We ate dinner together in front of the TV, and sometimes when he got up to clear plates, he would pause beside my chair and rest his hand on my head, not saying anything. That was how we lived until Leo.

The day Luli and I spent hunting for Evangelyne, I talked about Spokane. She had asked—a ComPA always ends up asking about this—and I'd spent that sleepless night with Maya and Micah, in which they told their whole life stories while I sat thinking mine. So I told the story gushingly as we drove through Greater San Francisco, often mired in the swarms of bicycles, scooters, and even pedestrians infesting the roads, gas being unobtainable then, me talking, talking, so a pedestrian keeping pace with the car sometimes looked intelligently at my window, having caught a patch of story. Sometimes, inexplicably, the road fell clear and we were freed, up and down the rearing hills and out to the delicate hem of the land with its vista of houses stacked on slopes in a seemingly two-dimensional array like a medieval drawing of a town, always one step behind Evangelyne. I kept talking while being mortified periodically by my strange affect: the chilly factual voice that cracked as I unexpectedly began to cry, the inappropriate laughter that bordered on cackling as I became more anxious. It's always been hard for me to communicate what Spokane was like, but once I begin I can't stop. As I create wrong impressions, I feel driven to correct them, creating more wrong, bad impressions—and meanwhile the car drove airily in the bright day. At last, in a desperate attempt to get Luli to like me, or feel bad for not liking me, I said that in college Evangelyne and I had bonded over our status as unspeakable. "Yes, *unspeakable*," I repeated when she looked skeptical; we were compelled to lie about our pasts to spare the feelings of other people. Of course I'd just been jabbering about my past, and Luli looked resistant, but I insisted that Evangelyne and I habitually silenced ourselves. We edited. We suppressed. For most social situations, our pasts were either too unrelatable or too triggering. We couldn't answer a simple biographical question without spoiling lunch.

Now Luli softened and said she understood because her father had been a hoarder. I nodded as if I believed this was equivalent, while trying to imagine the hoarding that might be done by an electronics billionaire. For a time we drove in silence, both preoccupied with this hoard, for her a real and painful memory, for me a fabulous dragon's treasure. Then the silence began to feel too prolonged; my mind strayed, and I realized with horror that Luli was seeing me in terms of Alain, as a human cunt, as—

She mercifully interrupted, asking me to try Evangelyne's number again. I did it gratefully, using her heiress phone, a normal cheap phone except you knew it was an affectation. I also knew we were wasting our time. Evangelyne always had her phone turned off and never answered texts or voicemails, unless she was fucking you or trying to fuck you. The phone was for the fucking girl only; for all other purposes, you had to text her acolytes. Still, she gave out her number, and people couldn't help trying it, then feeling hurt when she didn't respond. Now I texted to the heiress's dictation: *still in the car w jane, hot on yr trail. r u at the club yet?*

Then I texted some acolytes, without dictation, and the acolytes texted back that they hadn't been able to speak to E, but she would be at the club, and the event would run an hour.

The club was a former jazz club called Don't Cry with a long line of women outside who'd been idly enjoying the mellow sunset, many of them with arms draped around each other, some smoking weed, a peaceful assembly of happy, improbably sexy women in sarongs, ComPA T-shirts, party dresses. Among the women was one trans man, or what had to be a trans man, I decided. He was wearing chino shorts and holding hands with a slightly taller girl, who looked drowsy, not amazed to be standing with the last cis man on planet Earth. The wall behind them was plastered with a line of posters with the slogan XI VS. HUMANITY, showing the biotech CEO Karen Xi in a photo that was clearly intended to be menacing but in which she actually looked confused. Some posters had been partly torn away. On one a dissenter had written: QUEEN XI IS A GENIOUS! FUCK YOU HATERS!

As we pulled in, everyone in line looked up and followed us curiously with their eyes. Luli immediately took on a defensive air and parked the Tesla with the fuck-you competence of an unfairly maligned heiress who had actually earned that Tesla. We got out, me towering unnervingly over her as I do with most women. She led me right to the front of the line, where she flashed her ComPA ID and said she had business with Evangelyne. All the people perked up with enjoyable outrage. Luli and the bouncer had a long altercation, the bouncer saying obdurately, "Nobody cares," and Luli holding back my name, just scowling and referring to "personal business," wanting her own name respected. At last a woman in line recognized me. There was a flurry of excitement and commentary. I started laughing. Any positive attention gets me overexcited like a small child. But everyone now was in a good mood, laughing. Even Luli was freed from her touchy insecurity and nicely laughed. The bouncer declared a little "jailbreak" and let a dozen others follow us in, even though the building was over capacity and it was against fire regulations. Luli and I and the jailbreak dozen forced our way into the thick of the crowd with the cheerful assertiveness of a tribe.

Here I became vertiginously aware of my trajectory toward Evangelyne, my out-of-control careen toward Evangelyne, like leaping out a skyscraper window laughing, laughing like a real fool as I flailed and fell. I'd driven all night after ten days roaming the mountainside, filthy and unhinged. I hadn't slept. I hadn't eaten since the slice of pizza at Holly's, and I was still wearing the donated clothes I'd gotten there, sweatpants and a polo shirt. But Evangelyne was not a cruel person. I had no cause to be this afraid. Still, I couldn't stop smiling and shivering at everything: at the woman making jokes about fire risk; at the other woman explaining "jailbreaks" to a non-ComPA friend she'd brought; at Luli, who'd gotten snagged by an irritated colleague who wanted to nail down a meeting. I needed Evangelyne there already but also felt I couldn't face her. I was only here to find Leo and Benjamin. I had to remember that was why I was here.

On the little high stage where bands usually played, a woman in hijab had come out and was timidly introducing Evangelyne, her voice only gradually gaining volume so the crowd realized and quieted down. When she finished, a real hush fell, everybody dramatically intent on the stage as the woman turned, blinking rapidly. Behind her, a door opened. Before I was ready, Evangelyne was there.

She wore a flowing, floor-length silver halter dress like an Oscar nominee, but was barefoot. I made a yelp of emotion but couldn't hear it in the screaming crowd. There was a faintness through my body; it had been so long since I'd been close to her, to the preposterous hope of the world. My heart pounded with importance, while I was aware that everyone's heart was pounding. I gasped a deep breath as the whole room screamed her name.

Evangelyne's looks were unremarkable. She had chubby cheeks and a low forehead, a little flat nose that had been broken twice, a crooked tooth in front. She was considered overweight in the world before. She wore her hair natural but neglected it; often you could tell which side she'd slept on. Some women made a point of calling her beautiful, but no one called her pretty. She did have upright military posture, which, combined with her voluptuous shape, made an outline that drew the eye pleasantly. Her mouth smiled in repose and was subtly ungainly, the upper lip bigger than the lower. She was the most unforgettable-looking woman I ever saw, but men never saw her. They only saw Evangelyne's ass. She was tall, but not as tall as me. From a distance, she could seem average height, but when she walked up to you, you felt it.

I'd never known her when she wasn't someone's Chosen One. There were stencils of her face spray-painted on the walls of a dozen cities. I've never met a more intelligent person, so intelligent that knowing her gave me more respect for the capacities of human beings. People would start chatting with her and end up hunting for a pen to jot down notes. When she couldn't do something, it was jarring, even though there were many things she couldn't do. She combined the unworldliness of a scholar with that of a person who'd started a long prison sentence at a young age. She was helpless with a cell phone; all she could reliably do was answer it. I personally taught her how to use a corkscrew, a hotel key card, and Google Maps. I explained to her who Harry Potter was and introduced her to the concept that women's handbags are seen as fashion items. All her friends had a list like that. Still the tendency was to suspect that anything Evangelyne didn't know was trivial, that knowing such things might be the sign of a lightweight.

When she addressed a crowd, it was like listening to a great singer. You could tune out the words and still get high on the timbre, the melody, the heights and depths. She was always direct and emotional. Even when she was reading from a printout, it felt as if she were unburdening her soul to a beloved sister. She meant every word. Her arm in the air was swaying and beautiful, her voice beautiful. Her body was startlingly graceful for seconds at a time, then plain again and just that voice. She would stop, settle back on her heels, tuck her chin, and shut her eyes, estranged with thought. Then, when she raised her arms and spoke, the crowd fell apart. Girls wept and fainted. The world held still and people changed.

Now I watched her speaking at Don't Cry, making a plan for expanded bus service feel like the Second Coming of Christ, and I laughed as the other women screamed. I was dizzy in the hot, inarticulate crowd, insecure and suddenly grateful that Evangelyne was shortsighted and unlikely to pick me out—because Evangelyne had loved me, really loved me above all others, but the last time I saw her, she had called me a coward and said I'd chosen the life of a worm; she said I was a fucking nonentity and I should fuck off out of her world. Worse, I didn't try to change her mind. I never sent her an email or pounded on her door. Like a coward, like a worm, I had let her go.

She finished her speech about the buses and allowed a pause, a hush in which she smiled. We felt the real thing coming. It was the end of the set, when the band gives in to pressure and plays its greatest hits. She didn't yet raise her arms but crossed them, letting us guess which speech it was. Then, when she began, you felt the rush. Even I, who had never heard this speech—I'd been away too long—I felt the rush.

She was saying, "Now, you know a lot of Americans think of history as a story in a book. You close the book and it goes away. It's just a story, so if you're not interested in it, that's cool. It won't come out and bother you. You don't *need* to know about history."

Women around me were calling out, "Oh yes, you do!" and clapping, knowing their lines.

Evangelyne rode that wave and said louder, "The truth is, history is more like physics. The world is made of it. *We're* made of it. The city outside and the language I'm speaking and the clothes we're wearing and what this makes you feel. So if we're the ones supposed to change history—what does it take to change history?"

She nodded as the more seasoned members of the audience called out, "We gotta change!" in practiced antiphony.

She said, "That's right. We've got to change ourselves. And that's harder than anything else you'll ever do, because you're made of the past. You aren't made of the future, and you don't have any future here to start with. You have to make that out of nothing, from work and dreams.

"But now I'm going to say something . . . something people maybe aren't ready to hear. Because we all just changed. The whole world changed. We didn't have to do *anything*, and we changed. And that's what you call a *miracle*."

She paused to let us realize she was talking about the disappearance. Of course we'd been waiting for this. I'd been waiting and—like most people there—should have known what to expect. Still, I felt a shock of anger. She let it run its course, smiling at the stiffening in the crowd, the muttering, how we'd turned against her.

Then we saw tears had formed in her eyes. In a moment, she was weeping openly; I felt it like a change of temperature, how the people eased and settled as if a cool breeze had blown through. I was crying already—we were crying already—when she said in an altered, choking voice, "Some of you know I've loved a man. You *know* I know what you all feel. I'm not here to tell that story again, so you ask the person next to you if you don't know that story."

A woman in the crowd cried hysterically, "Tell it!" and Evangelyne laughed and raised her palm for silence, tears glittering theatrically on her cheeks.

"No, I'm not going to tell the story, but there's people here know I loved a man *for real.* I was ready to die for the men I loved, and I believe they would have deserved my life. They're gone. My brothers are gone, and my ComPA brothers are all gone, all men I loved. But we still have to live in this world.

"So today I'm here to talk about hope."

Then she told us how to live in this world, and we all breathed and sang that song in our heads. Tears glittered on our cheeks, and we leaned forward as if to lean on her. Women peered at each other: *Are you feeling this?* Women smiled back: *Oh yes. It's real.* And she expanded her theme, still weeping as she talked about her August 26, a night when police came to her house—multiple cop cars arriving over a trivial argument with a white neighbor—and she was frozen among them, terrified. But the night was silent. Nothing moved but fireflies lighting in the hedges. There were guns on the lawn that would never be used. In the morning, she'd collected them like Easter eggs. And now she compared our situation to the jubilee years of ancient empires, when all debts were forgiven and all slaves freed. She quoted from the poet Marie Kourouma: "And from our grief came water, and that water grew a forest, and that forest was a world redeemed." She raised her arms and settled back on her heels and talked about God in her unashamed way, daring anyone to think such talk was ignorant—because hadn't God shown His hand? Were we not all God-touched now? God-struck? God-robbed? At last she gave it back to the room, as she always did. She started the "I Am I" chant.

She began it with a demonstration, calling in her sweet river of a voice, "I am I, Evangelyne Moreau! Of all the people in the world, I am the best!" Then she said, "Now you shout that with your name, because that's *true.* I need you to say it, again and again, until you feel that truth."

Then she held up one hand to stay us. Music came over the speakers, a soupy R&B track that gave us a beat, and Evangelyne counted one, two, three, then raised both arms and the whole room bayed it, howled, Evangelyne's big voice leading us into the music so we chanted with it, all standing shoulder to shoulder so you felt the person next to you grow as they drew breath and felt someone's hot voice on your nape. We barged against one another with the force of it, deafened in the smell of us, inhaling bodyfuls of perfume, sweat, booze, and a hint of pussy—"I am I, Jane Pearson. Of all the people . . ."—my eyes deep in the goodness of her, Evangelyne of all the people in the world, when Evangelyne's face changed focus. Her body lost focus. She stepped to the front of the stage with a face like a heart attack. She had seen me.

What is your opinion of the Burning Girls conspiracy theory?

Top Answers

Jarray Montez, Ex-Rookie - Now: Bemused Quora user - 2 year mark achieved

Answered October 15

For anyone who's new to this, The Burning Girls is a conspiracy that asserts that the Disappearance was somehow caused by a handful of women around the world who set themselves on fire. Some believers think the Burning Girls saved the world from overpopulation or nuclear war. For others it's demonic and these girls died in a Satanist sacrifice. Either way, the conspiracy espouses a fiction and glamorizes the issue of suicide.

What's true: At least 200 women died of burning on August 26th/27th. But how unusual is this? It's hard to find numbers for how many women burn to death on an average day, but if you consider that 2,200 people commit suicide daily, it isn't that insane to see this as coincidence. Also it's likely a lot of these women were murdered. Given the lack of police investigations in the confusion after the Disappearance, we don't know all these burnings were suicide, or even that burning was the cause of death, where it might be a murderer disposing of a corpse. These are just some considerations why the Burning Girls is not based on solid facts.

Nimrat Singh, M.A., The School for Conflict Analysis and Resolution, George Mason University

Answered November 23

Many people make fun of those who are interested in the Burning Girls phenomenon, but there are good reasons to look at it more closely.

1. 271 women burning themselves on the same day as the Disappearance, with possibly many others that were never reported.

2. Some Burning Girls being connected to eminent figures (e.g. the niece of Mette Frederiksen, who is Danish prime minister, the daughter of Karen Xi, the GenPro founder, and there are others). I don't agree with people who call this evidence of conspiracy, but it is reason to stop and think nevertheless.

3. Several Burning Girls leaving behind writings that seem to show pre-knowledge of the Disappearance or other events. These kind of writings are also not typical for a suicide note, as many mental health professionals have attested.

4. Three of these writers (Adelgonda Tozzi, Maria Dietrich, Anonymous #2) talking about other women who will burn themselves and calling this a "sacrifice." Of course they are using different languages, but the translation is very precise.

5. Time of death for all Burning Girls (where this is known) within an hour of the Disappearance, with only a couple exceptions. These exceptions could also be unrelated people who decided to burn themselves that day by chance and not true Burning Girls.

6. An international cover-up, with e.g. the Chinese Communist Party banning all mention of the Burning Girls on the internet, and a near media blackout in many Western nations. Also, while I do not approve of all the actions of Burning Girls protesters, many have been arrested who did not set fires or threaten anybody, but were simply sitting in a park. When there is this violent crackdown on all sides over what is only an idea, it cannot help but arouse suspicions.

Rhiannon Bourghetti, Blocked by Condoleezza Rice on LinkedIn
Updated October 21

I think the Burning Girls crap is doing society a service by unveiling just how many irrational people we have amongst us. See, people like me always knew that the majority is dangerously irrational and useless, but now we finally have proof.

The thinking goes like this: One unexplained event happens (the Disappearance), therefore the world no longer has a cause and effect and make-believe reigns. And of course the make-believe is about Satanic rituals, because what in life is not Satanism, from mythical child abuse scandals in the nineties to the very suspicious fact of some Democrats ordering pizza in "Pizzagate."

TLDR: This sh*t is cuckoo bananas.

8

Ji-Won first heard about The Men at a truck stop in Battle Mountain, Nevada. It was October, and she was driving a mail route from Kansas City to L.A., in a truck she'd been given in those first months, when a trucker was anyone who volunteered, when the training was one long, grueling day, then they gave you a route and you left the next morning. The roads were still hazardous. Through Nevada and eastern California, there were towns with no food supplies or water, and some truckers had been ambushed and killed. Now everyone carried a gun, and trucks traveled in convoys of a dozen or more. Rest areas and truck stops were guarded by the military.

The truck stop where it happened was also a food distribution point, where locals came to receive potatoes, onions, blocks of government cheese. When there was cheese, people came from miles around. This was a cheese day, and Ji-Won and many other truckers were in the line too. It was early morning and still chilly with the dry Martian cold of the high desert. The low mountains along the horizon were black against the sun that was rising simple and blinding in cloudless sky. Ji-Won was wearing Henry's fat coat, a corduroy jacket with sherpa lining. She'd been driving six hours, long enough that being out of the truck felt unnatural. When she'd taken the trucking job, she'd shaved her head for practicality's sake, and now her scalp was cold. She had the feelings of a turtle coaxed out of its shell, or perhaps of a naked heart on a timid foray outside the body.

The line was the motley line of those days: some women had coats thrown over pajamas, their hair unwashed and faces deformed by grief; others were neatly dressed and made up, and these already appeared a little retro. People touched each other more, so it was difficult to tell which pairs were couples. And, of course, there were the wolf packs of little girls not obviously attached to any adult, chasing one another around the gas pumps and crawling underneath the trucks. Half the parking lot was covered with their chalk drawings of horses, princesses, rainbows, monsters. A few had gathered around the ComPA patrol at the gas pumps; one ComPA was holding her rifle aside to let a child tie a red satin ribbon around her waist. It was the first time Ji-Won had seen ComPAs this far east, and they seemed to have displaced the usual U.S. soldiers. There was only one soldier here, a poignantly childlike Black girl in bulky camouflage, looking bored and footsore, leaning by the bins of cheese. Sometimes she smiled wistfully at the ComPAs, who paid her no attention.

There was no particular moment when Ji-Won noticed the girl handing out flyers. Awareness must have gathered in the back of her mind; then she was suddenly watching nervously as people pointedly ignored the girl, some rudely turning their backs. The flyer girl went on doggedly, making each rejection last long enough to be uncomfortable. She was a heavy, earnest-looking white girl, red-cheeked in the cold of morning. At first, Ji-Won guessed she was asking for money; panhandlers often worked these lines. But her clothes looked too expensive, and the women in the line were being too rude. Everyone seemed to know what the flyer was and to have come to a consensus that it was offensive. It was the sort of thing Ji-Won didn't know about because she never talked to anyone, and when the girl with the flyers reached her, she accepted one out of curiosity. The people all around her subtly drew away. The flyer girl herself was so surprised she took a beat before she gratefully beamed. Ji-Won braced herself for conversation, but the girl just said, "Don't make your mind up until you see it. You have to see it for yourself," and carried on along the line.

The flyer said:

WATCH "THE MEN"!
SEEING IS BELIEVING!
THEY ARE STILL ALIVE AND
YOU CAN HELP FIND THEM!
MANY ARE FINDING THEIR LOVED ONES NOW!
Sons, fathers, husbands, brothers—
WE CAN HELP!

SEE AND BELIEVE: www.themen82019231.com
FIND A SUPPORT GROUP: findthem.com

Ji-Won read it twice, feeling weak all over, shivering now in the cold desert sun. She took a deep breath but still felt as if she couldn't breathe. She took another deep breath.

Suddenly the line began to disperse in front of her. The depot had run out of cheese. One woman paused beside Ji-Won and said, "You should throw that away. No kidding. You know what that sick crap is? Have you seen it? They're just exploiting people who are grieving. It's sick."

The woman lingered with a civic air. She was wearing a track-suit and fuzzy slippers that had once been white, and she had the dramatically chapped, reddened skin of a middle-aged white person who works out of doors. Her breath smelled of wine and toothpaste.

"Okay," said Ji-Won.

"No, serious. You don't believe me?" Then the fuzzy-slipper woman got out her phone as if she and Ji-Won had agreed this was what should happen. As she tapped at the screen, she said, "Some people say it's made by Russia. There's lots of conspiracy theories, but *I'm* pretty sure it's just a scam. If the government wasn't so effed up, they'd find the people doing it and shut them down. It's evil. I lost my two sons, and if I thought I could see them again? That's how they suck people in. And the people who are into it, it's like they're hypnotized. It's like an old-time cult."

Ji-Won should have made an excuse and left, but instead she waited, struck by the strange conviction that this was the solution to the mystery of why she'd come here, although there was actually no mystery to why she'd come here. It was her job to come here. She'd been standing in line for cheese.

"Okay," the slipper woman said, "feast your eyes. It's supposed to be a film of where the men are now, but it's just these actresses doing nothing, with a bunch of screwy CGI animals. *I* think it's actresses, anyway. Some people think it's real men. *I* don't."

She moved to stand shoulder to shoulder with Ji-Won. There was a moment when the pose distracted Ji-Won; it was the closest she'd been to a person in weeks. Then she registered what was on the screen.

Several men were shown kneeling in a grove of trees, all staring directly ahead. Their mouths moved in an uncoordinated way, silently gnashing at the air. In the far left of the frame was a gargantuan beast with the general appearance of an elephant, but with a rounded head and bright blue eyes. It was so large, Ji-Won thought it was a painted statue until it shifted its weight and shudderingly sighed.

What struck Ji-Won was not the image itself—a lot of video art was equally strange—but its quality. It was blurred, but only in patches, as if it had been filmed through a smeared pane of glass. The elephant-thing was much too big, but everything else was normal size. All the colors were off. The men's clothes and the sky had a Technicolor garishness. It had the extravagant palette of certain kinds of folk art—lime green, turquoise, chalk white—and was fraught with the bright melancholia of that art. Ji-Won should have known what kind of photographic process she was looking at. She'd lived among artists all her adult life and was familiar with every kind of video equipment. She'd even helped one man turn his van into a pinhole camera. She'd worked in dark rooms and had altered photographs both manually and digitally.

This image made no sense to her. The best she could come up with was that someone had doctored the image piecemeal, painting it in places and creating the elephant separately with animation software. But the men were men, not women or CGI. She couldn't see them as anything but men.

Then the clip changed abruptly to a lone man walking toward the viewer across a poison-green lawn that seemed to bulge with light. As he approached, his face came briefly into focus. Ji-Won was startled into speech. "I know him."

The woman flinched and hunched toward the phone screen, squinting. Then she scoffed and said, "You couldn't. Think about it. How many Chinese people are there? Like a billion? For that to happen like that? Plus you can tell it's a girl dressed up like a man. Look how delicate she is."

The man was Vietnamese. He had lived in Ji-Won's apartment building in New Hampshire.

The woman must have read resistance in Ji-Won's face, because she said, "I guess you better join those people, then. One more cracker for the cracker barrel!" She laughed angrily, then frowned back at the phone as if it had wronged her. The clip had changed again: two small boys were walking away from the camera laboriously, up to their knees in swamp.

"Okay," Ji-Won said.

The woman turned off the screen and said, "I got to watch the charge. We don't always have power here. Sorry what I said about the cracker barrel. But you don't want to get mixed up with those people."

Then the woman repeated all the things she'd already said about The Men, watching Ji-Won with wounded suspicion. Ji-Won nodded, pretending to listen. She couldn't remember the Vietnamese man's name, which she'd only ever seen on his mailbox. He'd worked at UPS, and in the film, he was still wearing his UPS shirt, brown and yellow.

At the same time, the phrase "cracker barrel" kept repeating in her head, with its overtones of "cracker" as a racial pejorative. The slipper woman was a cracker, but Ji-Won was not. There was a Cracker Barrel restaurant on Route 10 that was still open, though it usually had no food. Sometimes the women there just served hot water and called it "Venusian tea." All the truckers went there because every night the waitstaff hung a sheet on the wall and showed *Mad Max: Fury Road*. One day Ji-Won arrived too early for *Mad Max: Fury Road*, and they were showing *Abbott and Costello Go to Mars*, in which, through a series of misadventures, Abbott and Costello actually go to Venus, which turns out to be populated by girls in skimpy clothes who've never seen a man and are driven mad by lust at the sight of Abbott and Costello. The truckers all laughed their heads off. Someone yelled, "It's true! Costello's looking pretty good to me now!" and someone else said, "It's prescient fucking cinema!" The Venusian queen was named Allura.

Ji-Won could have talked about this to Henry for hours. Henry would have loved that scene at the Cracker Barrel. He would have believed her about the neighbor.

When the woman was gone, Ji-Won went to her truck, got out her phone, and watched The Men. She missed the next two convoys watching it. Then she went to FindThem.com and spent another hour looking through the classifieds. In the house share section, there was only one room available on Ji-Won's route. It was the photos of the mansion that decided her. She'd never lived in a beautiful house.

She took a selfie of herself with the truck, then added a photo of her unlimited gasoline permit. The subject line of her email was: *Good at fixing things, never at home.*

* * *

Ruth didn't see The Men for another two weeks. By then she was living in Los Angeles with her daughter, Candy, and fighting with her every night. The day it happened, Ruth had boarded a bus to go to a job interview in Santa Monica. She missed her stop, got off in a random place, and couldn't find the bus stop to go back. She ended up crying on a residential street while her thoughts crawled back and forth. There was no one around. Her footsteps and the wind were the only sounds. The sun was going down, the housefronts in shadow, but the yards to the east still blinding and golden. She was walking nowhere, in a strange L.A. desolation of apartment buildings everywhere and not a living soul.

She heard the ComPAs coming a long way off. It was audible that they were marching in step, but it didn't occur to her that they were soldiers until they appeared around a corner, nine women in cardinal-red uniforms, walking down the middle of the empty street. Ruth knew what ComPAs were from the news, but these were the first she'd seen in real life. They marched in solemn formation, faces forward, passing Ruth as if she were invisible. Most carried rifles, which were all different, but one of them carried a trumpet instead, and another a big-bellied Mexican guitar. At the intersection half a block beyond Ruth, their leader barked a word and they all halted.

Then the trumpeter raised her horn to her mouth. She blew a long, high, tremulous note, into which the guitarist began to strum. The other ComPAs raised their heads and sang, and all around, unseen, other voices joined in, countless feminine voices like flowers opening in a desert landscape. It was a song Ruth had never heard before, the kind of sentimental Mexican ballad she would normally ignore as having nothing to do with her. Doors and windows opened along the street, and women poured out, appearing on apartment balconies and porches and spilling onto the sidewalk singing. It was now revealed that this was a Hispanic neighborhood. For a moment, Ruth thought she was the only white person and felt a shameful jolt of racial paranoia. And maybe the singing was mandatory, Ruth thought; maybe those rifles weren't just for show?

But then three young white women came wandering along the sidewalk right by Ruth. They were staring at their phones, not singing. Ruth drifted toward them, embarrassed to be so comforted by their presence, as the song came to an end. All the people stood for a minute, silent, observing a somber pause in which the wind was heard once more. Then suddenly the crowd lost its coherence. Some women began to talk among themselves; others simply went back indoors. At their leader's barked word, the ComPAs shouldered their rifles and marched off down the street.

The phone girls looked at Ruth, then back at their phones. Ruth said in a soft voice, "Hey, I'm not from here. Could you guys tell me what that song was about?"

Still looking at her phone, one girl explained that the song was "Amor Eterno," often sung at Mexican funerals. In it, the singer was mourning a loved one and living in a loneliness like the grave, looking forward only to dying and being again with the one she'd lost. The ComPA patrols sang it every day at sunset to honor the men.

Then, seeing Ruth's eye drawn there, the girl turned her phone so Ruth could see its screen. She said, "And here are the men."

THE MEN (12/12 8:01:35 GMT)

1. This is the last of the "leading edge" clips. We start with an aerial view of the river, its mustard-yellow water bulging against its shallow banks. One shore is now covered with standing men, all motionless, facing the opposite bank. Only at the far left edge of the screen an empty patch remains.

From our vantage point in the air, it's clear that the men are gathered in discrete groups. Each group, whether of four or twenty, centers around a child. The men stand evenly spaced in rings of roughly ten feet in diameter, encircling a child but facing the river.

Filtering among the men are animals: lurching elephants, creeping cats. A swirl of white birds circles above. In the water, a creature occasionally surfaces, a pallid thing of indeterminate shape whose bulk extends massively, deforming the water.

This scene continues unchanged for several minutes. At last another group of men jogs into the last empty patch and halts, already in their bull's-eye pattern.

2. We're on the riverbank among the men, in a section where everyone is naked. They're all oriented to the opposite shore, at which they fixedly stare. One tiny infant, surrounded by four men in a neat quincunx, is on all fours with his head raised but unsettlingly still. Among the frozen humans, the horse-sized felines stalk restlessly. An elephantine behemoth switches its tail and turns its head as it daintily picks its way through. Even where the riverbank seems most crowded, the animals move unimpeded, inspecting the men with an air of anxious industry. The shadows of misshapen birds above cross and recross the image.

By the time this set of clips appear, the riverbank sequence has been playing uninterrupted for weeks, and the sense of tedium and paralysis is overwhelming. The only apparent development is that the men have grown visibly thinner. When they're clothed, the clothes hang loose, and in nude clips like this one, ribs can be counted and pelvic bones jut. Among the skeletal people, the health and sleekness of the animals strike the viewer as ominous. The impression given is that the animals are somehow feeding on the men.

3. As this clip begins, a grayish object rises from the surface of the water. At first it appears to be a rock that has uncannily begun to float; then two lumps on its surface move in tandem and become distinct as eyes. The object is a face, crowned with protruding eyes but otherwise featureless.

A moment later, another head rises near the first. Then another and another, until the river is pocked with floating heads. On the bank, the cats, birds, and elephants have fallen still. They stare at a point in the air, the same point toward which the aquatic eyes have turned their slotted pupils. The men are angled, equally rigidly, toward a different point.

Once all have fallen still, the image rapidly darkens until the screen is almost black. It sweepingly brightens again, then darkens. This repeats in phases that take about two minutes each. When it's dark, a pale moon flies across the sky; this appears to be our moon. When it's light, we see the shadows of the men and animals turning, lengthening and shortening. At the end, the men are visibly thinner than they were when the clip began.

4. This is the first "tsunami" clip. It begins unremarkably. We're among the men and animals, who are all stiff with attention. The darkening and brightening have stopped, and a minute passes with no change. The only movement is the trivial stirring of grass in wind, the slight changes of light on flowing water.

Then the group breaks into frenzied motion. It happens so abruptly it takes a second to see the human beings aren't involved. The men remain as still as furniture. Only the animals are on the move: cats springing and bounding past the camera, birds taking flight, an elephant charging with a hurried flounce, the water agitated as the aquatic creatures dive.

In thirty seconds, the animals have all vanished. The men remain as rigid as before, all staring at the opposite bank.

In the riverbank series, fewer people appear per clip. The credits are correspondingly short: between fifty and a hundred names. About a fifth of the names are followed by asterisks. By the time of this first tsunami clip, it's been determined that the asterisked names are those of children.

9

After I married Leo, there were four years when I did nothing but play wife, cook and clean, daydream, and it was all about the healing sex of love. I never watched the news. I never went on the internet. I baked every day, and the house was always filled with that narcotic smell. I met Leo at the door in lacy underwear. We made love and feasted on cakes and watched all Leo's favorite films. In the daytime, I read difficult books to be intellectual enough for Leo, did calisthenics on the living room floor to be attractive enough for Leo, and planned things I would say to Leo. I attended community college courses, during which I took notes that I colored and embellished with cartoons to entertain Leo. I believed my life had been an ordeal that had tempered me and rid me of ego, preparing me to be a saint of love. Nothing else in my life has made me as happy as those empty days.

Leo loved me too, more dilutely or reflectively, dim moon to my sun. He was easily happy, perhaps a little emotionally facile, as men can be emotionally facile. He was on my side but never really grasped my admittedly niche, not-relatable problems. For him, it was obvious I'd been Alain's victim, and no one could seriously think I was a rapist. Who actually thought it was abuse when a teenage girl fucked teenage boys? People might say ugly things online, but if you just ignored them, they would move on. He also didn't think anybody really cared that he was twice my age. Anyone who gossiped about that, Leo said, would have to be really bored. Until his family came from Madrid for our wedding, I thought this brand of unworldliness might be a quality all Spanish people shared. In fact, his parents saw me as a criminal parasite, and there were ugly scenes where they screamed the word *pedófila* and tried to get Leo to call the wedding off. Leo told me glibly, mistakenly, that they would learn to love me.

The plan had always been that, once I had enough college credits, I would transfer to a four-year university. That university was always going to be UC Santa Cruz, where Leo taught, and where I could get cheap tuition as a faculty spouse. I'd taken Leo's last name, Casares. In community college, that and a haircut were enough to make me unrecognizable. But everyone at Santa Cruz knew that Dr. Casares had married the ballerina from the child abuse scandal, so my anonymity would end. Around this time, I happened to encounter a lot of stories in which unlovable women were unmasked: a lovely immortal, on leaving Shangri-la, withers into a senile hag; a knight falls in love with a lamia, who is exposed at their wedding in her true serpent form; Caprica-Six reveals she is a Cylon just before her cyborg race exterminates humankind. But the story that haunted me most was from the medieval romance of Tristan and Isolde. It was the part where the lovers are banished and go into hiding in the wilderness, living in a magical cave hewn into a mountainside by primeval giants, one of many such caves the giants used for privacy when they made love. The cave's walls are round, smooth, and snow white. In its center is a crystal bed, and its entrance is guarded by bronze gates that exclude anyone who isn't there purely for the sake of love. Here, the lovers need no sustenance; they're magically nourished by love itself. But at last the king summons them back to court, where they will never again be alone together—and, remarkably to me, they obediently go. They return to their worldly honors but sacrifice their magical love forever, and that was how certain I was that I would lose Leo when I went to Santa Cruz.

I was sick with dreamlike foreboding the day I went to my first class. Entering the groomed green campus I'd been imagining all this time, with its polite trees and banks of flowers, its flocks of well-meaning, well-heeled students, I was already sweating. I was hoping to get lost and be too late to go to class, to put off my fate for one more day. But I'm compulsively efficient. I arrived early and had to walk around for ten minutes so as not to be the first one there. When I did go in, exactly on time, all the other students were already in their seats. It was a class called Approaches to Black Studies, one of three courses I could take to fulfill the university's Ethnicity and Race requirement. Nonetheless, I was surprised to see that all the other students and the professor were Black women. I balked on the threshold. All the students looked up. Seeing me, their faces soured and they exchanged significant glances. At first I thought I'd betrayed my bewilderment in some racist way. Then I realized I was me, Jane Pearson. I bumped into the doorframe coming in and made my way to the last free chair in a daze. The students had all looked away again, it seemed to me angrily. Most had phones in their hands. A flurry of texting broke out in the room.

There were three solid minutes of evil silence before the class began. In that time, I sweated through my antiperspirant and was conscious of the underwear I was wearing, already sodden with sweat. At last, the professor handed out the syllabus and began to talk us through it, but I couldn't concentrate against the hostility, against the certainty that I was detested, and that all my classes would be like this.

The instant class ended, I bolted from my chair, but as I hurried down the stairs, I noticed another student had rushed out after me. Where the stairs turned, I saw her above: a big, solid woman who looked about thirty, staring directly at me. That feeling of pursuit made me weak all over—*Jane, why don't you want to talk to me, Jane?*—and when I got outside, I broke into a run. Improbably, she broke into a run behind me. It became a real chase, us running and dodging other people on the sidewalk. There was a certain satisfaction in running full pelt the way I never could back in Spokane, when I'd been hobbled by that broken foot. Still, when I spotted a coffee shop, I ducked in. It was a trick I'd used many times before. If I stayed near the counter, harassers were deterred or muted by the presence of baristas. For the price of a coffee, I could wait them out in relative security.

So I joined the line for coffee with sweat coursing down my sides, reeking, my life with Leo up in smoke and all the people in the coffee shop noticing me, the stinking freak, the pedophile, the rapist. I had to leave Leo. It could never work out. I could never finish school or get a job. He would have to support me all my life, and he would lose his job the instant any rich parent found out I was on campus. We could never have a child, since the government could take it away for any reason or no reason, and I couldn't go within five hundred yards of a school, and I'd been kidding myself. I must have known I was deluded. Why else did I race to answer the phone so Leo never heard the obscenities and death threats? Why else did I monitor the mailbox, clandestinely destroying the letters I got from men who combed through sex offender registries for female names, letters full of violent obscenity and sometimes specific plans that involved breaking into my house when I was alone? Leo had done nothing to deserve this life. We could never have a child—

—and the other student entered the coffee shop, sweaty in the face and annoyed, and came straight up to me, saying, "Excuse me? I'm in your class? Could I talk to you a second? I don't want to freak you out, but if you just have a second?"

I said, "Okay," almost voicelessly, looking toward the baristas. The favor would be that I not rape kids. The favor would be that I hang myself.

She said, in the tone of a person keeping her temper to get something practical accomplished, that she and some friends had planned to make this one class all Black women. They'd wanted just one class with all Black women, and it wasn't that easy to find a Black female professor teaching a requirement. So they'd gotten together and planned it, and they'd all signed up the second registration opened, except I snuck in too. And she knew this wasn't my responsibility. No one was saying it was. But if I could just take a different section . . . it was important to them. She could explain if I wanted. She wouldn't ask if it wasn't important.

At first I couldn't switch gears. I was still looking for a barista to protect me, sick with adrenaline, dying in public. Then it all fell away. She kept talking, explaining, while I stared at her, almost crying. My body was cold with sweat, and the thought of the Black girls' classroom moved me so much I wanted to thank her on my knees. Even I could do someone a favor. I could help with a thing this pure. It was as if she had handed me a star. The instant she finished, I said, "Of course." I'm a practical person—I had been a Cleopatra—and I got out my phone and got it done in one minute.

When I'd finished, she was visibly stunned. She'd been braced for any white-girl bullshit; I'd literally run from her in the street. Then she said, "Hey, have we met before? I meet a lot of people, but I feel like I know you."

I said, "No, we've never met before."

"Not at a political thing? Do you live in Santa Cruz? I know I know your face."

"I do live here, but I don't go out much."

"Okay. I guess I must be wrong."

Her eyes had cooled, growing subtly sarcastic. It struck me suddenly that she was thinking I couldn't tell Black women apart.

I blurted out, "Or, if you recognize me, it could be from . . . because I've been in the news?"

She inspected me while my face grew hot. The coffee line moved forward a step, and I used the opportunity to turn away. When I glanced back fearfully, she was frowning.

She said, "No way. You're not Jane Pearson?"

For a final sick moment, I thought of denying it. Then I said, almost whispering, "I am. But—"

She cut me off with a shout of laughter. "No! No fucking way! You're *Jane Pearson*? *That's* what it was? You're fucking *Jane Pearson*? I heard you were at this school, but for real?"

She put out her hand. I flinched and only belatedly realized she was inviting me to shake. I took her hand gingerly as she said, "Evangelyne Moreau. And if you recognize me, it could be from, I killed two cops when I was sixteen. Girl, I'm just like you! I'm done! I could cure cancer tomorrow, I'll always be the cop-killing Black girl. I mean, you fuck one goat!"

Her laughter filled the room. After a pause, like a delay in transmission, I burst out laughing too. All the people in the coffee shop looked up and looked away. I realized they'd been eavesdropping all along. Nobody was typing or talking anymore. The whole room was about us.

But for the first time in six years, I wasn't afraid. We left the coffee shop together, talking, and everything was different from that moment.

Of course, I've often told the story of that meeting. When I do, two things predictably occur. First, the person I'm talking to, amazingly to me, doesn't know the "you fuck one goat" joke. (A Scotsman is guiding a visitor around his hometown, pointing out the landmarks he's built with his own hands: the pier, the bridge, the tavern. After each of these he says, "But do they call me MacGregor the pier-builder? No! Do they call me MacGregor the bridge-builder? No!" . . . until at last he bursts out bitterly, "But ye fuck *one* goat!") The second thing that happens is that people don't believe Evangelyne would make that joke. To kill two cops is one thing; to laugh about it and compare it to fucking a goat is another. Evangelyne was never disrespectful about the lives she'd taken, people said very stuffily, blaming me.

But when I met Evangelyne, she was fresh from prison, where she'd known a group of women who'd almost all been beaten, raped, and terrorized, who had lost loved ones to suicide and murder, and were changed, unhinged by grief and horror, so some nights the prison seemed more like a refugee camp where they'd all taken shelter from a terrible war. The people outside did not respect this pain. The people outside kept voting to hurt these women more and to hurt their children, who'd been left without parents in the world outside. Yet no one expected the outside people to express remorse. Add to that the fact that the two cops in question had shot Evangelyne's family in front of her. I thought she'd earned that joke.

For a long time, she loomed larger in my mind than in my life. I'd somehow assumed we would be instant friends, but Evangelyne was always besieged by people, all infatuated just like me. I followed her rise to fame online. I thought about her in the car. I was then an Asian Studies major, and, after I gave up Approaches to Black Studies, we had no classes together. Sometimes I saw her from a distance and felt a jolt as if something significant and dangerous had happened. Once or twice I joined a group around her, but soon felt uncomfortable and left without speaking. Her personality haunted me like a fragrance; Evangelyne the person now seemed lost.

Then one day, I saw her in a student parking lot with her inevitable entourage. This time she waved me over. They were talking about her book, which had just come out. She turned to me and promised to give me a copy, but the conversation drifted on, and I began to feel self-conscious. Of course she didn't really want to give me a copy. I'd somehow made her feel obliged. As I was thinking of slipping away, a girl casually lit a joint and offered it to Evangelyne. Evangelyne balked, then accepted it self-consciously, handling it like a dangerous insect.

She gingerly took a drag. I was already full of panic, as if the sky had been lifted off like a lid. I'd been off probation for a year, but the terror of crossing any line remained. At twenty-three, I'd still never had a drink in public. I hadn't smoked weed in seven years. Still, when Evangelyne passed the joint to me, I took it. As I lifted it to my mouth, a car pulled into the lot, and Evangelyne and I both startled, ducked, and stepped convulsively toward a nearby dumpster as if to take cover. I let the joint fall from my hand as the girl whose joint it was said, "What the fuck?" She stooped immediately to pick it up. Of course the car was nothing. A student.

I turned back, making myself straighten up, and saw Evangelyne's face, so angry and sensitive. That set me off. I started to cry.

The joint-giving girl saw my tears and said, "Oh shit. What's wrong?"

I said in a tense bitch voice, "It's just that I can't do anything illegal, even borderline illegal."

"It's not illegal here, it's California," another girl said.

"It doesn't work like that," I said. "Not for . . . Some people are vulnerable."

"No, wait, how are you vulnerable?" said the joint-giving girl. "I mean, you're vulnerable? What?"

She looked at Evangelyne for backup, but Evangelyne said, "Jane, hey. Let's get you that book."

As we walked away from the others, I was twisting in shame, still crying. What I'd said was crazy, and I'd said it that way, uptight and shrill. And the reason I was scared was that I was a sex offender, which I couldn't say, though they probably knew. Evangelyne knew. Evangelyne was about to tell me to leave her alone. She would say I had to stop acting like we were friends. I was a rapist, a pedophile, worse than a murderer. She was about to say the words.

By then we'd gotten to her car, her new Miata that was her earthly love, though she still only had her learner's permit and couldn't drive alone. For her, of course, this was no practical obstacle. She opened the trunk, which was full of author copies of *On Commensalism*. It was the first edition, where the cover art was a photo of a coral reef, and twenty of them scattered in a car's trunk made a striking, psychedelic array. I spontaneously smiled and wanted to compliment it, but I was still crying a little.

She started to reach for a book, then paused. She was struggling, as she did with anything personal. At last she said, "You were right. You can't smoke that shit on university property. You can't even smoke it in public. That's a crime. And you *really* can't give it to minors. Why I handed it to you? I know you're over twenty-one."

My tears had gotten worse. "Okay."

"No, I'm saying, I have to know all that. I have to think about it. They don't. A cop comes by and sees *me* with a joint? What you think's going to happen? You were right."

"Why didn't you say anything?"

"I don't know. I was embarrassed?"

"Okay."

"It's like you're asking, why am I a fool? I'm here trying to thank you."

Then she stooped and fished out a book. The dust jacket was already rumpled at the edges; no physical object could pass through Evangelyne's hands without sustaining some damage. At that time, she always carried a pen in her breast pocket, so as she handed me the book, she put her hand to her heart. Our eyes met. She said, "You want me to sign it?"

"No," I said. "I want to be your friend."

She smiled. I'd been smiling for a while. She got out the pen anyway and wrote her phone number in the book in place of her name.

On Commensalism, Evangelyne's first and most popular book, was written in the Chittenden Regional Correctional Facility, a medium-security prison in Vermont. She began it when she was just seventeen and finished it fourteen years later, just a few weeks before her release. It benefited from the reading she could do as a famous prisoner with friends in academia who photocopied articles for her, but also has the listen-up, real-talk voice of a jailhouse raconteur. Like many people, I read it in one sitting and was forever changed.

In biology, "commensalism" refers to any relationship between two organisms in which one organism benefits while the other is completely unaffected. One example is the cattle egret, which feeds on the insects flushed out as cattle graze, with no effect on the cattle. Another is the various species that take shelter in termite castles without harming or even disturbing the termites. In Evangelyne's political philosophy, many economic relationships we think of as parasitic are more correctly seen as commensalist. The most important example is progressive taxation. The wealthy may complain about being taxed to help the poor, but they live just as long and happily with marginal tax rates of 95 percent as they would with marginal tax rates of 0. Other examples are the squatting of buildings, garbage picking, and some kinds of theft. Whenever value flows from the rich to the poor, it's commensalist. When value flows from the poor to the rich, it's not even parasitism but *amensalism*—a relationship in which one organism harms another with no benefit to itself. This may seem counterintuitive. Surely the rich do profit from such relationships? Doesn't the slumlord who grows wealthier gain some benefit from that wealth? Evangelyne's answer is no. Even if we measure by subjective reports of happiness, the rich gain no benefit at all from their wealth. We must remember that rich people are just organisms and can benefit only *as* organisms. They aren't their fortunes, which are inanimate, insensate, and have no interests.

Of course the book is more complex than this, and in later chapters, Evangelyne gives a commensalist account of capital and markets, reinterprets various historical practices in the light of her theory, and introduces key concepts like "jailbreak," "jubilee," and "powerless relationship." But that simple idea of commensalism, where eating the rich is a natural process, accounted for the book's notoriety, for the disgust it engendered in its opponents, and for its forty-eight weeks on the *New York Times* bestseller list.

Those forty-eight weeks were the weeks of the Commensalist Party's first short, brilliant life. They were also the weeks of our friendship, when I was at Evangelyne's side while she made history, carrying my battered copy of *On Commensalism* to branch meetings when there was just one branch, designing ComPA flyers, working the laminator, working the phones. I neglected my studies to be her muse or amanuensis, or whatever I was. I neglected my marriage for her, though my marriage turned out to need not much, to get along fine without me. She and I were attuned to each other from the start, could spend long days in each other's company and act in wordless tandem. We talked things over frictionlessly, like a single person thinking aloud, or, in the car, were silent together and felt it as a fortified solitude. But in most of my memories, we're in a crowd. She was seldom alone, maybe couldn't be alone. Raised in a cult, then incarcerated, she'd lived among noisy crowds and slept in a dormitory most of her life. Now she lived in a cloud of acolytes, constantly talking and listening and writing down notes, until I started writing down her notes for her. She was never too busy to invite a roomful of strangers home, where she always had penniless ComPAs staying, whose inflatable mattresses appeared in random places as if adrift on tides and who came to the door to greet her like dogs, all jumpy and laughing with the pleasure of her, jealously eyeing their new rivals. Then she cooked bad spaghetti for everyone, drove people home in her car, and left them changed forever. By the end of my first year at Santa Cruz, she'd met everyone at Santa Cruz, so I knew everyone at Santa Cruz. They knew me, and, thanks to her, I was never the sex offender there; I was Evangelyne's friend who'd been unjustly blamed for the crimes of a powerful male. One memorable night we were invited to a party by a writer Evangelyne knew online, a party of mostly middle-aged people neither of us had ever met. When I arrived a half hour after her, Evangelyne introduced me to everyone, and they were all already outraged that I'd been blamed for the crimes of a powerful male.

Her history had left her with odd zones of secrecy, to me completely unpredictable. Even when I was her closest friend, I often learned what was bothering her by reading a piece she'd published in *Jacobin*. Once she went to Sacramento for the night and came back with a black eye and a broken wrist; she'd been attacked by racist thugs and spent a night in the hospital. She'd called me that night and spent an hour talking ComPA business, never mentioning that she was in a hospital, never mentioning the men with baseball bats. When I asked her why, she said, "I didn't think of it." She would entertain large groups with prison anecdotes but got annoyed if I asked about her time in prison. She also never talked about her family's murder. When I first heard her tell that story, it wasn't in a heart-to-heart conversation but in a speech at the California Democratic Convention.

The worst episode was the time she told a few of us about her first prison girlfriend, who called her "Angie" and got a tattoo of "Angie" on her ass. I asked thoughtlessly if Evangelyne had had a girlfriend before she went to prison. She looked at me as if she hated me. There was a chilling silence in which, to our horror, her eyes filled up with tears. Someone asked if she was okay, and she looked at them as if she hated them. Another woman hastily changed the subject, and that was the last time I asked Evangelyne a personal question.

I must have known she was in love with me, though I always dismissed the idea to myself, much as one might dismiss a common superstition. It was obvious and still very easy to ignore as a thing that shouldn't be true. For context, I'm good-looking in a commonplace way. I'm exceptionally tall, as mentioned before, and when I put on any weight I'm just titanic. Of course, that can be attractive; I decisively fill a bed. My hair is dishwater blond, which I now like, although for years I lightened it. I grow my hair to my shoulders. It's straight. It swings and pleasantly has no shape. I have blue eyes, a color I've noticed only idiotic women have in books. I do have a simple-minded face. The famous person I most resemble is Eva Perón, who had a very simple-minded, good-hearted face, incongruous in a fascist. My body looks good when I dress carefully, but is awkward nude, narrow-hipped with big, floppy boobs that look tacked on. When I was thirteen, I read a pulp science fiction novel called *Captive of Gor*, in which a fashion model is abducted and taken to a planet where the women are all sex slaves, and the sex slaves are all gorgeous so that the model is nothing special there, and in token of this, she's given a common slave brand called a Dina, a simple flower that is the mark of a run-of-the-mill, ten-a-penny sex slave, and girls with this brand are all called Dinas, a story that comes back to me whenever I look in a full-length mirror.

I have no idea why I would inspire erotic devotion in anyone. But I do. I unnervingly, reliably do. Many of the boys from Alain's time became unhappily infatuated with me, a part of the story I generally leave out. The Brazilian boy I often mention was head over heels in love with me, a fact I never mention. He continued to write me from São Paulo even after I was married to Leo, a detail I tend to conveniently forget. There'd also been a lonely deliveryman in Spokane who followed me all around town, attempting to explain his love to me. I dismissed this at the time and lumped him in with the men who harassed me. I still don't know if that was wrong or right. And Leo, and Evangelyne, and one of Leo's friends who had wanted to leave his wife for me, so I had to reject him whisperingly in the hall at a faculty party. It's always been easy for me to attract romantic love. Not friendship. Since I was sixteen, my core relationships have always been sexual. I can't change this fact about myself, though at that time I attempted to deny it and believe I could be something else, dismissing the many times Evangelyne fell silent, gazing at my face, and wistfully smiled or didn't smile, and the way it felt. I had needed a friend.

The next phase began with Lucinda Gar. Lucinda Gar was a white ethnic studies professor who'd been one of the first academics to answer the letters Evangelyne wrote from prison. Ultimately, more than two hundred scholars wrote back, including some household names, and Lucinda was one of dozens of people who sent Evangelyne books and articles. She was the only one, however, who raised funds for Evangelyne's legal fees, sent press releases to journalists making the case for Evangelyne's innocence, introduced Evangelyne to a magazine editor who published a selection of her prison letters. Lucinda also flew to Vermont to visit Evangelyne in Chittenden, bringing stacks of letters from Lucinda's students, who were all studying Evangelyne's case. When Evangelyne's release date was coming up, Lucinda fought to get her accepted at Santa Cruz despite Evangelyne's lack of conventional credentials. Many parts of Evangelyne's current good fortune were facilitated by Lucinda Gar.

But as soon as *On Commensalism* entered the *New York Times* bestseller list, Lucinda changed. Suddenly everything Evangelyne said was met with condescension or veiled hostility. Lucinda suggested Evangelyne see a psychiatrist to deal with her "issues," and when Evangelyne demurred, Lucinda wouldn't stop texting her the names of psychiatrists. Lucinda came to every Commensalist event and always sent a follow-up email suggesting how Evangelyne could improve her ideas, her presentation, and her appearance. Lucinda would invite Evangelyne to lunch, then make long phone calls at the table, and if Evangelyne asked what was up with that, Lucinda became sighingly patient, implying Evangelyne was a prima donna and everything with her was a minefield. Once Evangelyne mentioned dating a girl, and Lucinda made a sarcastic grimace. She said, "You forget I know you were straight before you went into Chittenden." This was absolutely not true, and Evangelyne asked where Lucinda had gotten that idea.

Lucinda said it was natural to be confused for a while after getting out of prison. At that point, Evangelyne stopped seeing Lucinda.

But Lucinda had just been warming up. She now wrote a long post on Medium claiming *On Commensalism* as her own work. It was derived, she said, from a series of letters she'd written Evangelyne in prison, with a few interpolations from letters Evangelyne received from "other prominent scholars." To any specialist, she said, it was obvious that someone with Evangelyne's meager background could never have written such a book, "however much that inspirational narrative has boosted its popularity." Then Lucinda Gar went through the text of *On Commensalism*, finding references she claimed were beyond Evangelyne, from articles she said would have been inaccessible to Evangelyne in prison. Many of these were articles Lucinda had personally printed out and mailed to Evangelyne.

Nothing in Evangelyne's experience had prepared her for this particular betrayal. She would call me in hysterical rage whenever there was any new development: an interview Lucinda had given to a journalist, an email from the lawyer Evangelyne had hired to handle the defamation suit, an op-ed written by a gloating conservative about how the Left was devouring its children. I would talk Evangelyne down from going to Lucinda's house and breaking her windows, and once I drove out at one A.M. to meet Evangelyne at the Santa Cruz Pie Shoppe and listen while she drank coffee after coffee and cried tears over Lucinda Gar and wouldn't take one of Leo's Ativans because she was afraid the cops would stop her and test her urine.

Then I went home to Leo. Or I know I must have gone home to Leo, although it feels counterintuitive, and I have no conscious memories of Leo during this time. I also must have cleaned the house and done laundry, although I have no recollection of this, and it strongly feels as if I didn't. I still had sex with Leo and talked to Leo every day, I know—but it feels as if the Evangelyne period happened to a different person in a different town, to Jane Pearson and not Jane Casares, Jane Pearson who could never have become a housewife.

Things had gone badly for a while. Evangelyne had to move out of her house because the landlord didn't like the ComPAs staying. The two candidates we'd fielded in local elections had lost their primaries by wide margins. The big book prizes had all been announced, and *On Commensalism* didn't even get nominated. All this made Evangelyne uncharacteristically short-tempered, mercurial, and paranoid. Sometimes she was rude to strangers, tainting the organizing she'd once done so well. The ComPAs were suddenly shedding members. Thirteen months after its inception, Commensalism already felt like a spent force.

One day Evangelyne and I went alone to Wunderlich Park, a small park in the redwoods with hiking trails and a riding stable. We'd booked a trail ride; it would be the first time either of us had ever ridden a horse. We'd planned this weeks before, in high spirits, but on the drive up, we were out of sync: she was out of temper with everything; I was conciliatory and chipper. Then when we arrived, the horse Evangelyne had reserved, Dingo, had a cold and couldn't go out. The staff was very apologetic and had already issued Evangelyne a full refund. Still, Evangelyne's state of mind was such that I ended up having to google *colds in horses* to make sure it wasn't a lie, that they weren't discriminating against the cop killer. In fact, horses get a lot of colds and then they need rest just like human beings. Of course the stable people still might have been lying, or (as I joked) Dingo might have been malingering. Evangelyne didn't laugh at that. She suggested we walk a trail on foot. On the trail we were silent and even saw a flock of turkeys without saying anything. We both just stopped on the trail and watched the turkeys passing through the trees for a very long time.

But the day it really happened, the day she called me a worm and a fucking nonentity and banished me from her life, was the day she met with the man from the town where she'd grown up. In that small Vermont town, Evangelyne's family had lived in a house with thirty to fifty other Black people, the numbers depending on the time of year, who were all members of the African Religions Research Institute, the cult in which Evangelyne was raised. Twenty-seven of these cult members, including Evangelyne's mother and two brothers, were shot dead by a SWAT team after their white neighbors told police they were Muslim terrorists. The man she was meeting with was one of these neighbors.

The man now wanted to make amends so badly he was flying in from Vermont to do it. For reasons she didn't explain, Evangelyne agreed, and I knew not to ask. But I had to be there to hold her hand, to be (as she said) her white-girl buffer. She didn't often bring up race with me, but this neighbor had called down murder on her family for being too Black in his white neighborhood, for worshipping Black gods in a Black way, and she'd been the one to go to prison, so in the forty-eight hours leading up to this meeting, which we mostly spent together, she talked about race incessantly. I walked on eggshells and was afraid to speak. When I did speak, my voice sounded jarringly white, white like a wrong note. I began to understand why certain ComPAs called me Ballet Becky. I remembered every race-related episode I'd been through as a white girl in the ComPAs: one girl told me my Asian Studies major was cultural appropriation; another girl called Alain a man of color who'd been imprisoned for my crimes; once at a party a Black guy said he'd just adopted a kitten and I expressed surprise, and he made a face and said, "Becky doesn't know a brother can have a cat," and the other people laughed, and I didn't know why I'd been surprised, so it actually could have been racist surprise. All this now recurred to me and made me defensive. Whenever Evangelyne talked about race, I froze up, then said the wrong thing, and she looked away from me, miserable and strange, like I was personally killing her.

When the day came, I drove her to the meeting, at that same Pie Shoppe. As we got out in the parking lot, Evangelyne said, very hostile and sensitive, "Don't fucking leave me." We'd been told to look for a silver SUV, and before we got to the Pie Shoppe door, a silver SUV pulled in. The SUV drove to the far end of the lot and fussily, very slowly parked, pulling out and back in again to get the angle right. When the driver's door opened, Evangelyne reached as if to take my hand, then didn't. A nondescript white man got out and raised a limp hand to us in hello. Then two other white men got out of the car. One was burdened with a video camera; the other, with a big handheld microphone. The neighbor had brought along a film crew. Evangelyne saw these people and shrank, stepped back convulsively as if to take cover behind me, saying breathlessly, "Fuck you. Fuck you. Shit, get me out of this. You have to get me out of this. I can't do this."

The neighbor was walking toward us with a big smile, waving like a nice guy certain of a warm welcome everywhere he goes. The other two men came behind him, unsmiling, raising their equipment into place. They could have been local news or InfoWars; I couldn't make out the logo on the microphone. I suddenly saw my place in the world and was filled with Cleopatra, with my old powers. I stepped forward and blocked Evangelyne with my body, saying, "It is *not* appropriate to bring a camera crew without telling us ahead of time. This conversation is over. Get back in your car. Go home, this isn't happening."

I turned back and found Evangelyne staring at me as if again seeing armed men surrounding her childhood home. Then she buckled and turned away too. Behind us, the neighbor was sputtering, apologizing. I could see her feel it like a rain of bullets. Still, she got into my car okay. I got in and we were driving with Evangelyne crying, her hands in tight hurt fists, saying, "Thank you. Thank you," then seeming to change her mind and saying nothing, us fleeing across those California hills, all sleepy grass in gold with a dusting of purple wildflowers in dry profusion, then on into the redwoods' darkness, which dabbled over us like water, to come out at the beach at last and fling ourselves out of the car and walk, laborious over the sand, nobody else there but one Latino man splashing through the shallows, running, flying a silly-tailed kite. We walked away from him, the shaggy cliffs over us morose and mossy, out to where huge stretches of kelp lay messily heaped like piles of ropes, and, in a jagged canal of runoff water, a scum of lime-green algae was startlingly bright among the rainy-day colors. Seagulls high-stepped among the kelp, occasionally sharply taking flight as if shocked by an unbearable memory and leaping to escape it, riding the air for a minute above it until the sea reached up and seized it away.

Then Evangelyne stopped. She waited for me to stop, to turn to her and feel the last thing come. And she asked me to tell her if she had any hope, while I kept my distance and couldn't meet her eye. Couldn't breathe. I was looking at the ocean.

I said at last, "Yes, but I can't just . . ."

"What?"

I didn't answer, so she said she loved me. She said I must have guessed, everybody else had guessed, and her voice was small in the ocean's roar. She said, "Jane, please."

When I looked, she was self-possessed, recovered from her weakness of the second before. I was terrified. I said in my worst uptight white voice, "I couldn't leave Leo right now. I'm pregnant."

Now I stood at Don't Cry with Luli, in the world where the men had all evaporated, facing Evangelyne and feeling it again. I was a worm, a nonentity, a coward. I had hidden behind my unborn child. I was now only ten feet from the stage. I'd stopped chanting "I Am I," among her followers who still chanted "I Am I," still deafening and heaving like a storming sea, and I was frozen by that self-loathing, when Evangelyne saw me and faltered. The women were chanting, "I am the best!" Evangelyne leaned forward, squinting. I strained both toward and away from her. I was aware of Luli looking back and forth between us with prurient interest and of the crowd's dimming energy, their confusion.

There was a full minute when I knew I'd failed. Our friendship had been six years ago. Any feelings she'd had for me were gone. She'd had a dozen girlfriends since, all hotter, better educated, kinder, more interesting, not freakishly gigantic, not famous pedophiles, not Becky-ish, and with firm, young breasts. She would ignore me or ask that I be shown out. I'd gambled everything and lost. I deserved to lose and I had lost.

Then her eyes opened wide and her whole face changed. Her body went happy all over. I made a little peeping noise in my throat. My heart was so affected, my vision blurred. When I could see again, she was reaching out to me, grinning. She was right at the edge of the stage, and she seemed to be about to jump but was cautious of the height—so happy, and about to, but no, too afraid. I started fighting toward her, my feelings silly and streaming like water, like an opened hydrant, anarchic in the sunshine of July. As I got close, she knelt and clambered down, and the very last people between us made way, the whole crowd deferring, deforming itself to give us space, so Evangelyne—big and real and smelling of good live sweat in her silver dress—was there and I had her in my arms. She kissed me full on the mouth, and I went out of my mind, my hands on her bare shoulder blades where the skin was so cool and tender. Without thinking, I kissed her like I would Leo, her tongue in my mouth and my body responding just like that, as the people chanted, "THE BEST! EVAN-GE-LYNE! OF ALL THE PEOPLE! IN THE WORLD! YOU ARE THE BEST!" and some women close to us had recognized me and were joyfully shouting my name to each other until the whole room shrieked with romance. They screamed for the victory of love as Evangelyne kissed me for the first time.

And I wanted her and didn't, no I did, with the pillowy feeling of her breasts against mine, and that silly spooked voice in my head, and my skin thrilling with surprised suppressed desire, and of course all the positive attention all around, and Evangelyne laughing in my face—her soft beer breath—saying, "Jane! Jane Pearson! Are you serious? Now?" The next thing I remember, we were outside, with the whole crowd that had streamed out with us, that had borne us out like a sea to take over the street and drink wine there and dance like witches. San Francisco! The good gay city! Ours! The heiress had opened her car doors and was blasting a jaunty country song as it gently began to rain, and we didn't stop dancing. I was hanging on Evangelyne's neck and kissing her throat as if I were drunk and crying as if I were here for her. I danced with her wet self in my arms, her drenched skirt clinging to my legs. I danced in the thickening rain, and since everybody there knew who I was, I could dance like a fool, like a former ballerina, making beautiful shapes and spinning on a toe, with Evangelyne laughing at my grace like it was the craziest thing.

And the next thing I remember is the pretty hotel. It had no towels at all. Its towels had all been looted and we would have to air-dry after the shower, the hotel woman sheepishly explained, but even this was like a holiday, a terrifying holiday, a holiday of clinging to a plank in the ocean, because the door was closing and then we were left alone with a king-sized bed. It was happening. Evangelyne asked me, "Are you okay with this? I know you've got to be in mourning," but I said, "Yes, yes, yes," and hurried it along and was pulling off her clothes, light-headed and scared, and her breasts were surprisingly beautiful: rounder than mine and somehow bright. I'd never touched another woman's naked breasts. I was conscious of not knowing if I wanted to, if they were a fascinating toy or a problem. She lay on top of the covers with me and stroked my breasts, her eyes half lidded, and I saw the faint bright stretch marks on her belly and was out of my depth, alight. I'd never thought this could really happen. I cupped her breast and it was indescribable like all sex. I really did want to have sex with her, but the feeling of having to do it right, but being out of my depth, was like Alain, like that first time in the Jokers Wild Hotel and Casino, when I'd thought I would die, when I was violently afraid.

I almost started laughing when she reached down and got a dildo from the side of the bed. She cocked it interrogatively, *Yes or no?* I wanted to ask whose place I was taking, who that dildo was lying in wait for, but I just nodded. I didn't want to laugh. It was one of those strap-on dildos made to resemble a dick with uncanny-valley realism, covered in something like and unlike skin—brown skin, a detail I'm ashamed to admit I first perceived as "political." Then she held me down and kissed me, and I moaned without thinking and prepared to be ravished. I didn't know if this was right, but when she touched me, when she entered me, I didn't dare open my eyes and it was good like sex, and it was, it really was, and I came. And came again and came. It went on a while before it seemed to be diminishing, hurting a little, and she stopped. She kissed my face, and I didn't dare open my eyes.

Then I sobered, faced with the task of making her come, which I went at first with my hand, too timidly, unconfident, plagued by terrible memories of boys and Alain. I was both grateful and annoyed that she'd taken the strap-on off and tossed it somewhere, that she didn't expect me to don the strap-on, which might have been easier but weird. And I was about to dive in orally (those words, "dive in," passing through my mind and being comical in a way that was unfunny), but she asked me in actual words, as I could never do, if I wanted a vibrator, and I said, "Okay." The vibrator she helpfully found almost instantly made my hand numb, and I kept thinking, *Don't cry, don't cry*, and this could go on forever, and I had to look at her cunt and it made me embarrassed, but soon she tensed all over and her legs straightened out, and the feeling of making a woman come, which was mainly the same, just relief that you'd succeeded. Then I didn't know if I should do it more. I did it more, just gently, trying to intuit it, but that terrible fear had returned. A hotel bed like the one in the Jokers Wild. I was touching another woman's cunt. But she did come again, less dramatically, almost resentfully, then took my wrist and moved my hand away. She kissed me on the head, and it was okay then. It was her, and I was able to forget it in kissing, in even feeling arousal again. So suddenly happy. Of course she was attractive to me. I loved her. My mind began to nervously chatter about why she even wanted me, enumerating my physical attributes and dissociating in a familiar way that was comforting. My body enjoyed the things and loved her euphorically, while I was elsewhere, worrying. It felt normal.

And the sex finished for real. She slept and I lay thinking in the bed with her. I was thinking of Leo and Benjamin. I also thought about my car, where I'd often been with Leo and Benjamin, a car I'd blithely abandoned to the twins, assuming I'd get it back "somehow." It would rust away at Micah's house with no gas. Another lost thing. My lost little boy. My husband who had really been the flesh of my flesh. I'd betrayed him. And nothing good again.

Evangelyne woke up and found me crying. She smiled and didn't make me feel bad or weird. She stroked my head and said, "Hey. Hey."

"Sorry. I know this is fucked up. It's not you."

"I get it." She smiled at me awhile. There was no one who had such a kind, smart face. Interviewers always called her "wise," which felt condescending when they did it, but was true. She was wise, kind, every way good. But, as I watched, she began to think. Her brow furrowed in a way that could have been adorable in anyone else. I felt it coming and quailed.

She said, "I've got to ask myself why you're here, though. I mean, I feel your hand in my pocket. That's a big hand."

She was smiling indulgently still, as if she thought my ulterior motives were cute. I said cautiously, "You know I had a son."

"I know you had a husband." She laughed to soften it. I laughed, but I was frightened. I took a deep breath. Then I had nothing to say but made a thinking face as if I might.

She laughed again, getting it. "You think I can fix that? Oh shit, Jane. It happened to me just like it happened to everyone else. I got no magic powers. You think I can bring the men back? Really? I hope that's not why you're here in this bed."

"But it's not as if you can't do *anything*."

Then I lay there exhausted while she really thought about it, staring at me as if using my brains. I hadn't eaten since the day before. The room was spinning. Her recklessness and gaiety, that witching aura she had, was everywhere. I felt her thinking my thoughts.

At last she said, "We're not even the government yet. Not close. You want something like that, maybe help me be the government."

I didn't try to hide my relief, and when she saw it, we both laughed. She shook her head and said, "Jane Pearson. What have I gone and done?"

"Yes," I said. "I'll help you. Yes."

Examining three strategies for recognition of individuals in The Men

Banu Ghoreishi, Nahida Siddiqui,
Caitlin Allbright, A. G. Sanchez

Introduction

The existence of The Men constitutes an unexplained phenomenon, assumed to be related to the events of August 26–27. In this study, 366 Men watchers in the United States and Canada were monitored for a period of fourteen days. Participants were recruited through online advertisements placed on the FindThem.com website. All agreed with the proposition "My primary aim in watching The Men is to see my loved ones." Each participant provided researchers with a target list of loved ones they hoped to see. The appearance of these targets in The Men was recorded for each participant.

The researchers identified three watching strategies: *viewing strategy* (n = 101), *group strategy* (n = 45), and *name strategy* (n = 221).

Viewing strategists watched The Men for as many hours as possible.

Group strategists collaborated in groups of five or more to watch for one another's loved ones, maintaining twenty-four-hour vigilance.

Name strategists did not watch The Men but relied instead on the lists of names that appear periodically in the footage. Name lists have been shown to reliably correspond to people shown in the video (Antin et al. 2020; Siddiqui & Antin 2020). Both major Men websites maintain searchable lists of names, with links to the corresponding footage.

These three strategies were predicted to be equally successful at finding people on The Men. This study demonstrates for the first time that this commonsense expectation is wrong.

For *name strategists* and *viewing strategists*, no targets appeared on The Men in the two weeks covered by the study. This was unsurprising, given the few individuals shown in that time: 382,201, or .001% of all people with a Y chromosome alive on August 26–27.

For *group strategists*, however, 115 targets appeared. The researchers were unable to suggest an explanation for this remarkable discrepancy.

Participants in the study also submitted to two medical examinations. No significant medical changes were detected in participants that weren't attributable to the extended periods of physical inactivity undergone by some watchers of The Men.

10

In late November, Ji-Won surrendered her truck and got a job in L.A. as an arborist, hanging from trees with a chain saw in the cool bright weather. It was municipal fire prevention work. She got picked up in a van every morning and was driven to some far-flung canyon, where the boss, Nana Pete—a stocky fiftyish woman who'd been raised in a forestry family and "had trees in her blood"—would inspect the place from a fire's point of view, pointing out the routes she would take and naming the neighborhoods she could wipe out. Nana Pete liked Ji-Won and would talk to her about Birth Zero Year and the end of humanity, ending each conversation by smiling ruefully up at the trees as if conceding victory to a worthy opponent.

Ji-Won came back to the mansion every night scuffed, bruised, stinking of sweat and sap, and carrying a fifteen-foot bouquet of interesting branches. Sometimes she started making art before she showered. She would have The Men on in the room, and art and Men mingled into one problem she was gnawing at mentally through the hours. She was feeling her way toward Henry, or possibly creating a machine to bring him back. There was one intuition still needed to turn the mediocre into the powerful, to make the object work. The men now stood very stiffly on the riverbank, as if ferociously concentrating, and their business was perhaps like hers, watching single-mindedly for that one thing.

For Blanca, it was the time Ji-Won was a crystallized ideal: the artist who had driven a truck through deserts with a gun on the passenger seat, who chopped down trees with a chain saw, who never looked in a mirror or complained or needed anyone. Ji-Won accepted Blanca tacitly and taught her embroidery and how to clean a gun and how to tie ornamental knots, The Men always silently on in the background. Blanca would talk about her father, to which Ji-Won said little. She'd never needed her family as Blanca did. Ji-Won had helped her family with money; she was strong. Blanca liked to repeat in her mind, *I learned at the feet of Ji-Won Park.* She imagined a future where Ji-Won was a world-famous artist and theirs was a legendary friendship about which documentary films were made.

After Ji-Won had gone to bed, in the long nights when Alma was out and it was Blanca's house, Blanca went out on the back porch and smoked Ji-Won's Newports. Often then she got down on her knees in the grass, while the starlit hills around filled with the zany howls of coyotes, and deer tiptoed out to graze on the lawn, all the world winding back to its pre-Fall wildness. She prayed and some nights lost her temper and ran around the lawn scaring off the deer, because no one got it. Even Ji-Won wouldn't read the Burning Girls materials. Even Ji-Won didn't see that The Men was an opening into a demonic place.

Alma sometimes startled those same deer, walking barefoot back from Aunt Christine's. Other times she stayed at Christine's overnight. It was an irresponsible spark thrown off from the first bad days with Blanca, when Christine would appear at the mansion to try to get Blanca to come home to bed, while Blanca screamed at her and called her a slut. Christine would bounce nervously on her heels and smile at Alma sideways, killing Alma. Then Alma went home with Christine one night and created a new equilibrium.

Christine liked to sit up after sex, sentimentally talking about her husband, often glancing at a framed photograph of Nelson Mandela he'd hung beside the bed, so Alma pictured the husband as Mandela, a handsome old man with a shock of white hair and a beatific grin. He'd been a piss-poor communicator but had a big heart, and that was what mattered, Christine said. Alma said consoling things, and it was dumb but nice. Christine always let Alma keep The Men on, and it was sweet how Christine slept with one arm thrown over Alma's waist, how she got up early and made pancakes from a mix, singing along with a Taylor Swift album.

At the same time, Alma had a frantic feeling of time being frittered away. Once Christine was talking about how she'd gone to a clinic for a sperm donation, though she didn't especially want a kid *now*, but she was scared there'd be a rush when people figured out it was their last chance. But it turned out she was the last to realize. Some women had gone to the clinic on the morning of August 27. That same morning! The waiting list was now seven years, and the actual supply would run out in two. Then Alma had to get straight up out of bed and run home and watch The Men. It was that feeling of sleeping on the job, not being at your post, getting left behind.

So when the Ghoreishi paper, "Examining three strategies for recognition of individuals in The Men," hit the news, it was Alma who watched the coverage with heart pounding, then found the paper online and read it three times, feeling sick with excitement. It made a kind of twisted sense to her that if you got a group together to watch the same screen day and night, you scored at finding people. She definitely got the feeling that what The Men liked was attention. She googled articles that claimed to find the flaws in Ghoreishi and laughed with relief when the "flaws" were that Banu Ghoreishi was a registered Republican and her family had worked for the Shah of Iran. Like, whatever, Republicans sucked, but this had shit to do with the Shah of Iran.

Once again, she posted an ad on FindThem.com. This time she took the task more seriously, cleaning the mansion's prettiest rooms before taking photographs and writing a description. She listed it as an open house and picked a date a week away. Only then did she go down to the library, where most of the watching happened now. Ji-Won had comprehensively trashed the room, so junk now filled three-quarters of the space, creating a chaotic frame for the flat-screen TV. The room always stank of cigarettes, foliage, mystery chemicals, sweat. Ji-Won and Blanca didn't look up. Alma paused in the doorway, annoyed by the mess, though it wasn't the time for that conversation, and she couldn't really talk when she was fucking Blanca's aunt.

At that moment, Alma's phone rang. When she looked, the screen said *Evangelyne.*

* * *

It took Ruth two buses and a ten-minute walk to get to the McCormick open house. She'd expected there to be a lot of people; the house was a mansion with pillars and verandas, like Tara from *Gone with the Wind*. You didn't have to care about The Men to want to live in that house.

Still, when a dozen women got off the bus with her, Ruth didn't guess they were all going to the same place. These others soon outpaced her—everyone in L.A. seemed to be twenty—and Ruth was left to walk alone and watch the nightmare slowly unfold: how the other women spread out along the route that Google Maps was telling her to follow; how they gradually started to talk to each other and cluster in groups, already making friends. As the house came into sight, she saw a litter of bicycles and scooters at the gate. There were even a couple of cars, which had to be using black-market gas; restrictions were still in place in every state but Texas and Louisiana. Then again, for this house, maybe people had come from Texas and Louisiana.

Ruth almost turned back. She'd read the profiles of the three group members here and had tried optimistically to think of them as being like Peter's nicer friends. But Ruth was fifty-three, broke, overweight, depressed, and her most glamorous ever job was managing a medical office in Chelsea. Fat chance those young girls would pick Ruth if they were able to choose from dozens of people.

Ruth stopped in the street, got her phone out, and watched The Men for fifteen minutes to calm herself. The tsunami series was still going. In clip after clip, the animals fled the scene, rushing through the men and vanishing. The impression was of a sifting process, as if the animals were lighter than the people and were being shaken free or blown away. On Ruth, it had the tranquilizing effect of playing a very simple video game; she felt a certain satisfaction every time the animals were cleared from the image. As she stood there, another group of young women passed, apparently coming from her same bus stop, and headed up the hill toward the mansion.

What ultimately made Ruth go on to the house was that she needed a bathroom. That got her to the front door, where two teenagers were balking, whispering together and giggling; they went blank-faced and silent as Ruth approached. One of them hastily opened the door, and both ducked in, seeming annoyed at Ruth for rushing them.

Ruth followed them into a kind of living room, two stories tall and the length and breadth of a tennis court. There were roughly fifty women scattered through it, mostly standing alone and frowning at their phones. The furniture was large but unassuming: a scuffed leather armchair, a long yellow sofa with a crocheted blanket thrown across its back. At the far end of the room was a massive stone fireplace, and over it hung a photograph of two men in suits embracing, laughing, with white specks of what looked like blossoms scattered in their hair. The photograph had been enlarged so the men were twice life-size, and some details were blurred, apparently by the violence of their embrace. Ruth hadn't brought her eyeglasses with her, and she'd been looking at the picture for some time before she realized it was a wedding photo. The white specks in their hair were rice. Then, with a different jolt, she recognized the woman standing below the photo as the oldest member of the watch group, Alma McCormick. Alma was holding forth to a little group of applicants who all stood with their phones slack in their hands. She was prettier than her profile photo and had a certain cowboy swagger, her back absolutely straight and her jaw square. A gap between her front teeth made her likably goofy-looking. She was smiling nonstop and checking her listeners' faces as she spoke. There was a vulnerability about her. Ruth decided she couldn't be the member who'd grown up in this enormous house.

As Ruth approached tentatively, Alma was saying, ". . . not in months. She hasn't been taking my calls since *August.* She just randomly decided to come today, because I really needed my weirdly famous ex to crash this event. I mean, she's not *trying* to mess with my head. She's actually not an asshole. She's actually—okay, I know I'm not supposed to say I'm still fucked up about her, but obviously I am. So today I'll be giving a live demonstration of lesbian drama. It's good, though. I mean, my ex is totally famous. *You're* impressed, right?"

The girls surrounding her laughed a little breathlessly, and each girl took turns admitting she was impressed, until one said serenely, "Fame doesn't matter to me. It depends on the person."

Alma's smile changed subtly at that, as if she were holding the smile in place. She said, "If it depends on the person, you're going to be impressed. I mean, the fuck."

The other girls around her laughed. Ruth had now drifted close enough to be in the group, and she was readying herself to casually ask who the ex was, when Alma looked around, checking on the listening faces with that happy, sensitive look, and her eyes passed over Ruth without seeing her.

The pain of it caught Ruth unawares. She turned away, humiliated, and went down a hall to find the bathroom she'd wanted. When she found it, she locked the door behind her, feeling as if she were barricading herself from an assailant, then pulled down her pants with the rote haste of a middle-aged woman who's taught herself not to look at her naked thighs. She cried luxuriously while she urinated. At the same time she distantly, bleakly noted the scum of hairs around the bathtub drain. That Alma was charming, but she was a pig. All the charming people were pigs, and the ugly, uncharming people cleaned up after them. It was a beautiful clawfoot tub, of course, and Ruth tried not to think about her daughter Candy's old shower stall with indelible mildew in every crack. This though Candy went at it with a toothbrush, Candy who was nice-looking enough but awkward and abrasive, who could never afford to be a pig.

As Ruth flushed the toilet, someone rapped on the door. Ruth startled disproportionately and cried out, "Just a second!" in a strained, frightened voice. She made a fist and stood there, wanting to yell at someone. At last she took a deep breath, ran cold water, and splashed her face. You got no peace. You were driven out. You were ugly and old and dragged into the light. But she dried her face with an already-damp towel and was keeping it together when she opened the door. Three girls were waiting there, blocking the hall in the direction from which Ruth had come. Ruth turned the other way, light-headed from tears, and walked as naturally as she could toward an arched doorway at the end of the hall.

The room through the archway was lined with bookshelves but dominated by a large flat-screen TV. The screen showed the men stock-still on the riverbank while the animals flew and flowed away. There were two girls watching it, sitting on the floor on a faded patchwork quilt. The walls and ceiling were covered with enormous snaking branches, inserted or attached so they appeared to be growing from between the books. Some were evergreen and still lush, some bare. The branches had been decorated with feathers, ponytail holders, scraps of tulle, a few bottles of Elmer's glue, wilted blue carnations, and tattered clothes, including a pair of gray cotton panties whose crotch was liberally stained with blood. Two dining-room chairs had been set up on either side of the arched doorway, and a length of bright blue rope was tied between them at knee height as a makeshift barrier against intruders, giving the whole room the look of an art installation in a museum.

With a peculiar shock like déjà vu, Ruth recognized the two girls as the two remaining members of the group: Ji-Won Park and Blanca Suarez. Ji-Won Park was exactly as Ruth had imagined her: a dumpy, frowning woman in a sweatshirt and basketball shorts, with a broad sad sensible face. She was the one whose photograph Ruth had liked, the one she'd imagined cooking dinners with. Ji-Won didn't look up as Ruth peered in.

Although the age in her profile had been fourteen, Blanca Suarez looked about twelve. She wore a men's white dress shirt and no pants, and had drawn odd symbols all over the shirt. The way she was sitting, you could see her pink underwear. Her face was set in adult rage, and her hair was in complex cornrow braids with red yarn stitched between them in patterns reminiscent of cat's cradles, a mature note if only because both braids and sewing were so well done. Ruth guessed instinctively—correctly—that this had been done by Ji-Won Park.

Both girls reacted to her presence: Ji-Won hunching away from Ruth, her jaw clenched; Blanca sighing with a theatrically disgusted grimace. Ruth began to cry again. She leaned in the doorway and stared at The Men through tears, the pain beyond her. None of this mattered. These people. This crap. On the screen, eight Asian men in dirty sailor uniforms encircled a tiny Black boy wearing jeans and an orange hoodie. The animals leaped, stampeded, flew, plunged beneath the water, and were gone.

Then silence grew in the rooms behind her. There was the ding-dong of a doorbell, followed by a jubilant commotion of greeting. All the girls in the hallway went to see, and a second later, the girl who was in the bathroom came out hastily and followed, wiping her wet hands on her jeans. Even Ji-Won and Blanca were whispering together, Blanca urgent, Ji-Won resistant. Ruth ignored them, watching The Men. She guessed it was the famous ex who'd arrived, and of course everybody flocked to her. That was what people did. That was what they were like. Well, Ruth was at an open house for The Men, and she was going to watch The Men.

Then Ji-Won and Blanca abruptly hushed. In her peripheral vision, their postures changed.

Blanca said, "Excuse me? Ma'am? Do you know what Evangelyne Moreau looks like?"

When Ruth looked, Blanca was gazing at her solemnly, with the pert face of a child accustomed to being admired by adults. It took Ruth a moment to understand. Then she said, "I suppose. I watch the news."

"If she comes down that hallway," Blanca said, "could you stop her? Tell her she's trespassing."

Ruth looked down the hallway dubiously. She was aware of her wet cheeks, but it didn't seem to matter. Maybe you could cry all you liked now. You could stick branches to your walls and hang trash all over them and cry.

"We didn't invite her here," said Blanca. "Only Alma did, because that's her ex? And did you know Evangelyne Moreau wants to stop gas stations from opening again? Like, she hasn't even been elected to anything, but she wants to tell people they can't drive *cars*. We don't want any communists invited to our home. Most Americans don't understand what communism is, but we're Korean. Do you know about North Korea?"

"Of course," said Ruth. "My first husband was stationed in Korea."

"Anyway," Blanca said, "Alma said Evangelyne Moreau could come here, but it's not even Alma's house. It's our house as much as it's Alma's house. I mean, legally."

"I don't know enough about this to have an opinion," said Ruth.

Ji-Won laughed, still watching The Men.

Blanca said, "First Alma decides to have this open house, which we agreed to. Like, I get it. But then she has that woman crash it and make it all about her and her politics? It's like, why even have the open house?"

Ruth said, "But you're not out there meeting people."

"We're not good socially," Blanca said. "We want them to *join* the house. I mean, we're not good salespeople, that's all. We're trying to do what's right for everyone. We don't need to be liked by everyone like Alma does."

"Smart," said Ruth.

"But actually," Blanca said, "Alma decides things totally on the basis of sex. She does lots of shitty things to people for sex. Do you think that's normal? Do you think most adults are ruled by sex to the exclusion of caring about hurting people?"

"Yes," said Ruth. "I do think that."

Ji-Won laughed again, still looking at The Men.

Blanca said, "I *know.* But *most* adults? Forget it. I'm just being stupid. I'm an idiot for thinking people could not be trash. I'm a child for thinking that."

Ruth was thinking how to respond, when the hallway women came back, chattering happily, and one of them went into the bathroom. Blanca said, "That's not her, is it? I don't want to get up. I don't want her to see me."

"It's not her," Ruth said. "But you don't want to meet the other people? It's your open house."

"It's not about the open house," said Blanca. "This isn't a joke. I don't know why people can't take it seriously."

A new girl appeared at the end of the hallway. She spoke to the women in the hallway, and they all gestured her toward Ruth. This girl was very tall with a gentle face, the kind of face that smiles in repose. She wore a gauzy green dress and high heels; perhaps she had thought this would be more like a party. She met Ruth's gaze and smiled, then came down the hallway a little tentatively, heels clacking on the marble floor.

"It's not Evangelyne Moreau," Ruth said to Blanca.

"Thanks," said Blanca, mollified.

For that moment, Ruth was so relieved to be accepted that she loved Ji-Won and Blanca. She smiled at the tall girl with that feeling as the girl came up, saying, "Hi. Is this where people are watching The Men?"

Ruth looked at Blanca, who shrugged theatrically. Ruth said to the tall girl, "Sure, you can watch here."

The tall girl peered into the room, still smiling. Ruth also turned to the screen, and there was a minute when Ji-Won, Blanca, Ruth, and the tall girl watched, in a pleasurable truce with the world. The men stood on the riverbank; the animals flew and flowed away. Then the tall girl shifted on her feet, losing interest. She was looking at the rope barrier, the branches on the walls. She smiled at Ruth again and said, "I'm Jane." Ruth was about to introduce herself when Ji-Won spoke for the first time.

"They're shaking. Look, the men are shaking."

Her voice was almost inaudible, and Ruth took a moment to understand. She looked back at the screen but at first couldn't see it. There were men in a circle as there always were. The clip changed, and there were different men in a circle—but in this clip the animals were already gone. Ruth felt their absence like a missed step in the dark. And yes, these men were shivering and twitching.

Blanca gasped and sat forward. The tall girl looked quizzically at Blanca, then back at the screen. Ruth was thinking how to explain why it was surprising when everything changed.

The men leaped. They moved so fast the image blurred, and they landed all together in a heap, as if sucked to one point by a powerful magnet. On the ground, they tangled, clawing one another, limbs hammering together in a frenzied mass. Without her eyeglasses, Ruth couldn't see details. She was leaning forward, heart pounding, telling herself it didn't have to be a bad thing. An area was darkening around the pile, as if a leak had sprung in the image, and still she told herself it could be good.

Then the screaming began. The screams came from the walls, as if the house were screaming in a dozen feminine voices. Both Ji-Won and

Blanca rose to their knees. Ruth might have understood then, but at that moment, two hallway girls barged past, leaping over the rope and standing right in front of her. Ruth swore and got on tiptoe, trying to see.

"What's happening?" the tall girl said. "Is this new?"

Blanca snapped, "*Yes*, it's new. Are you kidding? The men haven't moved for like a month, and now they're—what are they doing?"

"They're attacking the kid," a hallway girl said. "Can't you *see*? They're tearing him apart!"

The tall girl said in a solicitous tone, "So it's not always like this?"

The clip changed to a new group of men, still in their circle on the riverbank. Once again the animals were already gone, and the men were trembling from head to toe with slight spasmodic jerks of the arms. Only the child was as still as before. By contrast, he looked tranquil.

Now the tall girl cried out suddenly. She stepped convulsively toward the screen and tripped on the rope, falling forward on hands and knees. One chair toppled, hitting Blanca. She cried out angrily. By then, the tall girl had risen onto all fours, her face so altered that for a moment Ruth thought it was really a different woman. By the time Ruth looked back at the screen, the new men were in a struggling pile. Only one remained on his feet in the foreground, shivering against a milk-white sky.

Another scream came from the depths of the house. A door slammed, and Ruth heard the rich, familiar voice of Evangelyne Moreau, surreal outside of the context of the news. "Jane? Are you still here? Jane!" as the tall girl clutched her face and screamed: "What *is* this? Please! What is it? Can somebody tell me what they're doing to him, *please*?"

Ji-Won said, "I think she knows someone."

THE MEN (2/15 22:13:00 GMT)

1. This is the last tsunami clip. A group of fifteen men are in a circle on a riverbank, all facing in the same direction. At first I can't tell they're in a circle; the angle of the camera makes it unclear. The men in this clip are wearing soccer uniforms, but the child is a toddler in a faded onesie with a bumblebee appliquéd on the chest. The most uncanny thing in the image is the baby's ability to stand unsupported, absolutely still, for three straight minutes.

There are only two animals here, both cats. This was the first Men clip I ever saw, and the cats were what appealed to me. I wanted the show to be about their adventures. I knew The Men wasn't about them but wondered if the makers of The Men would be open to making a spin-off. At this point I still assumed it was made by a studio with a comprehensible financial goal.

2. In this clip, there are no animals. At the time, I didn't know this was unusual. I only hoped the cats were coming back.

Two adjacent circles of men are shown from the vantage point of the river. Shortly after the clip begins, they begin to tremble violently, vibrating like a plucked string. Only the two focal children are as still as before. There's a peculiar impression that they're causing the vibration.

3. This is the first of the massacre clips. It shows one circle, most of whose members will be eventually traced to Paris, though they're ethnically West African.

It begins with the men vibrating, then all the men spring onto the child. The area around them darkens, speckling and dimming the luminous colors. When I first notice this, I think, *That's meant to represent blood.* It's too maroon to be real blood, and the effect is darkly comical because the men all rear their buttocks in the air. It's like a spoof of nature programs in which wild carnivores feast on a kill. This makes it more macabre, not less.

Still, I'm startled by the extreme reaction of the other women—gasping, screaming, fighting to see. There's always been violence on television, and it's strange to respond so dramatically even to a scene involving a baby. I assume this must relate to some development in the ongoing plot. Perhaps a much-beloved character has been killed; perhaps someone has shockingly betrayed him.

4. In this clip, the child at the center is my son. He's in the shortie pajamas he wore to sleep on August 26. Although this isn't visible in the clip, I know they are Avengers pajamas, and on the front of the shirt is the slogan EARTH'S MIGHTIEST HEROES ARE STRONGER TOGETHER. Leo stands in the foreground, in the boxer shorts he wore to sleep. In the ring around Benjamin are twelve other men. I recognize them all.

Since there are so many, once they fall on Benjamin, nothing can be seen of him but blood. Here the blood is obviously real, perhaps because it is my child's.

Only Leo does not attack him. Throughout, Leo stares into the air, trembling violently. At the time, no one knows this behavior is unusual, that in most massacre clips where a father is present, he will take part in eating his son.

When Leo does break free, he doesn't move to rescue Benjamin. Instead, he lurches into the river just as the water's surface erupts in splashing, heaving movement. In the final seconds of the clip, we see that this is caused by the sudden arrival of dozens of huge aquatic creatures. In the last frame, the river has entirely vanished, replaced by a wall of seething tentacles.

I didn't watch the credits at that time. When I did comb through them later, I found what I already knew. Three of the men in the clip of Benjamin's murder were boys I'd fucked for Alain, now adults. Another was a juror from Alain's trial. Another was a pharmacist who'd filled a prescription for me once at a CVS, and another was my ninth-grade homeroom teacher. Two more were waiters from restaurants I'd eaten at, and three were men I'd seen around Santa Cruz but never spoken to. The twelfth man was my father.

11

This is how my father and I became estranged.

A year after Evangelyne stopped being my friend—a year in which I was pregnant and then had a newborn while still attending college, when I was engrossed and overwhelmed—Evangelyne wrote an essay about our friendship.

It was first published in the *New Yorker* and became their most read story of that year. It was later reprinted in various anthologies and in the *Evangelyne K. Moreau Reader*. After *On Commensalism*, it's the work for which Evangelyne is most well-known, and the version of Jane Pearson in the essay has gradually eclipsed my former fame. The essay is called "The White Girl."

It begins with Evangelyne's arrival at Santa Cruz and her first encounters with white students, which were almost uniformly bad. Some treated her like an unexploded bomb. Some familiarly patted her on the head. They were always asking her where to buy drugs. She told one white guy she'd been accepted at Santa Cruz straight from prison with only a GED, expecting him to be appropriately impressed. He said, "Well, the bar's way higher if you're white." The week her book deal was announced, a white girl told her it was ironic her career wouldn't exist without racism, since that was the subject of her writing. It wasn't the subject of her writing. This was where she was at when I walked into her Approaches to Black Studies class.

Here she told the story of our first meeting: how I'd run away from her in the street, and she'd felt like she was going crazy. She'd given chase and run me down as if she could finally corner whiteness, confront it and make it face its lies. When I agreed to withdraw from the class, she assumed it was just my way of escaping the class of scary Black girls. For that minute, she was in the dystopian world of the old Nation of Islam, where whites were perversities, the botched results of a malign experiment, eternal antagonists to real human beings.

Then I said the words "Jane Pearson," and the scales fell from her eyes. I was none of that, and she was a self-centered fool. On the spot, she fell in love.

Here in the essay, Evangelyne told my story the way she always told it: I was a victim of sexual abuse who'd been blamed for the crimes of a powerful male. Then she talked about our romantic friendship and how I'd haplessly broken her heart. In this section, I'm described through the eyes of love, which I find saccharine and mortifying. She uses words like "pure" and "gentle." There's a metaphor about a stained-glass window. She has us riding those horses in Wunderlich Park—in her version, Dingo isn't sick—so there's an image of me in sad, lost beauty, galloping on a horse with a streaming mane through a sun-dappled, primeval forest.

Predictably, this is the section from which people love to quote. I've even seen an Instagram photo of someone with the whole stained-glass quote tattooed on her shoulder. I didn't take this section at face value. I'd often helped Evangelyne with essays written for mainstream publications, and I knew what a tenuous connection there could be between the sentiments in an essay and an author's actual thoughts. Evangelyne knew white audiences craved forgiveness from Black people, and she could be very crafty about trading gestures of forgiveness for things of real economic value; she could easily turn a stained-glass metaphor into a stream of cash donations. The word "pure" was especially fishy and likely to be a practical joke on unsuspecting white readers, who wouldn't see anything odd in the association of whiteness and purity.

But the heart of the essay is the section that follows, where Evangelyne wrote for the first time about the murder of her family. Here she came to the titular White Girl, who wasn't me but a girl in the town where she grew up, Barclough, Vermont. Barclough was the kind of depressed rural town where rich New Yorkers have vacation homes and are broodingly resented by locals. Of course, Evangelyne's mother belonged to a cult, and the house Evangelyne and her brothers grew up in was a cult house. Still, they were basically more city people, current and former urban professionals, most with advanced degrees.

The cult was called the African Religions Research Institute and lived up to that stuffy name. There was no apocalyptic ideation, no promiscuity, no subservience to a ranting charlatan. They were just overearnest religion nerds, prone to interminable arguments about the worship traditions of medieval Timbuktu or whether Mambila spider divination required a particular spider species. They were adults who slept in dormitories. They performed goofy rituals and wore strange clothes. From the point of view of Evangelyne and her brothers, they spent their time devising ways to embarrass their teenage children. Their devotions were focused on the healing of this Earth—the defeat of war, injustice, and poverty—and their hearts were broken, little by little, because they accomplished nothing. They were an innocent thing in the world.

But they were Black. That meant the cult was suspected by its neighbors of every form of Islamic extremism and voodoo witchcraft—also of every unsolved home invasion and burglary in a twenty-mile radius. Some white locals spied on Evangelyne's backyard with binoculars to see the people bobbing up and down on prayer mats, drumming and chanting, dancing in masks, and occasionally sacrificing live chickens. One of the ARRI men sometimes took the older children out to teach them shooting, using bottles or (seasonally) pumpkins as targets; this was perceived as "military training" by the paranoid neighbors. There had been some calls to police already, and cops had come to the front door once but weren't invited inside. The more conspiracy-minded locals had drifted toward the belief that ARRI was a Muslim terrorist sleeper cell.

One day the nominal head of the cult, Malcolm Sundayate, went to the supermarket with the sixteen-year-old Evangelyne, her mother, and her auntie Noor. Sundayate was sixty-three. He had recently undergone a cardiac procedure and also had early-onset Parkinson's. He walked with two canes and wore a defibrillator vest underneath his faded dashiki. That day, he went along to the supermarket because he didn't trust the others to choose good fruit, and peaches were in season. He'd never been the popular idea of a cult leader, but rather a gentle, bookish man, a lay scholar and sometime tax preparer. What he most missed about Brooklyn was his hobby of going out at night to feed colonies of stray cats. In fact, when he was shot, it would be with an ancient three-legged cat in his arms, a detail that later featured prominently in articles written about the case.

This wasn't the day he would be shot. This day he was standing in the supermarket parking lot while the women put groceries in the trunk of the car, when a passing white girl stooped, picked up a half-empty soda can lying on the ground, and threw it at Sundayate. She ran away laughing at her own daring, pursued by a shrieking friend. The soda can hit Sundayate in the face. He lost his grip on one of his canes, flailed in surprise, and fell to the ground. Evangelyne crouched down hastily beside him. The other women started to crouch down too—they were initially afraid he'd had a heart attack—but then they grasped what had happened and started after the white girl, shouting angrily.

The white girl and her friend ran into the supermarket. A white man who'd been watching inside came out and stood protectively at the door, yelling at the women to leave the kid alone. The women turned back, helped Sundayate to his feet, threw the last of the groceries into the trunk, got in the car, and drove home.

The white girl went home and told her mother that five of those "Black Muslims" had chased her with canes, intent on beating her to death. The white girl's mother called everyone she knew, gathering an impromptu neighborhood meeting in her kitchen. A case of beer was shared, after which the mother made a call to the state police.

The following day, eighteen police arrived at the house where Evangelyne, her mother, and her two brothers lived. Ten minutes later, everyone living in the house was dead but Evangelyne. From her bedroom window, she'd shot two cops, for which she spent the next fourteen years in prison.

Evangelyne dreamed about the white girl all her life. In some of the dreams, she was in love with the white girl. In others, the white girl was in her cell and Evangelyne couldn't make her leave. In all of them, the white girl was there to murder her. There was always a seemingly irrelevant part in which the white girl ran and Evangelyne saw her streaming hair, unnaturally orange in a way that signified poison. This was the most terrifying part of the dream, expressing Evangelyne's realization that the White Girl was everywhere, eternal, and could never be escaped.

Evangelyne then talks about seeing me as White Girl, eroticizing/demonizing me as White Girl, and what this taught her about the nature of hatred. When she turned on me, she writes, she knew she was scapegoating me unjustly. I had a right to prefer my husband. Nonetheless, when she saw she'd hurt me, she was filled with the exulting malice of the victim who can at last wield power.

She ends the piece with a firework display of ideas, drawing analogies between police violence, erotic focus, and the fear of the Other. She says that loving a white when Black is a sex act committed upon a mass grave, a desecration or ritual performed to marry hell and heaven. She quotes from William Blake and Dante's *Paradiso*. It's brilliant because of the way it was done. It was rightly called a tour de force.

What I mainly got from it, though, was that she realized she'd been unfair to me and might want to be friends again. I instantly wrote her a sentimental email, gushing about the essay and telling her what it was like to be a new mother.

No answer came. She'd just transferred to Princeton and moved across the country, and I didn't expect a speedy response. But three months passed with nothing. It felt as if time were being more and more tightly wound on a mechanism not designed for the tensile resistance of that much time. This was when my father read "The White Girl."

At that time, my father had a new girlfriend who was teaching him to be more open about feelings. As expressed to me in a long, brutal phone call, his feelings about "The White Girl" were that he didn't appreciate being put in the crosshairs of a professional race-baiter, and he'd tried to be tolerant because he knew I'd been through a lot, no one knew better, but there were times he couldn't just stand by. I probably realized he'd been opposed to my marriage to Leo, a widower twice my age, which had frankly seemed like just another mistake, but he'd kept his mouth shut because I seemed happy. And he was proud I'd made the best of that decision. He was proud of the life I'd made. But now he learned—with the rest of America—that I was cheating on my husband, not just with a woman, which he wouldn't have minded, but a criminal, a female thug who had murdered law enforcement officers. Why do that? Could I tell him why? And don't try to tell him I wasn't cheating. He knew my fibs of old. What rankled most was that I'd let that woman write about it in a national magazine, and maybe she hadn't asked my permission, but you couldn't tell him I couldn't have stopped her. He was ashamed now to show his face in church. He was ashamed to go to work in the morning. With all he'd sacrificed, I seemed determined to pay him back by publicly humiliating him. It was the lack of consideration that galled him, after all that business with the Cornyn man. How much was he expected to take? Could he hope this would ever end, or did I have more nasty surprises in store?

I sobbed inarticulately all through this. I couldn't make sense of what was happening. I sniveled and gasped and wiped my streaming face. Benjamin was screaming in the background, and I finally hung up with the blurted excuse that I had to go change Benjamin. As soon as I hung up, Benjamin was fine. He was always a remarkably helpful baby: now he lay very peacefully with his wet face. I picked him up and paced slowly through the house, gently bouncing him to calm myself.

As my tears dried, I realized what I was feeling was rage. My father's response was really about the nasty lesbian as seen through the eyes of the bigoted members of my father's church, people who believed gays burned in hell and vaginas brought sin into the world. Never mind the "female thug" thing and how my father's reactions were tinged by racism. Even his thing about Leo was racist, since my father made sure to tell all his friends that Leo's last name was "Spanish from Spain," as if it preyed on his mind that people might think his son-in-law was Latino.

And as far as my happy marriage went, my father had it backward. I had never cheated; Leo had. What was worse, he had cheated with a twenty-year-old waitress from a local fish restaurant and even once brought the girl to the house when I was there with Benjamin, the two of them laughing at inside jokes and exchanging private glances in front of me, while I was aware I couldn't object. I sat up nights with my newborn thinking how to safely object, but came up empty. I couldn't risk anything that might end in divorce; no court would award a convicted pedophile custody of a baby. So I worked even harder to make Leo happy, to be sunny and unsuspecting, and ultimately the waitress faded away. And now that it was over, I still loved him and was mostly content with my life, except when I lay awake at night with my true thoughts.

But I *had* been nineteen at my wedding, and Leo *had* been almost forty, and my father could have spoken out then. Instead he'd given me away at the altar and washed his hands. He wasn't the ideal parent I'd imagined, but a cold, judgmental person who'd never understood a thing about me. He hadn't protected me from Alain.

So I was angry as I hadn't been in years, as I hadn't dared be since Spokane. I was enraged and it felt cleansing. Benjamin was happily content with my anger. He nursed and fell asleep, and that sensation of nursing an infant, which had sometimes felt invasive like tickling, or even like the boys in Alain's time, went clean through me like a wonderful knife, and I knew I was right. For a change, I knew.

Then more time passed, slack time. My father still came over to babysit Benjamin, to listen to the engine of Leo's car, to have Easter dinner. He came to Leo's birthday party, and we behaved around Leo and his friends. These normal things still happened, but I never spoke to him privately again. He made no attempt to speak to me. His girlfriend looked at me glitteringly, angrily—a hard-faced woman, I thought. A bitch.

Then one afternoon, six months after the publication of "The White Girl," it occurred to me to read the email I'd sent Evangelyne: perhaps it had been unintentionally offensive in some subtle way. But when I found it, I saw I'd never actually sent it. For days I'd rewritten it obsessively, but then I'd forgotten to hit *Send*. Seeing this, I was filled with peace. I wouldn't bother her now. It was the right outcome. We would both move on with our lives.

Four years passed. I brought Benjamin to class sometimes in the first year of his life; then I graduated and stayed home with Benjamin. I followed him around the house all day, seeing things through his intent, unfiltering eyes. That baby trance never really lifted for me. It was like being a monk, outside of life, every intimate task a rite of worship: rising for matins to be alone with God while the dull, profane world sleeps, and the menial labor made a song by His presence as the years pass grandly or enfold each other in days that cross each other at night, back and forth; and the baby growing, standing up on two feet, learning how to point and say the word "Look!" and the "Look!" month turning into babbling stories he tells about a dragon and a puppy, and my Benjamin was always an easy baby, a sweet little boy, good company. He loved books about polar bears and igloos. Once, when it snowed in the mountains, I put him in the car seat and drove him a hundred miles to see his first real snow, and Benjamin was always good in the car; he loved to sing and talk to himself in his car seat and needed no other amusement. I too have always found it easy to be happy if nothing interferes. I believe my father would have found it easy to be happy if nothing had interfered.

Then Benjamin and Leo and my father just vanished. Every person with a Y chromosome just vanished. Ten days I hunted for my family on the mountainside, fevered, crazed, half dying, then I drove all night to find Evangelyne. By the time she came down from the stage to claim me, I was purified. I was hers. I don't know how to explain her power. When we left the club en masse and were dancing in the street, in the rain, a woman passing with grocery bags strode over to Evangelyne importantly, interrupting the party to inform her that socialism never worked anywhere, and Mao had killed more people than Hitler, and the woman herself had relatives in Venezuela who'd almost starved to death under Maduro, and anyone who wanted to try that, well, they'd find an awful lot of people fighting them. I couldn't stop smiling foolishly, Evangelyne behind me, one arm confining me against her as she explained over my shoulder that commensalism wasn't exactly communism, though they did share a lot of common ground, and she did understand the woman's concerns, but she hoped the woman would read up and decide on the basis of full information. Then Evangelyne sketched some parts of her program, the woman interrupting to complain, until Evangelyne had grasped the woman's story and assigned someone to find the woman an apartment from newly vacant housing stock—a ground-floor or elevator apartment, accessible for the woman's disabled daughter. All around us, people fell quiet in the street and were lulled, brought safely to earth, enchanted by her good-witch powers, while the Venezuelan woman suffered. Her mouth worked and twisted as if she were gnawing a too-hard nut, and she seemed to live a hundred years as she thought this through and fought it, determined not to be taken in. But her body language gave her away. She was swaying to the music, lulled. In love.

And later that night at the pretty hotel, after midnight when we'd been fucking for hours, Evangelyne got up at last and went naked to the window. Of course people walked around naked then; the whole world was a girls' locker room, and you could walk your dog naked in the center of town, though you couldn't go into stores. She stood at the window grandly nude with the window open to the rainy night.

I said, "You look as if you're going to make a speech."

She said, "I used to not be able to stand at a window at all. I used to be scared."

"When there were men?"

She made a little shrug of yes. We both thought then about the siege of the cult house. The cops had fired almost two thousand rounds of ammunition at the house, and bullets had broken all the windows and even penetrated the walls, so the only room undamaged was the upstairs bathroom where Evangelyne was finally found cowering by police, who didn't at first connect her to the shooter. She was wearing pink scrunchies in her hair and a white flannel nightgown. Of course not a speck of blood on her. I was thinking of this and of Mussolini, who used to make speeches from a window, or, technically, a balcony. Essentially the same.

I said, "So you're not scared now?"

"Not of that." She turned back to me. "You know I could fill that street in about ten minutes? I've done it. Not here, but I've done it. Do you think that's weird?"

"Do you?"

"Definitely. It's weird, Jane. Like, you ever have something happen that's so exactly what you wanted to happen, it feels as if you had to have made it up?"

"No."

She laughed, then looked tentative. She might have told me something then, but a ComPA knocked and ventured in cautiously to give her the agenda for the following day. Evangelyne told her I was coming on the team and would be working on issues around the disappearance. The girl gave me a long, assessing look, then smiled as if thinking we might be friends. When she was gone, I said, "I can do other things too."

"You will." Evangelyne laughed. "Oh, you *will*."

The next five months were very peaceful and joyous. It was like summer camp, in the way that summer camp is like a vacation in someone else's life. I was keeping my side of the bargain, helping Evangelyne to power in those heady months of her annus mirabilis, when that job was easy. For most of that time we lived in a bus with a band of ComPA girls who were all overeducated, needy, riven by love affairs, too intense, someone's voice always raised while someone else said, "Damn, bitch, please calm down." It was speeches, interviews, town halls, meetings that metastasized into one-on-ones. All day we texted officials, wrote emails to supporters, made calls, while kicking or making faces at each other, all of America passing in the windows. I did the dull parts: arranged, kept schedules, made reservations. I was also the nice white girlfriend who could give white donors a feeling of safety, a girl with a radiant public goodness like a stained-glass window, like Eva Perón. In this connection, my sex offender status only seemed to add a little spice, as perhaps fascism had for Eva.

Those women were a priesthood and a pack of merry hounds. There was the blind redheaded Alabama girl, Deakin, who played the ukulele on long bus trips. There was Nell who knitted and Darrelle who was a birder and Minky who could fall asleep anywhere. Priya cast everyone's horoscope and told me my Sagittarius bluntness could be misunderstood by sensitive people. Our beauty, Kaitlyn, let us dress her and coo about the amazing results, and we had long conversations about whether that would have happened Before. Tasha and Yi were our tempestuous lovers who broke up and reconciled at every stop, Yi red-eyed, Tasha stony-faced and unrepentant. Hour by hour, the bus became a malodorous terrarium in which we were penned, condensed, overheating, until we tumbled out, weak as newborn foals, into a hotel parking lot whose silence hit us like deafness, like free fall. We all stretched, saying nothing in the simple hiatus in which no one else knew we'd arrived. Evangelyne was learning to skateboard then, so everybody had to have a skateboard, and sometimes in that first hour they all irresponsibly skated downtown while I stayed behind with Deakin, writing/dictating the *we're here* texts.

For those key months, we were a delicate, potent thing, we ten girls sweeping into town, sweet-talking America and conjuring heaven. We would walk at the roadside singing in harmony. In those scared post-August brownout towns, Evangelyne acted like a drug. She was the prophet of Saturnalia who'd introduced "jailbreak" into the lexicon, meaning the everyday crimes essential to every social system—the tax dodging, black markets, drug-fueled nights that were how a system stretched its limbs—and everyone turned wild with her. At Christmas, we led a drunken throng of locals through the empty streets of Memphis. We all packed into a tiny Indian restaurant, drinking bourbon we'd bought along the way, and made the waitstaff eat with us, we ComPAs helping to serve and wash dishes. A few days later, in a grocery at one A.M., the newly minted mayor of Galveston drunkenly shoplifted a six-pack of IPA, thinking to impress Evangelyne, and we drank it in her car in the parking lot, arguing about whether property was theft, until the police arrived and the mayor had to get out and explain. We left every town with bouquets and love letters. There were always girls who followed us onto the bus; in every city, we "stole" some Democratic activist or activist's daughter who lost her head. One nonbinary kid from Dallas stowed away in the luggage compartment and they cried with a suitcase in their arms when we told them they could stay. On New Year's Eve, long past the excuse of midnight, a party chair put me up against a wall and kissed me while I laughed into her mouth, until Evangelyne appeared and slapped her ass and said, "You'd *best* support me now!"

Often the bus became a day-long argument, with people dipping in during breaks, then going back to their work but making faces of agreement or dissent as the fight went on around them. We argued about whether August 26 was proof of God's existence, or whether the "chromosome line" was evidence it was the work of aliens. We argued about whether it was a lesson, an experiment, a punishment, or none of the above. Was it intended to throw a monkey wrench into our reproductive process to give Earth time to revive? Was it the work of the genocidal God who'd killed all the firstborn sons of Pharoah's Egypt and brought death into the world as punishment for eating a single apple? We also debated whether it was ever acceptable to call those who were taken "men" (as 99 percent of people did) when that erased all the trans women, intersex people, and nonbinary folks who'd gone. We agreed that the term "the disappeared" (which the left-wing media had now adopted) was insensitive too, akin to referring to Jewish people killed in the Holocaust as "the exterminated." We argued about whether this left us with no way of expressing our grief, or even talking about the people we'd lost, and we cried and called each other names, and repented and hugged, and started arguing again.

But a moment would come when we all fell silent. The phones all stopped and we looked up. Because our influence was growing exponentially. We were opening chapters in Atlanta and Chicago, then in Terre Haute and Laramie, then they were opening themselves. We found a hundred candidates for special elections, ran signature campaigns to get them on ballots, and won, all in the same three months. The *Atlantic* called us "The Anarchists Beating Government at Its Own Game." The *Wall Street Journal* asked: "Can Our Democracy Survive the ComPA Coup?" We were an idea people felt they'd had themselves while looking out their door one post-men morning at the weeds growing up in America's streets, a morning overfilled with cacophonous birdsong, as a neighbor passed in pajamas, undone and barefoot, weeping openly: a world of tears and springtime, a world made real.

I was the one who wrote the disappearance into the party platform. In the bus, I would put in earphones and scour the internet for research. When there wasn't enough, I got in touch with universities to prod them to sponsor more. From Evangelyne's email address, I wrote to scientific luminaries, nudging and badgering, calling it a ComPA priority. I signed everything as *Jane Pearson, for Dr. Evangelyne Moreau.*

This work was sometimes featured in our newsletters, since it was popular with the grassroots. Internally, it was not. On the bus, there was an ongoing argument about whether this focus bordered on "androlatry"—the religious worship of men that had become very common in those months. Many spiritually minded women saw the vanished men as ascended bodhisattvas, and some even claimed to be guided by them or healed by their masculine intervention.

Of course (the ComPAs said) the concept of "men" had always been religious. All women were sold the idea of men as superior beings, closer to God, and the idea of servitude to men as a pious duty of all females. God made man in His image, and woman as a softened, degraded form: the gift of a slave for Adam's birthday. Only men looked at heaven and saw a mirror. A girl world (said the ComPAs) might dispense with all hierarchical religion, might have no gods *above.* Even erotic love might lose its tone of upward worship. Trans men could be masculine without making sex into a two-tier system, as cis men always had. We could love one another face-to-face, where before we had loved only through a glass darkly: so the ComPAs said.

In the midst of all this, I thought about Leo and Benjamin less and less. I was always in a crowd, then in bed with her. And I was happy like an unhatched chick in a warm egg, waiting. If I sometimes had a flash of Leo during sex and was sickened by unbearable pain, or if I sometimes felt like the husk of a once-living organism without Benjamin, I put it in brackets. Kept going. Went to work. And Evangelyne was sympathetic to my pain but hadn't liked Leo and hadn't met Benjamin. Of course the pain returned in dreams, in which there was a baby I'd lost through negligence, and then I found him, mutilated but alive, and I knew I had to save his life, but would forget him again, then find him again, every time in worse condition, and I would flail in guilt and lose him again, and wake up crying. Then I went to work.

All over the world, women had these dreams and woke up crying and went to work. There was so much work to do. And I would have found it easy to be happy that way if nothing had interfered. It didn't matter that Evangelyne ordered me around and had no time to hold my hand when I cried about Benjamin—that meant nothing. Our relationship was charged and delicate; an ideal friendship touched by fire. Once she said to us all, "How someone treats you is nothing to do with how they see you—until it *becomes* how they see you." Then she asked, "Is that anything?" meaning, *Could it be used?* We pondered, the cozy, uncomfortable hum of the bus all around and a heavy East Texas rain making lines of wavy light on the windows, lines that trembled and were deformed in wind. It was the early days, when the water supply was still unreliable in many places, and the roofs of apartment buildings were covered in buckets, tubs, kiddie pools, trash cans—makeshift rain barrels of every color, shape, and size. Houston stood on the horizon with its unlit office towers already looking like monuments of a lost civilization. There were no cars on all the spaghetti loops of highway, nothing but rain and lightning, and in the bus, the light was moody and strange, the artificial bus lights overwhelmed by the gray light pressing on the windows. We have no real face; they are masks that are borrowed and passed on, that live for millennia and are what a human is. We didn't understand that then. I understand now. There is no truth about life.

But I loved her. Even if my love was a face I made, I loved her all the time and was out of my mind sometimes with the feeling and the rain and the lightning. I had no other face.

The day the Ghoreishi paper came out, Evangelyne didn't comment publicly. Instead, we scheduled a visit to a Men home. It was the home of one of Evangelyne's exes, a very common animal in lesbian circles, who happened to be having an open house. Evangelyne and I would fly to L.A. from New York—our first flight since I'd joined the team—do the visit, watch The Men at the house, then have a meeting to decide our position. As I understood it then, this appearance was a sop to Men believers, as an atheist politician might feel obliged to show their face in church at Easter; Evangelyne was publicly respectful to Ghoreishi but privately hostile to The Men. I still hadn't watched it for this reason. We had seen short clips on the news, but they always looked very clearly fake, or they did with Evangelyne there, disgustedly saying how fake they looked. I did want to watch more seriously but kept putting it off until I was alone. Now I put it off until the open house, when Evangelyne couldn't disapprove.

The day before, we were in Manhattan for a Conception Crisis conference. I hadn't gone to any of the morning events because Evangelyne and I had had a fight, after—for the first time—she'd mentioned "The White Girl," and I said I knew she hadn't been totally truthful in that essay. Evangelyne reacted with shock. I was shocked at how much she was shocked. We were silent for a full minute, sitting in front of a room-service breakfast in one of those beige hotel rooms with "art" photographs of the city on the walls. Outside the window, a sheer cliff of office windows faced us, and steely February weather that would pervade my memories of that day. She had the posture of a person facing a reckoning. I was afraid and began to haltingly specify that I meant the love stuff about the stained glass, the horse with the streaming mane, and "pure." At first she looked very relieved, then she frowned and said, "What? That was true." I said self-consciously that it just seemed sentimental. She scoffed and said, "So the essay was bad?" I pointed out that we hadn't gone riding that day because her horse was sick. She said, "They had more than one horse. We went out riding, Jane." I said, "But I feel like the word 'pure' plays into stereotypes about whiteness?" She said, "Now I'm racist? What?"

I started crying, which always annoyed her but which I couldn't help. I tried to explain that she was smarter than me, and it sometimes made her motivations opaque, so I naturally started imagining things.

She said, "That's bullshit, Jane. If a man had written that essay, you'd be able to hear it. It's not rocket science. It's love."

It got no worse than that because she walked out. She had a way of pulling the plug and leaving me alone and hysterical. That day, I knew I was wrong in a way that exposed me as rotten and deserving of hate, though we definitely hadn't gone horseback riding. I had still never ridden a horse. She must have gone back with some other girl and gotten the two events mixed up. She had a surprisingly terrible memory. I went to a mirror and watched myself cry and the ugly faces I made. I was a nonentity. A slave for Adam's birthday. A Dina.

At the same time, part of my mind was aware that she really was smarter than me, and she'd just kicked up a lot of dust. She'd been braced for exposure, then had looked relieved when I specified that I meant the love part. There was *some* lie in that essay, a lie she was afraid to face. Immediately I suspected it was in the story of how she'd killed the cops. In the essay, she'd repeated the version her defense attorneys presented in court. She'd been asleep in bed and was woken by gunfire. She'd picked up a gun to defend herself, because that's what Americans do. It was dark. She was unworldly and a little myopic. When she crept to the window and peered out in panic, she never guessed the attackers were cops. She fired on them in terror.

The cops, however, said that the first shots came from the house, that they hadn't fired until fired upon, that one of their men was killed before they fired. They said Evangelyne was the cause of the massacre.

Sometimes, when I was angry at her, I thought this might be true. At such times, I thought of my suspicion as a hunch. At all other times, I saw it as shameful malice, an idea I entertained only because it would hurt her if she knew.

As I thought about this, I got a text from the airline, saying our flight to L.A. had been canceled. On the heels of this, I got a text from Evangelyne saying I should come down to the lobby. I cleaned up hastily and went. She was there with some Lower Manhattan ComPAs and a bioethicist she'd met at the conference. She introduced us all, very friendly, as if there was nothing wrong. I was charming to them in my wife persona. They were taking a lunch break, talking excitedly about the morning's events. We all walked to Ground Zero, although it was really too cold for such an outing. At that time, people liked to be outdoors, as if we needed to inspect the world bequeathed to us by men, in this case the Financial District of Manhattan. Finance had just won its fight to be a priority sector in the Christmas budget, but the area still felt abandoned. With the people gone, it had a Skynet vibe, our tiny group dwarfed by glass-faced skyscrapers seemingly built to accommodate alien organisms of gargantuan dimensions. Or perhaps the buildings themselves were cybernetic giants on which we lived as fleas.

I was thinking this, walking just a little apart, while they heatedly talked about Karen Xi, the biotech executive who'd delivered the conference's keynote speech. Xi's company, GenPro, had recently succeeded at producing embryos with two mothers through the use of in vitro gametogenesis, a process through which an embryo could be grown from any cell. The first human fetuses conceived this way were already in their second trimester, and twenty-three of the initial ninety-four embryos were developmentally normal and healthy. The others had either spontaneously aborted or were aborted through the choice of the mother. The research team had already identified areas for improvement. A problem going forward was that, for reasons not yet understood, every fetus that remained viable was female.

Xi covered all this in her keynote speech before warming up with a crescendo of verbiage about innovation, American freedoms, and the pioneer spirit and announcing her presidential run. Now the ComPAs were irritably saying Xi might win. Voters were so naive, they would easily accept a biotech executive as an outsider candidate. And at fifty-two, Xi had a hard-edged beauty; she looked like the A-list actress who would play Karen Xi in an action movie. She had some previous political experience and, best of all, a tragic backstory. Her youngest daughter was one of the Burning Girls, the two-hundred-odd women who'd committed suicide horribly on August 26.

On the other hand, Xi's work in biotech, however necessary it now was, had a strong ick factor. For instance, because of past legal judgments, Karen Xi might *own* children born from IVG. She was also known for lobbying the government to relax regulations against "human-animal chimeras." These were just animal embryos with some human genes, and they had real medical applications, but it didn't play well with voters. Imagine a half-human, half-pig baby, born to donate organs—that alone ought to kill her electoral hopes, the ComPAs concluded gloatingly. The bioethicist said the joke on Twitter was that if Evangelyne Moreau and Karen Xi both ran, the election would be between one candidate named Dr. Moreau and another who literally was Dr. Moreau from *The Island of Doctor Moreau*.

They all glanced at Evangelyne then, checking hopefully to see if she'd decided to run. Evangelyne smiled noncommittally, looking at Ground Zero as we passed. She mentioned that she was flying to California that evening and had to keep an eye on the time. She used the first person singular—"I'm flying to California"—as if I weren't there. I remembered again that the Men thing we were supposed to attend was at her ex's house. Half the ComPAs in L.A. had dated her, of course, but in this context, it felt different.

I thus felt some satisfaction in announcing that our flight had been canceled, so time was not an issue. There were no other flights to L.A. tonight.

But at this, the bioethicist got excited and said she thought she could get us a private jet, if Evangelyne was interested. She knew a woman who'd inherited a jet. Evangelyne said, "Hell yes." Everyone laughed at her excitement. I too managed to laugh. One of the ComPAs put in shyly, "Wouldn't people think it was hypocritical if you flew in a private plane?" Another ComPA scoffed. "Come on. They call Evangelyne hypocritical for *breathing air*."

By that point, we'd reached the waterfront. Flocks of people were praying and meditating there, as was common in public places now. Perhaps because it was that atmosphere, we fell silent and drifted meditatively apart. The bioethicist was texting her friend about the private plane, while the New York ComPAs pretended not to be waiting on the outcome, demonstratively gazing at the gray river. Evangelyne and I walked off from the others and headed down a pier. The morning's argument was tangible between us, but neither of us mentioned it. We looked back at the wall of skyscrapers built from the sweat of millions of people, not just people here but all around the world, wherever money was made by sweat. The clouds had parted. Sun fell from on high. The day itself seemed to tower, and the praying women below appeared to be worshipping the buildings, even though they were facing away from them.

I said, "I just realized you're running for president." Evangelyne smiled and threw an arm around my shoulders, startling me. She seemed lighthearted suddenly, or perhaps the word is reckless. She stretched out a hand and swept it past the skyscrapers, saying, "All that stuff built by people thinking one way . . . we could get rid of it all. Do you believe I could?"

"You don't want to keep the private jet?"

We both laughed. She said, "Baby, don't try to keep me honest. I'm already honest. You don't even know how honest I am."

"Okay. But power corrupts."

"You think?"

We laughed again, so hard it felt performative. The fight of the morning was between us, the ghost of it, a gossamer, provocative thing, as Evangelyne grappled me to her and we kissed in the cold of the riverfront, aware of the others waiting for us and possibly watching as we kissed. And I was thinking of the people on the shore who weren't us, all the people living their real lives, who could never matter as we did. I was thinking of them enviously. I was remembering my life.

That night I found her a pilot. All the while I was out of sorts, unbalanced, scared like a person who hasn't worn enough layers for the weather and has forgotten what it's like to be warm. The fight and the waterfront scene had changed my mind about something, I wasn't sure what. But getting the pilot was just a matter of badgering people until it happened. Half of real power comes from badgering people, a very underutilized tool.

Evangelyne and I took no one else on the plane. It was our plane now: a low, oblong room with an anodyne Hilton aesthetic, a reminder of how unimaginative the very rich can be. Nonetheless, as it took off, we laughed in adolescent victory. Our own motherfucking plane!

Evangelyne led me to the bed and we had sex while the plane achieved cruising altitude. We hurt each other a couple of times with the occasional turbulence. Afterward we lay on a few stacked pillows and looked down on miles of rock mountains in moonlight, the details all picked out in snow, with plunging valleys where dark trees grew and a bright tail of water subtly moved. Against this was the prosaic white canister of the jet engine, snug beside the window, and its massive intimate noise.

This was when she first hinted at the truth, though I didn't know that was what it was at the time. We were talking about the plane and how much this was like a fantasy, and she said she'd long been dogged by the feeling that everything that came after August was a dream.

When I asked what she meant, she launched into the story of her August 26, a story I'd heard many times before. It was about a white Republican woman who'd lived in Evangelyne's neighborhood and led a campaign of harassment against her, mostly conducted via the homeowners' association. This HOA was always issuing fines to Evangelyne for trivial infractions, and sometimes for things she hadn't done. On the morning of August 26, Evangelyne went to confront the woman, and they had an argument on the woman's doorstep, in the course of which Evangelyne lost her temper and said she would like to punch the woman's teeth down her throat.

At 7:14 that night, Evangelyne was working at home alone. She had her phone off as she often did and didn't notice when the disappearance happened. At about eight P.M., she went out to take her garbage to the curb. On the street she found eight cop cars, all parked just out of sight of her front windows. All had their lights out. All were empty. It was quiet all around, not a cop to be seen. At her feet on the lawn she saw an object she would later identify as a high-tech battering ram. It took her a long time to trust her instinctive feeling that the policemen were all gone.

I'd always found this tale too good to be true. I half expected her now to admit it was a lie. But she told it exactly the same, with what was clearly genuine emotion, balking and sensitive, reliving that night. I realized with a tweak of self-loathing that it must have happened exactly that way—her rolling the garbage can out to the curb, the cars in her peripheral vision, the startled recognition, the terror. She'd been certain the darkness was filled with police whose guns were trained on her. She had stood in the road for fifteen minutes, paralyzed, hands in the air, not getting it. By the time she felt brave enough to investigate the scene, her clothes were soaked with sweat.

"But what I keep going back to," she said, "is the minutes just before they disappeared. I'm sitting at my kitchen table reading a letter, and I don't know these cops are surrounding the house. I don't know I'm about to be killed. Because you know that was what was about to happen. It's too easy for a cop to say I came at him, to say he had a reasonable fear for his life."

I said cautiously, "So, not the part where you're standing in the street?"

"Not at all," she said flatly. "It's the house."

"Why do you think?"

"It's what I'm telling you. I feel like this is a dream. I keep thinking I'll wake up back in that house, only this time there's no disappearance. The cops go ahead and break down the door, and nothing stops them. I mean, the men disappearing? That's not real life. Cops executing a no-knock warrant on a Black girl who threatened a nice white lady? A Black girl who happens to be a known cop killer? *That's* real life."

The plane had passed out of the turbulence and now felt unnaturally still, as if braced for something. She too seemed braced for something, though her voice was calm and clear.

"It sounds like PTSD," I said. "I mean, not to dismiss it."

"Yeah. No, I know it sounds like PTSD." She shrugged as if this were immaterial. "But I've also heard of people having dreams like that, extended dreams, when they're on life support. There was a woman in prison who'd been shot seven times, and when she was in the hospital, she hallucinated whole weeks of life. Like, getting up in the morning, making breakfast, dressing her kid for school—that level of detail. All the time, she's in a coma in an ICU. Did you ever hear of that?"

"I don't think so."

"I *can't* be alive. That's what haunts me. I've got no business to still be alive. So this trip? The Men? Baby, I need this reality to be *real.* I don't want to be dealing with unexplained videos. I don't want any spooky math that shows impossible things are happening. That Ghoreishi paper? That ruined me."

"So why are we going to a Men thing?"

"Because it's my job. Because I'm not a child. Shit, Jane."

Then she apologized and said we should get some sleep. She shifted to lie on her back. For a while, I kept thinking of things I could say about the way she treated me. I again suspected her stories weren't true, or at least that she was withholding something. The fight of the morning nagged at me. I'd really never ridden a horse. That wasn't true. At last I was distracted by the dawn, a colossal light coming over a bowed horizon of red Nevada desert. I remembered I'd be watching The Men in just a few hours, and my anger passed.

We landed at LAX and someone gave us a car. We went to the hotel to shower and change, then on to Benedict Canyon. Evangelyne drove because she knew L.A. In the car, she talked about what it had been like to live here, speaking in a self-conscious way that reminded me again that she'd dated the woman we were going to see. When she'd been looking at Men open houses online, she'd recognized the ex's name and called on impulse. Alma McCormick. Now I looked around uneasily at the assorted mansions, most a little unkempt now, their gardens brown, grown out of shape. If we ever broke up, Evangelyne might ask me for a favor and turn up with a new girlfriend. Evangelyne pointed out the mansion at the crest of a hill where we were going.

It was just us two, and walking up in the cool bright sun, I felt the insecurity of not being met by sympathizers, of not being in a ComPA phalanx. Did people support us here? Were we about to be surrounded by hostile Democrats? Inside, the house was like many houses where we'd done fundraisers: an atrium foyer with cozy furniture, a fireplace with a massive stone surround. The furniture was all too far apart because the room wasn't human-sized. I instinctively looked around for a place from which Evangelyne could make a speech.

Here I was hit by excitement, remembering I would soon be watching The Men. As I thought this, Evangelyne abruptly strode away and hugged a disturbingly pretty woman. Of course this had to be Alma McCormick. They laughed excitedly in each other's arms. I expected Evangelyne to look back for me, but she kept talking, shaking

Alma gently by the shoulders. The people all around smiled sentimentally. No one looked at me.

I was newly aware I hadn't slept. I decided to slip away before Evangelyne remembered to introduce me. I didn't feel up to that conversation. I crept off down a corridor and asked a few women by the bathroom if there was a place to watch The Men. They gestured onward vaguely to where Ruth Goldstein stood in a doorway. I felt that excitement again. I had the nonsense thought: *We're off to see the Wizard.* I went to Ruth and, although I could see the TV, I asked if this was where they were watching. Blanca Suarez and Ji-Won Park looked at me. I had a minute to think, *This is it*, though I was also distantly noticing the branches attached to the walls and the crude rope barrier. I was making a point of noticing them to hide my emotion. *Look,* I was trying to say, *I'm noticing the strange things here. I'm not the strange thing.*

Then I looked at The Men. I liked the cats. The men were less shocking than I'd expected. They were like men from any film made before August. Their jerky movements made it seem obvious the images were manipulated; it was hard to believe so many people were fooled. When the killing began, I didn't strongly react. I thought it was a typical scene from the show. Two strangers shoved past me into the room. There were screams throughout the house. I asked if this was normal for The Men, and Blanca Suarez snapped at me for the first time. I wanted to laugh. I was watching The Men and I was fine. I wasn't taken in. I was fine!

Then the clip changed.

12

When I first saw Benjamin killed on-screen, I screamed until I was breathless, until my vision swam from lack of air. I believed I would die. Evangelyne ran in and, for a while, there was chaos, people shouting all around while I sobbed in her arms. Blanca was the one who asked me questions, who needed to know who I thought I'd seen. When I begged to see the footage again, Ji-Won was the one who got a laptop and found the clip on FindThem.

The second time I watched it, I had cried myself out. I could answer Blanca's questions then. I wrote down the names of the men I'd recognized and details of those whose names I didn't know. Blanca posted all this on the FindThem site with the thread title *Mass Fucking Recognition!!!*

By then, I was afraid to move, to take my eyes from The Men. Alma wrapped me in a quilt. Ji-Won and Ruth went to the kitchen and made chili. I ate chili and drank beer in front of the flat-screen

TV, while the other people all gradually left. Ruth didn't. At the time I didn't know this was strange. I assumed she had lived there all along. We talked a lot that night, though I remember not a word of what we said; just talking, and running out of talk all at once, and the relief, as if we'd jettisoned some pointless ballast. Night fell. It never crossed my mind to leave. I was in the one place. We watched The Men.

By that time, Evangelyne had gone. I know now she left the room early on. She'd only watched The Men for five minutes, and had found herself irrationally terrified, sick with terror, like someone with a phobia of snakes watching live snakes writhe in an insecurely covered terrarium. She'd expected this reaction but had not been prepared for its power and persistence. Now she lived in a world that included the snakes. She would never again feel safe.

In the long hallways and unused rooms, she managed to escape the crowd. She slipped out to the back lawn and paced around manically behind the pool house, thinking. At last she lay down in the grass and shut her eyes. When she'd lived in L.A. before, it was a time of crisis and loneliness for her, and she'd sometimes lain out like this, and it had helped her. It did nothing now. When she shut her eyes, she saw the warped animals and the bloodied men on the riverbank. When she opened her eyes, the sky looked flimsy, the pool house and towering palms unreal.

After a while, she heard people leaving: voices in the street, cars pulling away. Then she got up, walked down the road, and sat in our borrowed car, which was now cold. She tried calling my phone, but it went to voicemail. She found some Men sites and checked what was happening now, though she had to stop from time to time and do the breathing exercises she'd learned long ago from a prison psychologist.

At last she came to a decision. She drove to our hotel, making calls all the way. That night, in a hotel ballroom, she held a press conference to announce the ComPAs' position that The Men was a pernicious hoax. She talked about what had happened at the mansion, how I'd been shown what she called a "deepfake video" of my own child being murdered—this on a day when our public schedule said we were attending a Men open house. It was clear, she said, that I'd been targeted as the girlfriend of a prominent politician and an emotionally vulnerable mark. She concluded by saying this species of harassment merited criminal investigation. Commensalist policy would be to stop The Men by every nonviolent means.

At the end of the conference, almost as an afterthought, she announced her presidential run.

She didn't return to the mansion at that time. I didn't miss her or worry about her absence. I lived in that room. We watched The Men.

The massacre clips all appeared to show the same two minutes at different points along the riverbank. The shadows were always the same length. The bright, cloudless weather was always the same. The aquatic creatures arrived exactly forty-two seconds after the adults sprang onto the child. In most clips, all adults took part in the killing, but every now and then, one person abstained. Then the aquatic creatures surged above the water; the abstainer fell into their reaching arms. If the clip continued long enough, we saw the tentacles surge back, bearing the little human figure across the river. They moved in concert, handling the person with what seemed like care.

I was still at the mansion on February 18, when the man carried over the water was Ji-Won's friend, Henry Chin. Two days later, I was there when it was Blanca's father, Alejandro Suarez. I was there when Ruth's son Ethan was torn apart by a group that included her husband, Tom, while her other son, Peter, stood by trembling, then took to the river a little belatedly, stepping straight into a tentacled mass. I was there on May 17, when Billy McCormick was the last to be borne across the river, and the images changed and those who'd crossed were shown sprinting over a cracked dead plain.

It was never clear how many crossed the river. What was clear was that the footage now focused on the loved ones of dedicated watchers. We saw our own men all the time.

They ran in a landscape where not a stick was alive, not a floating seed. The air was thick with dust or rain that glinted like cartoon radiation. There were forests of shattered, leafless trees and wetlands denuded of vegetation, where the water was thick with plastic trash. In a few clips, a half city stood on the horizon, a skyline of partial buildings that appeared to have been gnawed by fire. Some places had entirely lost the contours of our world. There were sculpted fields of orange dust that rose in puffs at every step; there were dunes composed of trash and bone. Once a black palace-like reef collapsed into whirling soot as a boy ran by. We understood: this was a future world in which the men had never disappeared. It was the hell to which we would have been condemned, the Earth they would have made.

We watched until it was real, until the room around us dissolved and became a figment. I would wake from sleep knowing Leo was coming, he was coming like a catfish swimming blindly up to the glass of an aquarium, and I stumbled out of bed, compelled, down the unlit stairs that gleamed resentfully by moonlight, and came in behind Ji-Won and Alma where they watched on the sofa with a quilt on their laps, as the clip changed and it was Leo. He ran among the thin, blackened trunks of a forest that had burned. The trees posed with a scarecrow air against a streaked yellow sky. Leo trotted, his face blank in an unfacelike way, blank like a demon's head.

The clip changed. I turned and went to the kitchen and put some oatmeal on to boil. Out on the lawn I could see the ComPA guards Evangelyne had posted by the gates; one girl glanced up to the window, sensing a movement, but didn't meet my eye. I turned back to the boiling water with its furtive scent of oats. I felt Alejandro Suarez coming to the screen, swimming up, and I closed my eyes and saw him run, in the mud and the rain, in the wind that sucked at the hot, gritty air, in the dark of shut eyes, he was coming to us. The clip changed. I opened my eyes. I got bowls from the cabinet. There was a hint of dawn in the window. I had lost a little time, but the oatmeal was still okay. When I got back to the library, Blanca had joined Ji-Won and Alma. We ate in a staggered formation that allowed us all to see. Upstairs, Ruth was showering. She was the one who never gave up on hygiene, who answered the door when the doorbell rang. All awake: a sense of time gone still.

And in a way, we were just watching television through the fall and rise of civilizations, as many other people do. We watched The Men while North and South Korea were unified, while the first female cardinals chose the first female pope. The day Evangelyne first drew ahead of the Republican in a three-way poll, we were watching The Men, and we were watching when she made the "For the Children" speech that cemented her position in second place. There were wildfires in Canada and drought in South America; refugees fled from cities where infrastructure had failed without male workers; and we watched men running through the dead land. Power plants and oil refineries closed worldwide from lack of skilled workers and diminished demand, and a climate agreement was reached that reflected these new, more permissive realities. Fish populations rebounded in the Atlantic and moose appeared in the streets of Moscow. People talked unironically about Gaea, Themyscira, Eden. We five watched our screen. Spring turned into summer, and now our ComPA guards ranged freely throughout the house. They cooked elaborate feasts in the kitchen, fucked in the beds, spoiled the dog with treats. Laughter rose outside as they splashed in the pool and ran through sprinklers, young and cloudless. It was as if a new, pure generation had arisen in the months since we'd started watching. And we were watching when an objectively different generation was born, the first human beings conceived without sperm, without sin.

The last weeks moved like rock underground, the tectonic grind of unseen things that only change through violence. Outside it was June, it was July, and our curtains were full of troublesome sunlight. In The Men, soot, dust, and scalding air. And we talked sometimes in the worst of the night. Blanca talked the most, about her father and the house they'd had in El Paso with a tall dog gate around the kitchen, where Blanca would lurk and wait for her father to come home with women late at night. He always spotted her and ordered her to bed, but let her shake hands through the bars. She never saw the same woman twice. They were tired, annoyed women wearing too much makeup; nice women who asked her questions in Spanish but kept looking uncertainly at her dad; teenage girls who giggled soundlessly, carrying their beat-up shoes in their hands. One white lady flinched from the sight of Blanca, saying, "What's *that*?" and her dad just laughed. Blanca had always thought her father was rich; then she went to a private Catholic school and found out that was wrong. He would have been rich if it weren't for Blanca's medical bills, he'd said once; then he corrected himself and said he *was* rich, because he could afford her care. Once Blanca had a colostomy bag for months while she healed from a bowel resection, and her dad wouldn't hug her all that time. But he always came to the hospital and wore his lucky sweatshirt. It wasn't his fault she was born a mutant. She should want him back.

And Alma said she now resented her brother, though it wasn't his fault he was the prince of the family, the chosen one who could do no wrong. Maybe he hadn't stood up for her, but they were kids when their mother threw Alma out, and with his gentleness came a kind of weakness. He bent whichever way the wind blew. It was true that, in Alma's many rock bottoms, he never let her stay at his house. But he drove her to AA meetings and rehab. He wouldn't give her money, but he talked her down from ledges. She should want him back.

And Ruth talked about how Peter had consumed her life, never gave her a break from pain. She was getting old and had a young son, but Peter still had to be the star of the show. He would lose his job and get kicked out in the street and find some lowlife to break his nose just so Ruth would come and kiss it better. All the phone calls from hospitals, the suicide threats; he had to make everyone who loved him hate him. She wanted Peter safe with every cell of her body, but she didn't want him back.

And Ji-Won remembered a night she'd been driving to Henry's apartment, and just as she pulled into his parking lot, he called to say she shouldn't come. At that moment she saw a boy—a shining, beautiful, deerlike boy—get out of a pickup truck and sprint up the building's outside steps to the second-story balcony. Before the boy reached Henry's door, it opened. In the lit doorway, Henry still had the phone in his hand. He was wearing a flowered shirt Ji-Won had found in a thrift shop and tailored for him, and he was transfigured by joy. He hung up without saying goodbye.

I had never hated Leo. He had been there when I had no one else, and it's hard to forget that kind of love. We'd fucked so many hours, days, weeks. We had a child, and that child was Benjamin, who cried when Pinocchio turned into a donkey, who was frightened of trees falling on him but believed if one of us stood beside him, we could stop the tree. My son had Leo's face. There's a thing that happens when a man lifts a child in the air, and the child screams ecstatically because it's safe. Leo Casares could be that man, not only for Benjamin but for me.

But in these weeks, my feelings changed. It was the clip of Benjamin with men swarming over him, painted in blood—and not just Benjamin, but three months of men tearing children to pieces, painted in blood. Not one man fought. Not one saved a child. Perhaps this was compulsion or automatism—but what in life is not compulsion and automatism? When was I free from compulsion and automatism? Still I am my life.

A real man would have saved his son. That was what men did. So I'd been taught. So I'd fatuously believed. It was instinctive in a man to defend the weak, to protect the ones he loved. My father and Leo had kept me safe—so I'd been told. So I'd believed. But I watched those murders and considered my life and found not a single instance of a man protecting me, only countless instances of men who *talked about* how they *would* protect me: Leo saying he would like to beat Alain to a pulp; my father wishing he could be there for me in Spokane; all the boys who had said they would fight for me, but they'd fucked me for Alain and said not a word in my defense when I was prosecuted for rape. All the world of men was a vast Spokane, where women and children were abused, and men blamed the women or wrung their hands and said they *would have* stopped it, *if.* It was good cop/bad cop: one cop made you give him a blow job, the other deplored it after the fact and said, "Take care of yourself, you're a lovely girl." It was Alain, who expected you to treat him as a kindly father while he orchestrated your serial rape, and he could laugh at himself when exposed as a sham but never change, never stop devouring children.

Evangelyne came back on the final day, when the wasteland footage gave way to clips of towns. These could be identified as real geographical cities, but with the buildings derelict and overgrown, the trees in parks dead and swathed in dead moss, the roads all choked with drifts of trash. Here the men, the adolescent boys, the trans women and girls, were seen to be coming home: the Japanese shown in streets with faded Japanese signage, the French in Paris and Rouen, an old Siberian man walking down an overgrown road through muddy taiga. We felt we were nearing the end. The colors were milder and the images clearer. They walked instead of running and appeared to have human joints, to weigh what humans weigh. Even the beasts had a valedictory air and moved with a tender solemnity, like parents shepherding their children to their first day of school, or to an abattoir.

It was also in these hours that watchers of The Men began to vanish. They melted into air. They disappeared like men.

Evangelyne came into the room, then balked. I noticed first of all that she'd been drinking. She was wearing rumpled campaign-trail clothes, her hair lopsided from dozing in the car. She'd taken off her shoes to come indoors, and I could see the raw, abraded patches the shoes had made across her first two toes. I couldn't speak. I have never loved anyone else; that was what I felt. I wasn't going to speak.

She asked if I was all right, but absently, preoccupied by something else. When I didn't answer, she sat on the floor in a corner, angled away from the screen.

We already knew, because we lived among ComPAs, that Evangelyne had surged ahead in the polls. Karen Xi had been set to comfortably win: donors were flooding her campaign with money, and her lead had stabilized. Some pundits were already calling the race. Then Xi's former company asserted property rights to the genetic material of infants born by IVG, meaning every baby now being born. Xi reacted to the resulting uproar impatiently, saying it was a technical issue relating to DNA sequences and would never affect those children's lives. An email was leaked in which Xi told a staffer she couldn't stand by and let her colleagues be burned at the stake by Neanderthals when they'd just saved the human race. She wrote, *If the voters are that fucking stupid, they should vote for Evangelyne Moreau.*

In the course of a week, Xi's numbers tanked. There was now no realistic chance Evangelyne would not be president.

Evangelyne didn't talk about this. She sat on the floor, exhausted and silent. In the television light, she looked very soft: a heavyset woman of almost forty, her posture bent with worry, in a dove-gray vintage suit with dark embroidery around its lapels. Still, even sitting slumped on a floor, there was intelligence in every line of her body. She was great as Napoleon might have been great, with a potency that came from the blood, from the gods, from being born to rule. And it struck me that she'd burned every hour of her life as fuel for one endeavor. Before she could have one scintilla of peace, she'd demanded that the whole world first be good, and she'd doggedly believed she could make it good—an incarcerated Black woman who had no conceivable means to change the world, much less make a bad world good. Yet here we were.

Still I couldn't turn to her, not fully. I had to look at the screen, at the street where a man named Yaniel Arias was walking. He was the only dwarf who'd crossed the river, the husband of a watcher in Havana, a neat nude figure who now marched tirelessly in a miasma of ash. Evangelyne was indistinct in the corner—we were all dark and indistinct in that room with only the flat-screen light, and even Yaniel Arias was a shape in a darkness—but Evangelyne was dark like a path.

And she said she had come to tell me the truth. It was a truth she'd hidden so long, it felt like it belonged to death, not life. But when she was done, we had to leave this place. We had no time to spare.

THE MEN (8/26 22:41:03 GMT)

1. This is the first of our homecoming clips. By the time we see it, a hundred watchers around the world have already vanished, erased as their homecoming clips ended. In some cases, a family member or friend came in to find the viewing room empty. In some, there was a visitor in the room at the time who went into a fugue state in which they were dazed by euphoria. When they came to, they were alone.

Henry Chin is first seen a long way away, approaching the camera in real time at a leisurely walking pace. In the foreground is a shopping street in Durham, New Hampshire, a few blocks from Henry's old apartment. It's identifiable by the remains of signage, though none of the storefronts is intact. The road is overgrown and littered with trash, scattered bones, and the rusting heaps of military vehicles.

Henry negotiates this terrain with the usual blank unconcern of the men. His clothes are still soiled with the dust of the journey and spattered on one side with a child's blood.

2. This is the last clip I saw of Leo. He approaches the camera through the black masts of a burnt forest in a violet dusk. The light is poor, and the feline creatures walking beside him shrink and grow like shadows. At a certain point, all the feline shapes peel away and he is left alone.

Still the clip continues. He comes closer and closer, until his face looms startlingly into the screen. I'm intent as if I need to understand his expression; there's something threatening about his face. When the clip ends, I want to think about this, but Evangelyne is still speaking. I'm trying to hear Evangelyne.

3. Here Alejandro Suarez is shown from above, walking in ankle-deep water on what was once a three-lane highway. Cars are scattered across it as if hurled there at random. Some are crumpled. Some lie on their sides. Again it is night, and Alejandro walks effortfully, unsteadily, like a drunk staggering home from a bar. Occasionally one of the bird-things passes by, its wings spread stiffly, crossing the screen with startling speed.

Gradually we notice the surging of the shallow water, the odd impulses of light that cross it in waves. A large piece of metal like a car fender cartwheels down the street. The silence of the image has fooled us. We are watching not a drunken man, but a man walking in a gale-force wind. Smaller scraps of wreckage fly past his head, but Alejandro continues undeterred, not ducking or flinching from the storm of debris. There's a doggedness in his movements. We feel the great distance he has come.

4. This clip is very brief. It shows Peter Goldstein swimming in an oil-slicked canal that flows between tall mounds of rubble that sparkle with shards of glass. His dark head surfaces for a moment, then dips again and he's gone. Behind him a wave recedes—a surge of tentacles that seethe, then submerge, leaving only shivering moonlit water.

There's something poignant about the clip's brevity. It's one that would often come to mind when I thought about The Men in later years, when we could no longer see the videos.

5. This is the last clip we saw. It shows a patch of brown land strewn with burned debris. At its center is the crisp outline of a rectangular pit, filled with trash and murky water. The skinny trunks of three burned

palm trees are identifiable by a fourth unburned tree in the same line, its waving yellow crown looking softly colorized in the hazy air. The background of the scene is lit by the blackish orange of fire still burning. Specks of soot fall constantly through the air. For a moment, the shape of a gargantuan elephant fills the frame. Its hide is smeared with soot, and its outsized humanoid eye seems swollen.

Then it's gone. In its wake, the earth is suddenly green with healthy grass. A change of light strikes the pit. All the trash disappears, and the pit is glowing and sweetly blue, the underlit blue of a pool. At the corner of the image, where there was previously a litter of woody trash, there is now a dainty white cabana—the same cabana visible from the window of the room we're sitting in. As we grasp this, Billy McCormick walks into the frame.

13

The white girl who taught Evangelyne what white meant, and who would star in Evangelyne's nightmares all her life, was her first girlfriend, Poppy Beacham. Bizarre though it might seem, she was also where The Men began.

It was the year Evangelyne turned sixteen, a year she spent a lot of her time alone, out walking, thinking, looking for her life. Poppy Beacham was then twenty-two. She talked to Evangelyne in a 7-Eleven, then they walked around town together for hours, both giggling like much younger girls. That day Poppy confessed her mental illness and said she still heard voices, but the voices were comforting. A psychic had told her they were like the demons that had spoken to Socrates. "And if I want to make them go away, I just take meds. The meds work perfect for me." Then Poppy led Evangelyne to a field and knelt at her feet in the grass. From that position, she told Evangelyne she was gay and had a big crush on Evangelyne already. Evangelyne got down in the long grass with her, and there, out of sight of the road, Poppy Beacham held Evangelyne's hand. That was all. But that night at ARRI, the phone rang for Evangelyne. It was in the front hall, where coats were hung, an open public area, and Evangelyne covered her whole head with a parka to muffle the sound while she talked to Poppy Beacham—the most important thing she'd ever done.

Poppy was a real out gay girl with match-straight cherry-red hair she cut herself and piercings in her nose and lip. She was beautiful in an alien way, her pale eyes spaced wide apart, her body so skinny it read as an absence of body, her skin bright white. When she said she was a changeling, she meant it. She believed it was in her astrological chart. It was true that her sweat smelled better than other people's, that her hair was peculiarly silken, that she had a physical intensity that was transfixing if sometimes jarring. Poppy Beacham ate meat with her hands, went swimming in her clothes, touched everyone familiarly—she would rest her hand on the shoulder of a store assistant to ask where the toothpaste was. All the men in Barclough, Vermont, knew who she was, even if they didn't know her name.

At first, theirs was just one of those mismatched lesbian relationships made possible only by youth and a lack of more appropriate partners. At sixteen, Evangelyne had just discovered Foucault and was preparing as a homeschooled student for early admission at Cornell. Poppy had dropped out of high school, and the only books in her house were about astrological signs and easy macramé. Evangelyne dreamed of studying at the Sorbonne but worried it would seem too snooty to voters when she eventually ran for office. Poppy worked as a veterinary assistant and lived in fear of the introduction of certification because she would have to pass a written test. At twenty-two, Poppy still lived with her mother, who worked at a Safeway bagging groceries and was on a methadone program. Evangelyne's mother, before she got her job as manager of ARRI, had been an adjunct professor at NYU.

In the early days, Evangelyne found Poppy's white-trash side exotic: her smell of weed and Jean Naté after-bath splash; her cooking that always started with a can of Campbell's cream of chicken soup; the bright-brown laminate floors in her house, covered here and there by warped offcuts of carpet; how Poppy and her mother, Debbie, both slept in stretch polyester nighties and unironically thought they were pretty. Poppy had five grubby rescue dogs who followed her around in a lovelorn pack and unapologetically slept in beds. Whenever anyone made a move toward the kitchen, the Dalmatian leapt to the kitchen counter, which Poppy and Debbie both considered hilarious. Trashiest of all, the house belonged to Debbie's uncle by marriage, now also Debbie's boyfriend. Poppy complained about him behind his back, always calling him "Uncle," but treated him with casual friendliness to his face. Uncle was on disability and took what Poppy called "the A to Z of pain pills." He was often at the house, lurking in the shadows of a bedroom in a thin gray bathrobe that seemed perpetually poised to fall open, but he never spoke to Evangelyne. Poppy's breezy acceptance of him was one of the jarring notes of those early weeks.

But at the time it was the sex that was the thing, the incredible fact that eclipsed other facts. It was lying really naked, kissing everywhere, the sensitive point of a tongue that focused the world. They could talk in between, well enough, and Poppy was the first one who called Evangelyne a genius, pouncing on top of her and yelling, "How'd you get to be so smart? Did you get struck by lightning or something?" And Poppy wasn't just a real gay girl but a grown-up.

She'd been to lesbian bars in New York. She had had a real relationship with a woman old enough to own a house. Evangelyne was still a kid, and nobody knew—her mother couldn't ever find out—she was gay. Most ARRI people saw homosexuality as one of the perversions of European culture. She walked around in a trance, aflame, dishonest, transfigured, damned. It had to be love.

The first shift came the day Evangelyne told Poppy about Yoruba funeral rites. Poppy was fascinated by everything Evangelyne said about African religions, which Poppy saw as previous to other faiths and closer to some primordial truth. It was the only area where she seemed to have real intellectual curiosity. Though Evangelyne kept trying, Foucault and Fanon left Poppy cold.

This day Evangelyne was explaining how the Yoruba king was buried with scores of other people, who were sacrificed so they could continue to serve him in the other world. There were many titles at court that required a person to die with the king, and the strange thing was that people fought for those titles. They would happily pay for high status with early death. Of course, sacrifice was part of their culture. For important rituals, Yoruba royals would sacrifice a series of creatures: a cow, then a dog, then a snail, then a bird, and a boy and a girl to round it out.

Here, seeing Poppy's face, Evangelyne balked and said human sacrifice was creepy, but it wasn't just African. Most people knew about the Aztecs and the Incas, and Slavs and British Druids did it too. Even ancient Greeks had done it. They had a thing called a "hecatomb," which meant killing a hundred cattle as a sacrifice, and some scholars thought those sacrifices were originally of a hundred people. By this point, Evangelyne wasn't sure what she was saying was true. She just needed to change Poppy's face.

They were having this conversation in Poppy's bedroom, lying on her mattress on the floor, hemmed in on two sides by dog crates, one of which served as a table and was covered with empty cans of Diet Sprite. Through the poorly sealed window came the sounds of wind, twittering birds, and passing cars; through the door, the too-intimate sounds of the house—the drone of Debbie's snore and the occasional jingle of dog tags from the excluded dogs.

Poppy said, "Is that what you believe?"

Evangelyne started to answer, but Poppy cut her off, saying, "Because I don't feel like you should do that just to keep some king dude company."

Evangelyne laughed, but Poppy didn't. Evangelyne said, "This was two hundred years ago. It's not about *me*. Come on. You're part English, so your people . . . I mean, the Druids did it too."

"What's worst is the dogs. And the cows."

"Cows? What?"

"They didn't volunteer to be sacrificed. The cows didn't do it for a job. They didn't even understand."

Evangelyne wanted to laugh again but was made uncomfortable by Poppy's rigid face. She said, "We still sacrifice cows. I mean, we eat meat. Those cows aren't sanctified to a god, but the cow doesn't care."

"I think I'm going to be a vegetarian," said Poppy. "Don't look at me like that. I mean it."

"Okay."

"Do you do that at your place? The cows?"

"At ARRI? Sometimes with chickens. You eat chicken."

"So you're doing . . . what did you call it? The heck thing?"

"Hecatomb. No, that's—"

"I always thought a hecatomb was a square with six sides."

Evangelyne laughed then, and Poppy laughed too. The atmosphere eased, and Poppy entwined her legs in Evangelyne's.

"You goof," said Evangelyne. "That's a hexagon."

"Hexagon, isn't that the military place?"

"I think you're thinking of the Pentagon."

Poppy nodded, but already she'd stopped listening. She fell back on her pillow, squinting in thought. Evangelyne was studying her face, finding the beauty in it that would make this feel good again, when Poppy gasped. "Oh shit! What if human sacrifice is all that works? What if you *have* to do a hexatomb or else God doesn't answer your prayers?"

"What?"

"No, I'm serious! What if all the things that are wrong with the world—it's all because we're not sacrificing people?" At this idea, Poppy shrieked. She grabbed Evangelyne's arm and said, "I'm being scary, right? It's scary? I feel like I just had revelations and I don't like it!"

For a week after this, no worse thing happened. She still went to Poppy's every day but left earlier. Evangelyne felt Poppy's strangeness more keenly without understanding it any better. She took care not to mention African religions or ARRI. They had mediocre sex predicated on the good sex they'd had before.

Then on the Sunday, when she walked up to Poppy's house, Poppy dashed out and intercepted her in the driveway. Poppy said, laughing breathlessly, "Today we got to go somewhere else. My god! My mom just *totally* freaked out about your folks. You're gonna lose it when I tell you."

Evangelyne looked at the house. She wanted to turn around and go home.

"It's cool," said Poppy. "I know where we can go."

"I don't know."

"No, it's cool. We could just—"

The door of the house flew open, and Debbie plunged into the yard, crimson-faced, and screamed, "You fucking leave my daughter alone! She's not well! And tell your fucking Africans to leave her alone!"

Poppy shrieked, hit Evangelyne on the shoulder, and took off running. Evangelyne was lost for a second, but when Debbie charged toward her, she panicked and chased after Poppy.

Almost immediately, Poppy veered off the road and ran directly into the woods. Evangelyne followed, conscious of her slowness. She was chasing Poppy's red hair among the trees, ducking branches, clumsy on the uneven ground. She called out, but Poppy didn't seem to hear. By the time Poppy stopped in a clearing, Evangelyne was out of breath. Poppy ran back to hug her, laughing and elated. She tried to swing her around, but Evangelyne resisted.

"What's happening?" she said. "What was that?"

"Look!" Poppy pointed up to a weather-beaten tree house just a few meters overhead.

"I see it. What happened with your mom?"

"Could you believe that? Fuck! It's because I told them what you said? About the hexagon?"

"The hexagon?"

"Uncle lost his shit. He says, 'That's Satanism, that's demon worship,' like he's suddenly a Christian? What?" Poppy laughed. "And my mom's all crying, like she only now discovered I'm a lesbian, and maybe *that's* Satanic? Says the lady who sleeps with her uncle!"

Evangelyne tried to smile, but she felt nauseated from the run.

"I told them what you said about eating chickens, and Uncle's like, 'Eat every damn chicken in the world, but if you burn it to an idol, you're a Satanist.' He thinks every cult is Satan worship. Like, I asked him if the Moonies worshipped Satan, and he says, 'Hell yes.'"

"You're talking about . . . You didn't tell them about the human sacrifice?"

"I said how you said ancient Greeks did it, and I'm pretty sure he thinks ancient Greeks are a cult now."

"You know we don't believe in human sacrifice. You told them that?"

"I know you don't."

"Also ARRI's not a cult." Saying this, Evangelyne felt a scruple. She herself had often complained to her mother that ARRI was a cult. They were people trying to change the world by chanting in languages they didn't speak and praying to statues they'd ordered from a catalog. All her life, she'd been ashamed to bring friends home.

But now she said what her mother had always told her: "If believing in the power of ritual makes ARRI a cult, then most of the world's in a cult. I mean, think about Catholicism."

Poppy shrugged. Her mind had moved on to something else. "I was saying to my mom—this was what she freaked out about, okay?

So, in your religion, do they only sacrifice their own, or would they sacrifice someone like me?"

"Now I don't know what you're saying."

"I mean, she's the one who's scared. I'm not. I know you'd protect me, but she's afraid you're bringing me to them."

"You don't think ARRI is *doing* human sacrifices?"

"I'm just asking. Just so I could tell my mom."

For a second, Evangelyne couldn't speak. Her mind was trying to put this together with Uncle, with methadone, with Debbie screaming, "Tell your fucking Africans to leave her alone!" At last Evangelyne said, "I mean, my people are . . . we've got some weirdos there, but we're not *killing* people. My mom has her PhD, she still writes articles in journals. That's what you think my *home* is like?" Then she felt something fall into place and said, "You've got to know that's racist."

At this, Poppy turned away from her with an offended smile.

Evangelyne said, "No. You have to take that back. That's my family."

Poppy said, in the voice of a person being patient in the face of unreasonable treatment, "I don't want to hurt your feelings. But what Uncle says—and some of his friends are retired police, and they say it too—there's people in your house who came here to prey on girls. Because a lot of your men are criminals from places like Baltimore, where it's part of life? They sing *songs* about being pimps. And those men are abducting girls, even kids, like I don't know how young, but kids. That's what *cops* say. So it could be human sacrifice or just a normal criminal thing. Or the two could be connected, because . . ." and Poppy went on talking, as if Poppy, not Evangelyne, knew who

Evangelyne's people were, while Evangelyne was paralyzed by rage. She was unable to speak. She was unable to even make a facial expression. Her heart rate spiked, and a feeling swept through her like a piercing noise that kept increasing in pitch.

It should have ended there. There was a blank in Evangelyne's memory where she saw herself going home, a clean break. She should have never seen Poppy Beacham again. There was a gap in her memory where that could have happened.

But she also remembered staying there all day while Poppy raved about being sacrificed—hours of holding Poppy and soothing her, lying on the old musty mattress on the tree house floor. That day Evangelyne explained again and again why it didn't make sense to think people sacrificed their neighbors in Vermont in 1997, why it didn't make sense to believe ARRI men were pimps from Baltimore, why Poppy shouldn't go around saying these things—just the first of many days Evangelyne spent trying to talk Poppy Beacham out of being insane.

Looking back, there were two reasons Evangelyne fell into this trap. The first was that she didn't yet understand racism. To her, it was a dubious entity, something exaggerated by adults to stop kids from going out and doing things. When Evangelyne and her brothers were growing up, there was a neighbors' house they were banned from because the parents were supposedly racist; Evangelyne and Giovanni sneaked there once to hang out with the sons of the family and found it thrillingly had MTV, Nintendo, deviled-ham sandwiches on Wonder bread, *Playboys*, and a picture of Jesus with a glowing heart visible through his clothes. There was a thing going on (Evangelyne and Giovanni agreed) where the adults were afraid they would hang with redneck kids and pick up their habits, and so those people got called "racist." It was true that local kids had called them racial slurs, but kids said every nasty thing, even when they didn't know what it meant. One white girl had cracked Giovanni up by saying his NYU hoodie was "ghetto." And maybe that was racist, but it wasn't *real* racism, not the kind that hurt people.

The second thing was that Evangelyne had lived around mental illness all her life. Places like ARRI attracted troubled people. One visitor spent his whole time there facing Mecca as he moved about the rooms. Another built shrines in the woods to his own shoes. Cowrie shells were ubiquitous at ARRI—if you walked barefoot, sooner or later you stepped agonizingly on a cowrie shell—and one woman had to be expelled because she wouldn't stop eating the shells clandestinely, believing they would cure her cancer. Evangelyne was raised with the belief that madness could be revelation—God's strange voice—or else a manifestation of pain. Either way, it could happen to anyone, and one of the beauties of African cultures was that they didn't lock people up for being different. The best cure for ailments of the spirit, Evangelyne was taught, was unconditional love.

So Evangelyne kept going back to the tree house, bringing herbs to burn, vitamins, spiritual books to read aloud. And it worked, or so she believed at first. Poppy started back on medication and got on a waiting list for therapy. She admitted it was her "demons" that kept telling her about human sacrifice, and maybe they weren't so benign. Sometimes she even talked about her sickness with humorous chagrin. Once she told a story about a man who came into the vet's office holding an elderly dachshund in his arms and asked, "Do you treat spiders?" Then all the people waiting with their pets had looked at the dachshund in revulsion, thinking it had spiders. Really the man had a sick tarantula at home; he just happened to have the dog with him. Then Poppy said, "I've got spiders. *Head* spiders." She made a goofy, cross-eyed face and, when Evangelyne laughed, was innocently pleased and burrowed her head into Evangelyne's shoulder. Evangelyne loved her then, or wanted to love her. She wanted her to be okay.

But there were whole days when Poppy was delusional, and her delusions were still focused on ARRI. She would ask if the ARRI people burned people alive or killed them first. Once she saw a stick in the woods she thought was a "baby bone" and started to cry and tremble. Poppy thought ARRI men were following her in cars, waiting for a chance to seize her. Her demon voices muttered to her that Poppy had to burn, that only her death could save Earth.

Worse in a way were the things Poppy told Evangelyne that might be true. Was it delusional when Poppy said Uncle tricked her into taking extra sleeping pills so he could have sex with her? When she said she'd once woken naked and both Uncle and his friend Roy were standing over her in their underpants? When she said once she didn't want to take an extra pill and Uncle said, "Oh, you're no fun," as if he thought she was in on the game? Was it true that, when Poppy tried to tell Debbie, Debbie said Uncle kept a roof over their heads, and Poppy would have to toughen up? Poppy made Evangelyne promise to save her if Uncle "got really bad again," and Evangelyne promised—couldn't not promise. But she wanted to say, *I'm a kid, this isn't my responsibility, I can't do this.*

Then Evangelyne walked home down an empty country road and thought, *But I love her*, and was afraid. Too much had happened, and the world had become too big. It was the year Sundayate had his heart attack, so all the lectures and workshops were canceled, and the ARRI house was hushed, half empty. The adults were preoccupied, furtive, in the mood of a people whose king is sick and all the land is sick. When Evangelyne got home, no one knew she'd been gone. She went to her bed in a six-bed dormitory, tiptoeing past a woman already sleeping, and crawled into her upper bunk that was always full of books. Now it also had a shoebox of Poppy memorabilia: a Bic lighter, an empty vial of Lorazepam, a blue silk flower, a Siouxsie and the Banshees cassette Evangelyne listened to only in snatches because she didn't like the music. Evangelyne lay with these relics all around her on the bed and cried. She'd long ago learned to cry without being heard, but now for the first time she resented her proficiency. She needed to be caught. She needed to escape from Poppy Beacham and she didn't know how.

What broke this spell was that Evangelyne's older brother, Giovanni, came home from college for the summer. Evangelyne instantly confided in him about being gay, about Poppy's mental illness, Uncle, everything. If it was a bid for his attention, it succeeded. As their mother commented, all that summer she and Giovanni were "thick as thieves." Giovanni told her it wasn't her fault and that bitch was an adult and she should "lose that bitch." He also took on a big-brother role toward two teenage brothers staying at ARRI, Jay and Paul, who'd been left by family who thought they were getting into trouble in Philadelphia. That summer they all became best friends. Giovanni had just bought his first car, and they would drive around for hours, explaining their true selves to each other, singing to the radio, laughing at anything, Jay ambiguously flirting with Evangelyne, and the boys all smoking while Evangelyne sat blissfully breathing their smoke and the wind, so excited and so safe. She came out to Paul and Jay, and they were overawed at first, tongue-tied; as Giovanni later said, "rabbits in the headlights." But soon they started teasing her about it shyly, and Evangelyne could tell tales about her crazy ex, which Giovanni used to interrupt with little falsetto cries of "Oh no!" Paul had a beautiful singing voice, and the others tried to harmonize with him sometimes, failing and laughing and blaming each other as they barreled down an empty highway. Only one night they succeeded, a night they were stuck in a blinding fog and driving with dreamlike slowness on a winding road, seeing nothing but the closest branches and a faint apparition of road ahead, their voices magically interwoven, turning and turning, singing slowly,

If you get there before I do
Coming for to carry me home
Tell all my friends I'm coming too
Coming for to carry me home . . .

until a sudden shock of light hit, a car with high beams on their side of the road. Giovanni braked, swerving so the wheels left the tarmac and a tree trunk loomed, the song smashed every way: yelps, shrieks, swearing. Then they were back on the road, the lights gone, song gone. They all laughed explosively, clobbering each other. Evangelyne said, "Oh shit. We're alive!"

In this time she didn't see Poppy. She'd asked Poppy (borrowing not just Giovanni's language but his tone of voice) to respect her boundaries. She did agree to call Poppy once a week, which she justified to herself with the fear that Poppy would kill herself.

In these calls, Poppy swore she was doing way better, and the new meds worked, and she was eating and even picking up shifts at work. Evangelyne explained why they couldn't be together, and Poppy agreed, expressing admiration for Evangelyne's maturity. "You're my one true love," Poppy said, "but I know if I love something, I've got to set it free. So I'm sticking to my once-a-week, and I'm so, so grateful you didn't slam the door."

This was bait, and Evangelyne knew it. She also knew she was creeping toward seeing Poppy, allowing herself to remember Poppy's gentle hands, her otherworldly face, the all-day glow of having a girlfriend. She would find herself thinking it could still work out. Bipolar was an illness, and you didn't abandon a person for having an illness. And soon Giovanni would go back to school. Jay and Paul would go home. She'd be left here alone.

Then one Saturday night Poppy called, hysterical and sobbing, to say that Uncle was "hurting" her again. "I didn't want to tell you, but he's getting so bad. He puts the pills in everything. And Roy, that friend of his, is always around. They started drugging the *dogs*. I was sleeping with the dogs in my room, and last night I couldn't wake them up. I couldn't wake them up!"

Evangelyne was in the ARRI front hallway. She could see through the window into the dark front yard, where she could just make out Giovanni and Paul smoking at the edge of the road. Now she kept her eyes on her brother, letting her sense of him guide her responses. "Okay. So maybe you could call the police? If you could prove it—"

"I *can't.* The cops are all his friends? A few of them are. And I don't know if it's *true*. Like, the whole point is, I don't know. And all they have to do is say I'm crazy."

Evangelyne kept her eyes on Giovanni. "Do you think it could be that?"

"I don't know. I wake up, and it's like, I have a top on and no bottoms. So I could have gone to sleep like that, but I don't *feel* like I did? And now it's the dogs. I can't be crazy if I can't wake up the dogs?"

At that, Evangelyne started crying herself. "You have to get out of there. For real. Is there someone from work? Because I can't—"

"No. Listen, I worked it all out."

"Because you need a place to stay. Long term."

"Yeah, a place he can't get at me. I worked it all out. I'm going to go to a hospital."

At this, Evangelyne relaxed as if an agonizing pressure had been released. She even smiled, gazing out at the dark yard. "Of course. You need a hospital."

"Yeah, I mean, right?" Poppy laughed a little nasally. "Like, we're so dumb. Not you, but I'm dumb."

"Okay. So you're going to call an ambulance?"

For a long time, Poppy didn't answer. Waiting, Evangelyne felt a peculiar heaviness in her stomach. Poppy might really need her to come. If Poppy needed her, she had an excuse to see Poppy. Outside, Giovanni had stooped down to look at something in the grass. She could ask Giovanni for a ride. If he said yes, that would prove it was all right.

At last Poppy said, "I could call an ambulance. But if they come, my mom's just going to get rid of them? She's so shit scared of getting stuck with the bills. If you came, I was thinking we could walk to Dunkin' Donuts. There's a pay phone there. Then I know I'd really do it."

Evangelyne gripped the phone. "My brother drives. I could ask— "

"Oh my god! You're an *angel.* Oh my god, *thank you.* Just get me out of here, and I swear I'll never ask you for anything again."

Evangelyne ran out onto the lawn. By the time she reached Giovanni and Paul, she'd already decided they had to go. She told the story in that mood. She used the word "rape" and talked about the dogs being drugged, about Poppy waking up half naked.

She was ready for Giovanni and Paul to resist and dismiss this as more crazy shit. But both boys became very serious and noble. Speed was of the essence, they agreed. It was perfect that Poppy was going to a hospital; it would keep her safe and away from Evangelyne, plus she could get real help. Paul ran into the house to get Jay, and before Evangelyne was ready, they were driving to Poppy's, through a night that now felt wild and warlike. They were heroes on a rescue mission. It was real.

They parked a little distance away from the house, and after some disagreement about how to proceed, all four of them got out and gathered to observe it from a copse of trees. It was an ordinary white one-story house with weeds grown up all around it so it had the appearance of sinking into the ground. Later, they all agreed you could tell bad things had happened there. The penumbra of skunk reminded Evangelyne of the dogs, who mustn't be woken. She crept forward alone from the trees, but not far enough to get out of sight of the boys, picking her way on the littered grass. It took a while to find something to throw—the broken shell of a ballpoint pen. She was afraid it wouldn't make enough noise against the screen, but when it hit, Poppy's window immediately opened. The screen came up, and Poppy crawled right out as if this were all prearranged. Even in that act, she was graceful, and perhaps it had been her athletic nature that had initially cloaked her illness and made her seem not sick but elfin. Poppy dropped lightly to her feet and turned to Evangelyne with a broad, thrilled grin. Then she noticed the boys and stiffened. Evangelyne whispered hastily, "It's cool, it's just my brother and—"

Before she could finish, Poppy was screaming.

Because they were teenage kids, they laughed. It was a nervous giggling they tried to suppress, and it terrified Poppy more. Poppy leaped back for her window, clinging to the windowsill a moment, shrieking, "Help! Help!" like a cartoon character. Lights went on in the house. There were voices and thudding footsteps, a cacophony of furious barking. Then Poppy flung up a leg, hoisted herself with startling sudden power, and vanished. Evangelyne still hadn't moved. She had some idea of confronting Debbie and Uncle and telling them Poppy had to go to the hospital. With the boys there, she felt safe.

The front door opened. Giovanni was already pulling at Evangelyne's arm when Uncle appeared on the doorstep, wearing his familiar gray bathrobe, with a pistol in his hand.

Evangelyne never saw where he aimed. She was running with her brother, her skin all afraid, her whole body feeling how the bullets would hurt. When the gunshot actually came, she tripped and almost fell. She wasn't hit. Paul shrieked, an unnatural sound that went through her like a saw. But he was running, not hit. At the car, they were panting and muttering swears as she realized how slow and ponderous a car door is, how long it takes to crawl inside. They ducked down in the seats as they pulled away, veering off the road because Giovanni hardly dared raise his head above the dashboard. They only sat up when they got out onto the highway, heading any direction, away. Then they all burst out laughing, shouting the story at one another, asking questions and talking over the answers, pounding fists on the upholstery, imitating Poppy's shriek of "Help! Help!"

They were too excited to go straight home, so they drove around for an hour like that. Evangelyne cried a little, and Jay was crying too, or anyway wiping his eyes. He talked about seeing a guy shot once in North Philly. They agreed that fucked you up. Whole communities were being fucked up, and not only in the city. What about these crackers here? Even having a gun was fucked up, but they should maybe start carrying, just to be safe. They laughed about how they didn't want to even open the windows, it was like you'd let a bullet in. As if a window would protect you! Jay said, "Like you wearing a *hat* and think you safe." They riffed on the idea of what they'd be like in World War II, all racing to hide behind a tank. A tree. A hat. "Help! Help!"

They agreed they'd better not tell anyone. They were world-class fools for believing in all Poppy's psycho shit. Giovanni said, "Tell me that's not all lesbians." At this Evangelyne laughed so hard she keeled over onto Jay, who laughingly shoved her away, saying, "I don't want *no* lesbian on me! Y'all got crazy cooties! Help! Help!" They all started shrieking "Help! Help!" again, laughing, while Giovanni weaved all over the empty road for no particular reason, honking the horn.

Evangelyne felt restored to life. It was done. She'd tried, and Poppy had screamed and run away and almost got her killed—almost got her *brother* killed. Evangelyne was free now. Giovanni forgave her. In a year, she would go to Cornell.

The incident in the supermarket parking lot in which the soda can was thrown at Sundayate happened exactly as written in "The White Girl." The mother of one of the girls really did call the police and make wild claims. But by that time, police had been investigating ARRI for weeks, ever since Uncle called 911 on the night Evangelyne tried to rescue Poppy. The police spent that night in Uncle's kitchen, listening to Uncle's and Debbie's stories about human sacrifice, child abduction, and criminals from Baltimore. Two dozen other people would later make statements to police in a similar vein, giving depositions in which they said they'd heard screams coming from the ARRI house and witnessed rocket launchers being unloaded from trucks. Of course other neighbors dismissed this as ridiculous gossip, but the police soon stopped interviewing those neighbors, considering them "dead ends."

During the weeks of the investigation, local attitudes toward ARRI hardened. The darkest rumors were now widely accepted as confirmed. Now there were hand-delivered threats in ARRI's mailbox every morning. Once there was a noose, and another time someone shot at the house from a passing car. The police were called after that incident but said there was nothing they could do. In the final week, ARRI posted armed guards at front and back, which were seen by law enforcement as a red flag. Police plans for the raid on the house took on a military aspect.

Meanwhile, Poppy Beacham had become nonverbal and was finally admitted to a hospital in Burlington. Debbie told the jury at Evangelyne's trial, "My daughter always had problems, but nothing like that. Nothing like, she can't talk. So I'll never know what those animals did to her, but I didn't want it happening to anyone else."

And one summer morning, just before dawn, Evangelyne Moreau was woken by gunfire. She would remember scrambling out of her bunk into darkness, noise, glass shattering, air filled with plaster dust. She was blind and gasping, crawling on all fours with plaster raining down on her head. After that, her memory was patchy. She wouldn't remember how she got up. When she tried to remember killing the cops, the image would always be of a cartoon cop who evaporated neatly as the bullet hit. But she knows she didn't initiate the gunfire, because she took the gun she used from the body of her brother Giovanni. Jay lay beside him, screaming; one of his eyes and a chunk of his face were gone. The window above them was shattered, open to the air. As she rose into it, she was thinking, *As if a window would protect you.*

She saw armed strangers on the lawn. She aimed. She squeezed the trigger and became a different person.

14

About the prison years, there was little to say. The first year she was almost comatose with grief, to the point of once needing to be force-fed. The doctor recommended heavy meds plus electroconvulsive therapy, which she accepted, and it probably saved her life. But if she had problems with her memory, that was something ECT could do. It also took the last remnants of her faith, which was mostly a relief. She had suffered at the COs laughing and mimicking her when she tried to chant in Yoruba. She also spent a lot of that year crying about her problems to other inmates, which went surprisingly well, considering that 90 percent of them were white and 100 percent had their own problems. A lot of COs taunted her and kicked her around—she was a cop killer, after all—but there were prisoners who treated her like their own child. People are a lot of things.

She'd been in that prison about a year when she got a letter from Seattle, Washington. The envelope was covered in Forever stamps, though the letter was just four sheets of paper.

Poppy wrote:

> I moved to Seattle (do you think it's far away enough?! haha!) but the mail works just the same here. Been in the hospital a looong time. Then it took a loooooong time to find you because I'm dumb and no one wanted to help me! But I been writing to the government and newspapers and everyone to tell them you never shot anybody. Don't they know those cops are the same lying dumbasses who bought my crap about how you were sacrificing kids to Hoodoo??? But nobody listens I guess when they see the letter's from a loony bin. Like a crazy bitch can put you in prison, but the same crazy bitch can't get you out! So I maybe can't make it better what happened BUT I'M CRYING FOR YOU ALL THE TIME.

The last three sheets of paper were covered on both sides with hand-drawn tears.

Poppy would continue to write to Evangelyne for thirteen years.

For the first three years, Evangelyne read the letters, although she never wrote back. This was also when she started work on the book that would later become *On Commensalism*—at first a thankless task. The COs were always tossing her cell and scattering her pages to the four winds. She had no research materials at all; the prison library was a set of encyclopedias and a few shelves of tattered romance novels. When she was in gen pop, she had to concentrate against the pandemonium of radios, TV, chattering, whistling, snoring, and even the occasional cellmate fart that interrupted a crucial train of thought. In seg, the only writing implement she was allowed was a tiny golf pencil. But she ground on, and slowly the work became her lifeline. She weaned herself off medication, and when the mother of an ARRI victim sent her commissary money, she ordered a clear-case typewriter. In the fourth year of her sentence, she finished a draft. It was then a Frankenstein book made up of half-baked jargon, flights of sentimental prose about "daughters of a world in chains," plus a few of the ideas that would later make her famous in embryonic form. She typed six copies with carbon paper, and soon half the prisoners were avidly reading it: Evangelyne's first fame.

She was planning to send a copy of this mess to Cornel West. She knew he taught at Princeton and thought a package addressed to "Cornel West, Princeton University, New Jersey," had a chance of being delivered. She'd even convinced herself the typewritten pages would impress him with their authenticity. Then she thought again and mailed it to Poppy.

At the time, Poppy was already infamous in the LGBT community of the Northwest. She was everyone's worst-ever girlfriend, a universal muse and stealer of hearts who periodically went catastrophically mad, ran amok, and left scorched earth. She dated a celebrated artist, then a restaurant owner, then two poets in a row, then a journalist, and ruined all their lives. Everyone in lesbian Seattle had a story about calling 911 on Poppy. Often she peddled books and junk in the street, and once she built an imposing art structure in Discovery Park that she said was a "religious machine." There was a brief controversy about its removal until Poppy set it on fire herself and was carted to a psych ward yet again.

When she was on her meds, she attended community college and worked as a dog walker or veterinary assistant. She functioned well enough in those roles, though she was never exactly sane. Even at her best, she heard voices, which she believed came from a demon realm. A typical letter from Poppy opened with the news that she'd gone to the zoo and received a message from the zebras, but the message was incomplete, so she went to the aquarium, where she was arrested for fighting the guards because she didn't have the entrance fee. She would apologize for writing "loony stuff," once excusing herself by saying, "I got to get back to taking meds, but if I take them I feel like shit, like when Wily Coyote swallows a canonball." Under this, she'd drawn a picture of a coyote with a massive cannonball in its stomach and the caption IS THIS HAPPYNESS? She wrote a lot about gender, most of it unhinged. In one letter, she said men didn't have souls and that was why they grew so large; in another that sex roles were demonic and therefore only "animals, amoebas, plants, and mushrooms" could know God. She was obsessed with climate change and pollution and believed she could hear trees screaming in pain because the earth was poisoned. Human sacrifice was another preoccupation, and she sometimes talked about the preparations for her own sacrifice. She now called this "the Miracle" and believed that when it occurred, the world would be "delivered from evil men."

From the letters, Evangelyne knew Poppy was currently going out with a local journalist. She now sent Poppy her manuscript, along with a letter curtly asking if Poppy's girlfriend could read it and maybe help get it published.

For a few weeks, nothing came from Poppy. Evangelyne couldn't sleep for rage. In the never-dark prison night, she stared at the ceiling of her cell, thinking about the deaths at ARRI, about sacrifice and whose human sacrifice mattered, about Poppy's cheery, babbling narcissism that Evangelyne could not switch off. She thought about Cornell and the beautiful life she could have had if Poppy had never crossed her path. In the nights, her anger turned to fear, which made the prison feel like the last safe outpost on a haunted Earth, and Poppy the evil that stalked outside, a demon from a hell realm. Even Uncle's abuse now felt like part and parcel of Poppy, as if there were an Uncle-and-Poppy entity that had fouled Evangelyne's mind with rape and incest, then gone on to butcher her family.

Then, after three weeks, a package arrived from Seattle. In it were three photocopies of the manuscript Evangelyne had sent. All over each copy were notes: one set from Poppy's girlfriend, one from Poppy's English professor, and one from Lucinda Gar, whom Poppy had met in a coffee shop and enlisted to help. Poppy enclosed a letter that said, "Let me know if you want ANY more help! WE ARE ALL HERE FOR YOU!!!"

From this time, Evangelyne's fortunes changed. She spent the next ten years in prison doing research, completing her education, and writing and rewriting *On Commensalism*, provided with every resource she needed by scholars nationwide.

She never wrote to Poppy again. She destroyed Poppy's letters unread, though the prison officers wouldn't stop delivering them, saying that would be interfering with the U.S. mail. After her release, she cut off contact with anyone who might be in touch with Poppy. No letters came, and eventually she stopped expecting Poppy to turn up at her door. In the meantime, she went to UC Santa Cruz, then transferred to Princeton. She wrote three books and earned a generous second income on the paid speaker circuit, spreading her wings. In all this time, she didn't hear from Poppy. She even found a way of talking about her history without the mention of Poppy. Only once she tried to write about it, in the "White Girl" essay, which was originally all about Poppy Beacham, but she ended up cutting those sections before it went to the editor. When it was published, Evangelyne was terrified that Poppy would come out of the woodwork to set the record straight. When that didn't happen, she felt safe for the first time since she was sixteen.

This sense of freedom continued until, in December 2018, she accepted a post at UCLA. She was hoping to revive the languishing ComPA organization in California; she felt she'd transcended the emotional problems that had undermined her first attempt. In Los Angeles, she bought her first house, a midcentury modern bungalow in Santa Monica, not far from the mansion where we were now sitting. The house represented a hope for selfish happiness, a thing Evangelyne had been afraid to imagine and never really thought could be. In fact, it turned out to be her fatal mistake.

The problem was the homeowners' association in her neighborhood, which kept fining her for violations like having pumpkins on her step at Halloween, allowing a guest to smoke in the driveway, and having an "inconsistent carport." Evangelyne could never make it to the meetings, so the HOA remained an enigma to her, though she knew the unfriendly woman who lived on her right was the president of the board. She asked her only Black neighbor if he thought she was being singled out. He said, "Oh, hell yes," and told her that woman was a Republican activist who'd gone around asking people if there was any legal means to stop Evangelyne from moving in. "Because you're a criminal, you understand. Of course she didn't ask *me*." The crowning insult was when the HOA issued Evangelyne a citation for having an unreported dog. Evangelyne had no dogs, while the Republican neighbor's dog barked all night. When classes ended for the summer and she had free time, Evangelyne hired a lawyer to file suit against the HOA for harassment.

The papers were served on the HOA on August 25. On the morning of August 26, police appeared on Evangelyne's doorstep to say they'd received a call about an African American female breaking into a home. Even though Evangelyne was in a bathrobe, they insisted on seeing ID and a property deed before they would agree to leave. Once they'd gone, Evangelyne got dressed and went to knock on the door of the Republican neighbor, who admitted she'd called 911 but didn't see why there had to be so much fuss about a simple misunderstanding. The woman was disarmingly tiny and seemed alarmed by Evangelyne's presence. Evangelyne began to explain why people shouldn't call the cops on their Black neighbors, but when she got emotional, the woman looked panicked and slammed the door in her face. Then Evangelyne heard—or thought she heard—the woman calling 911 again.

Evangelyne only lost herself for a few seconds. In that time, she beat on the door, kicked notches in its paint, screamed threats. Then she came to her senses. She was a Black woman in a rich white neighborhood, shouting about beating a bitch's teeth down her throat *while* the bitch called 911. Leaving, she tripped on the step and almost fell. In that jolt of lost balance, she knew.

Evangelyne didn't even go back to her house. She got in her car and drove. In traffic, she called a ComPA friend, who volunteered to meet her at Bed Bath & Beyond to help her pick out a security camera. When Evangelyne arrived at the store, three ComPA girls were waiting for her. She'd calmed down enough by then to joke about the meltdown she'd had on the nice white lady's doorstep, acting it out with funny faces and making the others scream with laughter. The girls googled what she'd done and decided that, in California, she was only guilty of vandalism to the door, though in Florida the woman could have legally shot her. Then they wandered the store for most of an hour, engrossed in an emotional conversation about police murders, the carceral state, and white women who dialed 911 whenever they saw a Black person looking happy. They traded stories of bad encounters with police, and the tone was one of sisterhood, but Evangelyne started to feel estranged. Police racism was real—no one knew that better than Evangelyne—but these girls weren't facing what she faced. She wasn't just Black. She had killed two police. She knew how she would die.

Instead of expressing these feelings, she ended up buying a home security system in addition to two outdoor security cameras. Then she lingered in the store with the ComPAs while one of them considered buying venetian blinds. Evangelyne was punch-drunk by this time and joined with the others in making lame jokes about Commensalist window treatments, laughing performatively loudly. When a white sales assistant hurried toward them, they bristled, thinking they were going to be asked to leave, but it turned out the girl had recognized Evangelyne and wanted a selfie. While Evangelyne was posing with the girl, feeling better (maybe being famous would protect her from the worst), her phone rang with a number in Reno, Nevada. Not recognizing the number, she didn't answer. A minute later, the phone buzzed with a voicemail, which she also ignored.

Evangelyne drove home alone and spent the rest of the afternoon writing. She'd gotten the worst of the terror out of her system and actually had a productive day. At about five thirty, she took a break to install her new security equipment. It took almost two hours because Evangelyne had never learned how to do anything handy; one of the notorious defects of women's prisons was a lack of educational programs. By the time she finished, she was physically exhausted. She might have gone to bed without knowing what had happened if she hadn't remembered that, with all the disruption, she hadn't checked her mail that day.

In her mailbox were the usual journals and one book for peer review. There was also a fat manila envelope, postmarked from Reno and forwarded from Evangelyne's old department at Princeton. From the handwriting on the envelope, she instantly knew it was from Poppy.

For a minute she was paralyzed, sweating by the mailbox, searchlit by her new motion-sensor light. When the light went off, she instinctively waved to get it back on, then felt more afraid when it worked. Walking back to the house, she was conscious of being filmed by her own cameras. She glanced at the Republican neighbor's house, of which she could see only the long driveway. Evangelyne was gripping that manila envelope so hard all her fingers hurt. She told herself she would throw it away immediately without reading the contents. She thought this even as she got inside, slammed the door, dropped her other mail onto the floor, and tore the envelope open.

It contained roughly fifty pages of psychosis. At first glance, this looked just like the letters Poppy had written her in prison. Evangelyne started to leaf through rapidly but almost immediately stopped at a drawing of beakless birds labeled DEMON FREINDS. She'd never seen a drawing of Poppy's demons, and she started to read the writing below. It was about how Poppy was fated to burn to save the dying Earth. She was the first sacrifice required by the demons of earth and sky. A thousand other women would burn with her; their names were written in light. The sacrifice of the Thousand would open a Door to the demon realm. "Then the Evil will be pulled through that Door and the demons will Take them for their Keeping. This is the Second Sacrafice, a Sacrafice as aweful as the time of Noah."

Evangelyne almost stopped reading then. She had wandered into her kitchen and glanced at the trash can. Still she didn't throw the letter away. Instead, she sat down at the table and turned on a lamp. She read on about how, through the grace of the demons, the world would become a haven of peace, ruled over by wise queens. Pollution would be cleaned up, and the "genecide of Earth" would come to an end. But the Door would be left open, and some "Lot's Wives" would look back through it, feeling pity for the Evil Men. The Evil would sense them there and start to march toward the Door, "like dogs on the scent." If the Door wasn't closed, these Men would find the opening into the world and flood back in. Then everything would go back to before. The Thousand would have burned in vain.

Poppy was writing to ask Evangelyne to remember this letter and close the Door. Poppy would tell her how, and it would be easy for someone as smart as her. The time was not yet come; all Poppy asked was for her to read this and remember. Everybody else thought Poppy was crazy, but Evangelyne was raised in the Ancient Wisdom. She knew sacrifice was real. Her people had—

Here Evangelyne turned a page and found a crude drawing of a group of men on hands and knees, who seemed to be tearing apart a child. One of the child's arms had come away, and streams of blood were shown in red ballpoint.

This image put Evangelyne over the edge. She started to leaf forward hastily again, now looking only for any indication that Poppy knew where she lived. The fact that Poppy had sent the package to Princeton was comforting. Still, Evangelyne was wondering if she ought to warn UCLA security. She looked at the Reno postmark again and was about to check Google Maps to see how far away it was, when she thought, with a cold, hard shock, of that phone call from Reno, Nevada.

She found and listened to the voicemail. It was from the Washoe County Sheriff's Office, calling to speak about Poppy Beacham.

She opened a bottle of wine and drank a large glass. When she called the number, it rang and rang. She might have given up, but as it rang she heard the voice of her Republican neighbor outside and froze. The woman was shrieking, sounding hysterical. At first Evangelyne was trying to remember where she'd put the property deed, but she slowly realized the woman was screaming a name. She was calling her child to come in.

At that moment someone answered the phone, a girl who sounded brusque and defensive but softened when Evangelyne identified herself. The girl said she was just a volunteer and she would go find an officer. Rattled, Evangelyne poured another glass of wine and ended up spitting a mouthful back in the glass when a new woman came on the line. This woman introduced herself as Officer Meg Herrera and asked if Evangelyne had someone with her. Evangelyne began to cry immediately, knowing Poppy must be dead.

When she could control her voice, she lied that she was with her roommate. Herrera said she was sorry to have such awful news on such a night, but Poppy Beacham had passed. She'd been found this afternoon by hikers in the desert north of Reno, where Miss Beacham appeared to have doused herself in gasoline and set herself on fire. She was still alive when found, and the hikers had managed to get her to the hospital in Gerlach. From there she'd been airlifted to Reno for emergency treatment, but her injuries were too severe. She had been pronounced dead an hour ago.

"Of course a lot's happened since then, and things have been in real chaos with . . . what happened with the men there. I guess you'll understand. So I have your name written down as next of kin for Miss Beacham, that's all I know. There's only four of us here, and that's including volunteers, but if there's anything we can do . . . I'm not finding many people tonight I can help."

While Officer Herrera spoke, Evangelyne was pacing with the phone, sometimes stopping at the wineglass and drinking more. She didn't understand all she was being told. She understood Poppy Beacham had made her next of kin, Poppy Beacham had had her phone number. When Herrera finished, Evangelyne stopped her pacing and was staring out the glass doors to her backyard. An animal ran past, which she first took for a coyote. But it was dragging a leash: a dog. The neighbor was still calling in the night, monotonously now. The name she was calling was "Thomas."

Without thinking, Evangelyne ended the call. She spent a minute trying to figure out how to block the number, then turned off the phone entirely. The voice of the Republican neighbor grew louder, then fainter, then stopped. A door slammed; she had gone inside. Meanwhile, Evangelyne stood over her garbage can and tore up the pages Poppy Beacham had sent and shoved them down into the wet trash with her fingers. Then she washed her hands, tied up the trash bag, and took it to the bin in the garage. She rolled the bin out to the curb, though it wasn't scheduled to be picked up for another day. In the event, it would not be picked up for a week. When it was, it would be because Evangelyne herself had reorganized Los Angeles trash collection.

Leaving the bin at the curb, she was worrying she wouldn't sleep that night and wondering if another glass of wine would help or make it worse. She only slowly noticed a change in the landscape, which then became intelligible as a number of cars parked in the street, not in front of her house, but at a little distance in both directions. The closest car had its inside light on and both front doors open. It was strange enough that she walked down the road to get a closer look. As she went, her vision adjusted to the darkness, and she suddenly saw it was a cop car. Altogether, there were eight police cars, parked along the road in both directions, all just out of sight of Evangelyne's windows.

That story, of course, was one I knew. Evangelyne had told it all the time: how she'd seen those cop cars and found the battering ram on her lawn; how she'd been the focus of a raid that had vaporized, raptured, turned into air. She'd told that story a hundred times. She'd told it to rallies of thousands of people.

But of course she had left Poppy out. She had lied about Poppy Beacham all her life, Evangelyne said, tired and hoarse. She sat in shadow, leaning back against the one bare patch of wall, Ji-Won's branches projecting all around and above her as if protecting her, like the forest around Sleeping Beauty. We hadn't moved. We hadn't physically responded to her. We watched men marching, almost invisible in dust, and Evangelyne was bright among us, fragile.

She said, "You know I fought against believing this. Even after I saw those videos that looked exactly like Poppy's drawings—even then I wouldn't say, *Okay, The Men is the Door. Poppy's right. It's all true.* So even when I was trying to stop The Men, I was acting as if we could fight it rationally. Like, maybe there's a Disappearance, maybe The Men looks just like Poppy's drawings, but this is still reality. There are still limits. If I jump from a roof, I break my back. The sun still rises in the morning. And if it's the real world, there's somebody making those videos, and we can find their computers and shut them down.

"But all that time, I knew. This isn't that kind of real. This is the reality I learned about when I was a child, where you get things done by prayer and ritual and, yes, by fucking sacrifice. So I'm pretending to be rational, but all I really want is to have Poppy Beacham's letter back, to read it to the end and find out how to shut that Door. Because I believe if I can't shut it, I'm going to wake up back in that house, and the cops will break in and shoot me down.

"So I'm thinking, what would Sundayate do? What would Sundayate believe? What did *I* believe, before they put me in prison and burned it all out of my head? And I'm here because I once believed in love as a holy thing, as a power that maybe created the world. And if I were still that pure and stupid, I would know the answer is love. If I could convince you I'm enough, that this world is enough, I think that Door would close.

"I don't even know if you're hearing this. If you are, I don't know how to convince you. I get that you lost your family. You're not Poppy Beacham. You don't owe me this. But if I'm right, you're not just killing me. You're killing all the work we did. We're so close to getting there, Jane. We can make this world everything humans ever dreamed of—all the wildest dreams anybody ever had, that's all within our reach. I love you more than that Leo loves you, *and* I'm going to be president. What is he? What did he ever have to give you? I don't want to be offensive, but in that world, you're a housewife with no skills and no options. Think what you can do here. Think what you can be. Don't be a goddamned fool. Choose me."

Of course, all the time she spoke, we watched. We watched strangers arrive in shattered houses, dead woods, flooded streets. We watched one man reach home and the land come to life all around him and the sky turn blue. We watched Henry Chin on the street outside his apartment building in Durham, New Hampshire. We saw Leo walk back to the campsite and Alejandro Suarez struggling back to the hospital complex where Blanca was having surgery. We watched Peter Goldstein swimming in the flooded street of a shattered New York City.

And as Evangelyne asked me to choose her, Billy McCormick stepped on the dead earth outside our window and it shimmered and grew green. The water of the pool clarified and became bright blue. A coyote ran past.

Behind me, Blanca got to her feet. The colors on the flat-screen TV silvered. I saw this even as I looked away. They were the colors of the room, where the light had changed. It was dusk. I couldn't see Evangelyne.

Time might have passed. I would never find out. I would never learn more about that world.

Ji-Won had gotten to her feet.

I got to my feet.

Ruth and Alma got to their feet.

The screen had gone tiny behind me, and all around the forest was jarring green. It was spangled with dew and moonlight, and the hushing sound of trees was oversewn with the cries of insects.

I took the first step away. I saw the flank of the tent, with a faint spot of electronic light in the tent's mesh window. The others were there and gone. I was lying in a hammock with my boots still on, skin sticky from mosquito repellent and the unwashed sweat of a long day's hiking. The large night around me made this feel clean. I remembered it all, every molecule and trembling of air: I had had an idea about watching the stars come out and feeling wild and solitary, bound to no one else. I had wanted to indulge my fantasies in which I'd never married and Alain hadn't happened, in which I had my whole life free. It was dusk, and the sky was all one color: grayish violet, silken, dim. There had been times I'd been frightened in the world, bad times. This was not a bad time and I was happy.

I opened my eyes. The lime-green leaves of the alder above me were trembling and luminous, brighter than the sky. I could see the tent. My son and husband were here.

15

I felt the compulsion from the first moment, but lay staring at the tent for a long time. The faint light from Leo's tablet went out. The shining in the leaves, which I'd taken for moonlight, turned out to be the last of the dusk. Real darkness fell. When at last I got up, my phone fell out of the hammock. I'd forgotten it was there beside me. Then I thought of looking online, of checking to make sure what world this was. I picked up the phone but didn't yet look.

The mesh flap of the tent was zipped shut against mosquitoes. I hunkered down beside and listened. Both Leo and Benjamin seemed to be asleep. I unzipped the flap very slowly, being as silent as I could. When I could see them, I had to grit my teeth. I clutched my throat with my hand as if choking off the sound I would have made.

Benjamin's head was tucked into Leo's side. His pale hair was clean and unharmed, his legs casually splayed. He was wearing those red Avengers pajamas, which were wrinkled but unharmed. They looked soft. I was amazed by his small body as if I'd never seen a child before. He was astonishingly beautiful—alive. My boy was alive. I had saved the world.

At first Leo was less striking. I'd been watching a version of him for months, and physically the two were identical. But even asleep, this Leo was clearly sentient. It gave him a strange appearance. It was as if a shoe, on closer inspection, were not inanimate but dozing; as if an armchair gently breathed. I didn't like to look at him. I found myself afraid he would reach out and touch me.

The feeling spread to Benjamin. Nausea swept through me like heat, most intense in my head. I shrank back.

For a long time I sat on my heels. The nausea waned, but the uncanny feeling didn't. I knew I should zip up the tent again but couldn't make myself touch it. At last I gave up trying and rose unsteadily to my feet.

There are feelings so painful they make you bigger. You grow to accommodate the pain. I walked down the trail I knew intimately from my ten days looking for Leo and Benjamin, a trail I could easily navigate in the dark. Despite everything, it felt good to be outside after all those housebound months. As I went, the wind died, and in the new silence, my footsteps sounded amplified, too close, like breathing inside a helmet. The car was where it always was. When I unlocked it, it chirped piercingly. I got in, and there was the chill and airiness of a car that's been left outside at night, like the air in an abandoned home. I remembered driving to San Francisco with Maya and Micah, and Maya's musky perfume, which had bothered me but which I'd complimented out of a compulsion to be liked. Now the car smelled of Leo's occasional cigarettes, plus a sour note from a ruptured juice box. These particular smells transported me back to a moment in time, a moment which must be now.

I laid the phone on the passenger seat where I could easily get it if anyone called. I took a swig from the bottled water that had been left in the beverage holder. I rolled down the window and started the car.

On this leg of the trip, I remembered Evangelyne's story of singing in the car with Giovanni, Paul, and Jay. I considered singing, but it seemed sad to sing alone. It was a wavering road that seemed to run into blackness, the forest deepening and deepening, then occasionally flashing on open sky. My husband and son were still terrible in my heart. I'd left them on that mountainside. This was myself. I had broken the world.

Perhaps because, for me, a year had passed, I'd assumed it was very late at night. But when I drove into the town where I'd met Holly, the pizzeria was still open. I noticed, as I hadn't noticed before, that its name was Kingdom Pizza. I thought this had Christian overtones, until I remembered the town's name, Redwood Kingdom. I was able to park directly in front, where I could see into the dining area. Of course there were no throngs of women outside, no crates of provisions, no tangles of power cords. Holly wasn't there, and the place was empty except for a woman and a little boy eating in a booth. Two TV screens were prominently mounted inside the pizzeria, both showing Fox News. They must have been there before, turned off. I hadn't noticed them then.

The woman and her son were both looking at their phones, eating pizza mechanically. On Fox News a host I didn't recognize was grinning at the comments of a guest; both were men. I kept willing the woman to look up at the screen in startled fascination or to gaze at her son with wonder. She continued paging through something on her phone. Her son said something and she answered without looking. She picked up a crumpled napkin and wiped her hands.

In this world, nothing had happened. In a minute I would go in to get a Diet Coke for the road, and it would be as if nothing had happened. I would buy a Diet Coke in a world with men.

As I thought this, a man got out of a car behind me and walked into the pizzeria. When the door closed, I smelled pizza suddenly. Holly came out from a door at the back to serve him, and I had a physical reaction to seeing her. Then belatedly I had a physical reaction to seeing a man. Specifically, I felt a rush of sexual attraction, ridiculous in these circumstances. I laughed to myself in the darkness of the car. I picked up my phone.

I still had Evangelyne's number in my contacts, but I also knew it by heart. In our Santa Cruz days, I always typed it in manually, feeling this gave it power. If I remembered the number, she would answer the phone. Now it meant that she would still be alive.

I entered it slowly, conscious of the minute movements of my fingers. When I hit the Call button, I felt chilled although the night was warm. While it rang, I started crying. I needed to talk to her so badly it seemed inconceivable she might not answer, but also inevitable. When it went to voicemail, I couldn't speak. I hung up and dialed the number again. This time I prayed silently, moving my lips. I was promising to work here as I'd worked there, to help Evangelyne to power. If I started driving now, I could be with her by morning. Some brilliant people need a wife; maybe everyone, to optimally function, needs a wife. I could end her problems with the HOA in a day. I could be at the door if cops came. I was thinking of the dead lands in The

Men. We had to act or the oceans would die, the temperatures would rise until terrestrial life died, plastics would accumulate in our lungs and blood until all life was gone. I was back by the grace of real gods; surely that must have some meaning. All resistance to us must fail like a failing wave that crumples against a shore. She had to be there. We could still save this world.

It went to voicemail again, and my mind was racing. This didn't have to mean she was dead. She only answered her phone for the girl she was fucking. In this world we hadn't spoken in six years, and my number might even come up as *Unknown Caller.* Police murders, while high as a number, were rare as the result of any given arrest. She was too well known to be murdered like that. It was natural for her to be afraid, but it wasn't likely cops would murder her, not for kicking someone's door and yelling. She was not now being shot or choked. Evangelyne never answered her phone.

Still crying, I hung up and typed her a text: *This is Jane Pearson, please reply. It's important.* I sent it and stared at the screen. Nothing happened. I typed, *Just tell me you're all right*. Then I deleted it without sending. She wasn't dead, but I was angry, buzzing with anger. My feelings were focused on this phone, this appliance that wouldn't do its job. It had to find her now and it wouldn't. It was killing her.

I called once more before I tried Google. In that state, it was difficult to type her name into the search bar. At first I made so many mistakes it kept auto-completing to *Elvis Presley*. Then I had to add more words—her name alone brought up nothing but magazine profiles from the last ten years. The search term that finally worked was *Evangelyne Moreau Santa Monica shooting LAPD.*

The video shows a residential street in Santa Monica. It's nighttime. The lighting and the colors are unstable with pulses of police car lights. Police barriers hold the camera at a distance. About a dozen cop cars fill the street haphazardly, at every angle, as if carried in on a tide. A few are parked directly on a lawn, and officers stand in clusters on that same lawn. More cops stand in a spaced line at the barrier, facing toward the camera. These hold shields and wear helmets with bulbous plastic masks that obscure their faces. Some carry rifles; one has a bouquet of white zip ties at his belt. All the police wear so much equipment and body armor that their black shapes are distorted. They are outsized creatures not quite like men. They do nothing at all and don't speak. They stand. This too makes them seem not human.

On our side of the barrier is a thin crowd of people. One elderly woman stands with her hands folded, held to her nose; she is praying. The others are in constant motion, milling around and shouting, sometimes briefly joining in a chant. The focus of attention is the lawn and, behind it, a one-story house in the modern style. This house is lit spectrally by what is probably a motion-sensor light. One of its windows is broken. The front door is entirely gone, and the gap is crisscrossed by police tape. On the doorstep, something is sloppily covered by a white plastic sheet: a body. One bare foot is exposed, turned sideways. In the weird light, Evangelyne's sole looks red. I can't tell if this is blood or an effect of the light.

Nobody goes near her. Minutes pass and the sheet doesn't move.

I turned the phone off and sat for a long time staring at the pizzeria. The Fox News screens were now showing footage of a forest fire: a towering mass of smoke with a slender leading edge of orange. The little boy in the booth was holding obediently still while his mother used a napkin to clean his face. By this time, I was very dissociated and my mind kept trying to think of jokes about search engine optimization for police shootings. I was sobbing. Like many people with a history of trauma, I cry a great deal. I can cry while feeling nothing. It cheapens the experience. It confuses it.

The man who had entered the pizzeria came back out, shouldering open the door and sliding across it to maneuver a large pizza box out with him. He came across the parking lot toward my car. He was looking directly at me, and my hand automatically went to the ignition. It still sometimes happened that strangers confronted me, called me a pedophile, filmed me on their phones while they told me to shoot myself. But as he came closer, the man put on an exaggerated face of concern and cocked his head. He was checking that I was all right.

I smiled and raised my phone to communicate: *I'm talking on my phone*. This seemed to be enough. He smiled back, looking as if a weight had been lifted, and turned away. Some men are instinctively compassionate, as women are; this was something I'd forgotten and it took my breath away. I started the car again.

When I got back to the trailhead, I parked in the same space, and, walking up the mountain, I made myself think up a story to explain my absence. I practiced it mentally, my face forming friendly, candid expressions as I imagined lying. But when I got back, the campsite was silent. I stood alone beneath the dark trees. I thought of going to look at Benjamin again, but both the craving and the fear were gone.

Not everyone is meant to change the world. We let the world change around us. We let it die if it will. We live small lives, constrained by habit and fear. I climbed back into the hammock and found the stars among the branches. I remembered my nightly meditation and repeated it mentally to calm myself. I felt my husband and son there and loved that they were there. I was in love with them. I had more than most people had. It was enough. There had been times I'd been frightened in the world, bad times, but this was not a bad time. I was happy.

That night I didn't sleep at all. Several times I decided to leave, and once I got as far as the trailhead before turning back. I searched for the others on my phone and was able to find Ji-Won and Blanca. I didn't write to them but composed the emails in my head. I checked my bank account and tried to think of cities where I could afford a first month's rent and deposit. I looked at jobs in those cities on Craigslist. I hated Leo and even Benjamin. I knew I could not go back to that life.

But I was still in the hammock at sunrise. I watched the stars fade into dawn.

Acknowledgments

Thanks first of all to my always amazing and often magical agent Victoria Hobbs, who's been with me from the beginning, gets smarter every year, and is a constant friend as well as being the best representative anyone could wish for. Thanks also to Jessica Lee, Alexandra McNicoll, Prema Raj, and Tabatha Leggett at A. M. Heath for all their stellar work.

Thanks to all the remarkable professionals who worked on this book at Granta in the UK and Grove in the US: first of all to my genius editors Peter Blackstock, Anne Meadows, and Rowan Cope, who dealt with an often baffling and wayward project with sensitivity and acuity, and exceeded all reasonable expectations by finding solutions I could not see. I'm also constantly grateful for my publicists, Lamorna Elmer and Kait Astrella, both for their outstanding work in getting *The Men* out and finding it friends in an uncaring world, and for always being fun to be around through the often trying work of promoting a book. Thanks also to Jason Arthur for his many contributions to the project, and to Emily Burns for her constant support and great work. At Grove, thanks also to Morgan Entrekin, Deb Seager, Judy Hottensen, Julia Berner-Tobin, Sal Destro, John Mark Boling, Deb Seager, Gretchen Mergenthaler, Henry Sene Yee, Nancy Tan, and Alicia Burns; and at Granta, additional thanks to Jason Arthur, Sarah Wasley, Arneaux, Simon Heafield, Dan Bird, Bella Lacey, Christine Lo, Noel Murphy, Phoebe Llanwarne, George Stamp, Pru Rowlandson, and Sigrid Rausing. The world of writers is full of horror stories, so I'm reminded every day how fortunate I am to be working with such brilliant and dedicated people.

Thanks to friends who were early readers: Lauren Hough, David Burr Gerrard, Tim Paulson, and Catherine Nichols, for their enthusiasm and often life-saving advice. Every single thing anyone likes about the book is their doing and the errors are mine.

Thanks to the friends who gave me places to stay and work while I was writing this book, with or without cats, frogs, lizards, etc. to keep me busy: Ellen Tarlow, Gina Guy, Jim Gottier & Andrea Ball, Arlene Heyman, Clare McHugh, Peggy Reynolds, and Mandy Keifetz. I feel an urge to thank the cats now too but honestly I don't want to thank the frogs.

Thanks to all the online friends who were my daily company while I wrote this book, and who got me through the bleakest days of 2020, especially the members of Small Twitter and the Echo Biosphere, but also my infinitely extended Twitter family. And thanks to Anita for being the wise, smart, generous IRL friend I needed in the worst moments.

Thanks to writers of feminist utopias who came before, especially Joanna Russ, Alice Sheldon, and Sherri Tepper, women brave enough to say, unapologetically, in a far more patriarchal world, that there should be no men. Their work made a crucial difference to me long before I ever thought of writing this book.

And thanks always to Howard, for reading every version of this book and being my first editor, literary collaborator, best friend, husband, boyfriend, thing that is there when nothing else is there, voice of reason, companion in unreason, home, favorite sweater, boat, water on which that boat is floating, multitudinous fish beneath, abyssal depths, have I left anything out?